HURT MACHINE

HURTMACHINE

A Moe Prager Mystery
Reed Farrel Coleman

TYRUS
BOOKS

a division of F+W Crime

Published by
TYRUS BOOKS
an imprint of F+W Media, Inc.
4700 East Galbraith Road
Cincinnati, Ohio 45236
www.tyrusbooks.com

ISBN 10: 1-4405-3202-8 (Hardcover)
ISBN 13: 978-1-4405-3202-3 (Hardcover)
ISBN 10: 1-4405-3199-4 (Paperback)
ISBN 13: 978-1-4405-3199-6 (Paperback)
eISBN 10: 1-4405-3200-1
eISBN 13: 978-1-4405-3200-9

Printed in the United States of America.

10   9   8   7   6   5   4   3   2   1

Library of Congress Cataloging-in-Publication Data
is available from the publisher.

This book is available at quantity discounts for bulk purchases.
For information, please call 1-800-289-0963.

0 3 1 4 8 6 3 0 9

Novels by Reed Farrel Coleman featuring Moe Prager:

Walking the Perfect Square
Redemption Street
The James Deans
Soul Patch
Empty Ever After
Innocent Monster

featuring Dylan Klein:

Life Goes Sleeping
Little Easter
They Don't Play Stickball in Milwaukee

as Tony Spinosa:

Hose Monkey
The Fourth Victim

with Ken Bruen:

Tower

For my late friend and publisher David Thompson and for Coleman Vance, born to carry on.

ACKNOWLEDGMENTS

I would very much like to thank my cousin Paula R. Schwartz, MD, who, in the course of giving technical advice, shared the most bizarre phone conversation with me I think I've ever had. As always I owe a great debt to my first readers Sara J. Henry, Ellen Schare, and Judy Bobalik. Thanks to Peter Spiegelman for his patience and advice. Props to Ben LeRoy at Tyrus Books.

As always, to Rosanne, Kaitlin, and Dylan, without whom none of this would be possible or worth it.

Death is not an event in life:
we do not live to experience death.

—Wittgenstein

ONE

Death, not time, is probably the only lasting remedy for hurt and even that's just an educated guess. Maybe it was wishful thinking. I'm not usually prone to wishful thinking, but since walking out of my oncologist's office, I'd given myself license to wish away. What damage, I thought, could wishful thinking do to me that the tumor couldn't?

Death and hurt were pretty present on my mind. I wondered when the former would come and if the latter would ever really disappear. I wasn't so much concerned with *my* hurt. I'd been long-hardened to the slings and arrows. No, I was more focused on the hurt I would leave in my wake, the damage I'd done and left unaddressed or unrepaired. Humans are like hurt machines. No matter how hard we try not to do it, we seem to inflict hurt on one another as naturally as we breathe.

"Hurt, pain . . . they're God's way of letting you know he loves you," my late friend and Auschwitz survivor Israel Roth once said to me, a wry smile on his face.

"Then God must really love you a lot, Izzy."

"More than some, less than others."

"So God invented tough love. Who knew? Good thing I don't believe in him."

"Is it a good thing, you think? For your sake, Mr. Moe, I hope *he* believes in you."

"We'll see, I guess."

1

"Yes, someday."

Well, suddenly, that someday felt very much at hand. It's funny, but I couldn't make sense of what the doctor had said to me. I mean, I understood the individual words and phrases. *More tests. A second opinion. Malignant. Metastatic. Surgery. Chemo. Radiation.* But somehow they didn't hang together. They didn't add up. I couldn't do the math. One thing he said required no math, no intricate equation. *Maybe it would be a good thing to get your house in order.* The one euphemism he used, I understood. That needed no further explanation. Problem was, I was at a loss for how to go about it. I could barely organize my sock drawer. How was I supposed to organize my future and my past?

One thing I was proud of: I hadn't walked out of the doctor's office asking, "Why me?" I had since learned not to ask that one. You ask it once and you never stop asking it. Besides, in a Godless universe, the answer starts fourteen billion years ago as a pinpoint in the void and I didn't have that kind of time. None of us do. I actually preferred icy randomness to thinking of God as the universal hurt machine. Still, I suppose I might have asked the question had the doctor said I would die before Sarah's wedding.

Sarah's wedding. There's a phrase I used to dread—now, not so much. As a matter of fact, as phrases go, it beats the shit out of *You've got a golf ball-sized tumor in your stomach.*

I liked Paul, Sarah's fiancé. More than that, I trusted him. He was solid, a state prosecutor in Vermont, and he loved my daughter so that it ached. He would take good care of her. I knew it was old-fashioned to see any woman, but especially my daughter, as someone who needed taking care of, but in a world so full of hurt, everyone needs taking care of. Anyway, since my trip to the oncologist, I didn't give a fuck about my thoughts being out of step with the times.

Not only did I like Paul, we were connected. Paul was the biological son of Rico Tripoli, my precinct mate at the Six-O in Coney Island when I was on the job in the seventies. Rico had once been my best friend, closer to me even than my own brother Aaron. It was Rico who, back in '78, had gotten me involved in my first case as a PI: the search for Patrick Maloney, a college kid gone missing after a school fundraiser at a Tribeca bar. While searching for Patrick, I fell in love with his sister Katy. Katy and I were married for twenty years and Sarah was our only child. So although Rico had pissed away his gold shield, committed slow-motion suicide with drugs and alcohol, and betrayed our friendship more than once, he was, in his way, responsible for both bride and groom.

At the moment, I was too busy checking my watch to worry about the train wreck that had been Rico Tripoli's life. Pam was late for the pre-wedding party and that was pissing me off to no end. It was actually comforting to be pissed off, to be able to focus my anger on something or someone other than the fucking cancer. I reached into my pocket for my cell phone, but stopped as I noticed a woman turn the corner, heading for the restaurant. I put the cell phone back, not because it was Pam. It wasn't. No, this woman was a piece of my past, someone who had first come into my life in 1972 and walked out of it eight years ago, taking a chunk of my soul with her.

TWO

Carmella Melendez and I had gotten married for all the wrong reasons, but with the best intentions. Perhaps it might have worked out better the other way around. The fact is, it didn't work out. Thankfully, we dissolved things before we could chew each other up or do any lasting damage. Well, before I could do lasting damage to her. I hadn't been lucky enough to escape unscathed. I'd been a father to Carmella's newborn for the first year of his life and although Israel—named for Mr. Roth—wasn't mine, I was the first man to change his diapers, to dry his tears, to tickle his belly. I didn't know what the now nine-year-old Israel remembered of me, if anything, but I could still hear him coo and feel his tiny fingers latch onto my nose as I cradled him in my arms.

My heart was thumping in my chest. My throat was dry. I hadn't seen Carmella for the better part of a decade and we'd barely spoken since she moved up to Toronto. The one conversation we'd had was about her changing Israel's last name to hers, thereby erasing all traces of me in the boy's life. Yet the sight of her still made me weak, the hurt and baggage being beside the point. The nearly twenty years in age that separated us was as meaningless now as it was the first time we met as adults. She was a young precinct detective in those days and I was investigating a corruption and murder case in Coney Island's Soul Patch. I didn't know then that our paths had crossed before, when she was a little girl with a different name and that I had saved her from certain death. Then it struck me that I hadn't saved Carmella from it at all. I'd only given her a temporary reprieve. I guess every day from the day we're born is a kind of reprieve. I wondered if I too might get a reprieve or if my ticket had already been punched.

We hugged. It was a silent, awkward embrace, both too long and not long enough, too distant, but too close. I recognized the once familiar feel of silk when the wind blew her hair against my cheek. The back of her cotton floral-print dress was damp and the raw scent of her perspiration cutting against the grassy fragrance of her perfume was intoxicating. It made me want to give in to the moment. Still, as willfully indulgent as I'd been lately, this was neither the time nor the place. And frankly, I was pretty curious about what she was doing here at all. I put my hands around her bare, light brown biceps, gently pushing her away. I needed some distance between us and, at the moment, arm's length was the best I could do.

And for the first time since I noticed her rounding the corner, I saw Carmella Melendez with my eyes instead of my heart. Her hair, once so impossibly black, was now salted with threads of gray. She was still fit and as perfectly curved as she had been in her mid-twenties, but some of the fierceness in her eyes had vanished and the sun-darkened skin of her face showed age beyond her years. There are all kinds of aging. Time ages us more gracefully than heartache. The lines in her face, around her eyes and mouth, were etched in tears, many tears.

"I hear Sarah is getting married," she said, her voice flat and distracted.

"In Vermont in a few weeks, yeah. This party is for the people who can't make it up there."

"You must be proud."

"Of course I am. I've always been proud of Sarah."

"She has forgiven you for Katy's death?"

"Let's just say that the last case I worked helped Sarah understand that the fault lines can get awfully blurry and the closer you are to things the harder it is to assign blame."

"That was the case of the little girl, the artist? You rescued her the way you rescued me once."

"That's the way the media played it, but it wasn't like that at all. I'm not sure she wasn't better off away from her parents. But what's this got to do with anything, Carmella? What are you doing here? How did you—"

"It's Carmella now, not Carm?"

"It stopped being Carm the day you left for Canada."

"I had to go, for all of us. You know that. We were starting to hate each other and I could never let that happen. You only married me to get over Katy and to give Israel a name. Somewhere you know that is the truth."

"How is he?"

She was young again, a beatific smile washing over her face. "He's amazing, so smart, so handsome." She reached into her bag and came out with an envelope. "These are pictures of him for you to keep. I could have emailed them, but I know how you are old-fashioned."

"No, Carmella, not old-fashioned, just old. Thank you for these." I slid the envelope into my suit pocket. "But you haven't answered my question. What are you doing here?"

"You have not changed, Moe. Still persistent." Her smile changed, turning to rueful and sad. She was older again. "I always

admired that about you. You never lost track of things no matter how confusing the situation would get. No, you have not
changed."

"Do any of us change, really, even if everything else changes
around us?"

"You are very philosophical today."

"I have my reasons."

"With Sarah getting married . . ."

"That too," I said.

"What does that mean?"

"Carmella, for chrissakes!" I clapped my hands together in
anger.

Her face turned dead serious. "I want to hire you. I need you."

I laughed. "You don't need me. You proved that when you moved
up to Canada. Besides, you were the best detective and PI I ever
knew. When we were business partners, you always did the heavy
lifting. And if you can't do it yourself, hire Brian Doyle and Devo.
They run their own shop now."

"No, not them. You."

"Sorry, I can't help."

"You have to."

"What the hell is so important that you come to me after all this
time?"

I regretted asking almost before the words were out of my
mouth. She took a small framed photo out of her bag and handed
it to me. The woman in the photo looked a little like Carmella. She
was older, heavier, but with the same fiery eyes and rich mouth. I
handed the picture back.

"She's lovely," I said.

"My big sister, Alta."

"I thought you didn't have any more contact with the Consecos."

"I did not. I *don't*."

"Look, Carmella, what's this got to do—"

"I thought you might have heard. Alta was murdered last month. She was stabbed dead in the street outside a pizzeria in Gravesend."

I'd grown up in Coney Island, not too far from Gravesend, and I don't think I'd ever given the name much thought. Gravesend was just another neighborhood. I mean, you don't say Sheepshead Bay, Brighton Beach, or Brownsville and contemplate the origin of the names. They were neighborhoods with names, names like any other names . . . until now, until I found out there was a time bomb ticking in my belly. *Tick . . . tick . . . tick . . .* A long time ago in a cemetery, Mr. Roth told me that he didn't want to be buried, that to be cold in the ground wasn't for him. And now the time had come for me to think about that. I didn't suppose it mattered. When you're dead, you're dead, but when you can see the end in sight, it does matter. *Gravesend.* For as long as I had left, I wouldn't be able to hear the name again without considering its implications.

"I'm sorry about your sister," I said.

"I cut my family out of my life so many years ago and now . . ." Carmella was crying. "Here, take this." She handed me a slip of paper. "Get back to your party. Give your family my love and wish Sarah all happiness. Call me, please."

She was in my arms again and I was stroking her hair. When I looked up, Pam was standing a few feet away, glaring.

From the *Daily News*, May 6, 2009
Cold-hearted EMT murdered in Gravesend, Brooklyn
By Henry Leroy

One of two FDNY EMTs accused of ignoring a man who died of a stroke at a Manhattan bistro was stabbed to death outside a popular Brooklyn eatery. According to a spokesman for the NYPD, Alta Conseco, 48, of East New York was accosted by an unknown assailant or assailants in close proximity of the Gelato Grotto on 86th Street in the Gravesend section of the borough. Stabbed several times, she managed to crawl to the famous pizzeria where she collapsed. No further details about the attack were released. She was off duty at the time of the assault.

Conseco was taken to Coney Island Hospital where she was pronounced dead. On March 12, Conseco and another EMT, Maya Watson, made international headlines after witnesses claimed the EMTs ignored pleas for help from the bistro staff after Robert Tillman, a cook at the High Line Bistro, seemed to faint. When they were asked to help, the two off-duty EMTs are reported to have told the bistro staff to call 911 and then left. Both EMTs have consistently refused comment.

Conseco and Watson have been vilified by New Yorkers for what many perceive as a callous decision and a dereliction of duty. They were both suspended for thirty days and put on desk duty upon their return to active status. Both the Manhattan district attorney's office and the FDNY have investigations pending.

THREE

I had to wade through a lot of shit before I could get to any credible media reports on Alta Conseco's murder. During the last case I worked—the abduction of Sashi Bluntstone, an eleven-year-old art prodigy—I'd learned some hard lessons about the ugly side of the worldwide web. The internet could be a magical place, but it was a sewer too. It was a place where people with axes to grind could hide behind screen names and ceaselessly vent their spleens in the most vicious and brutal ways imaginable without ever having to justify their points of view or answer for their screeds. Sashi had been a particularly favorite target of a group of frustrated art bloggers who posted invective-laden rants and altered photos of her being crucified, raped, and flayed alive. All of that aimed at a prepubescent girl because she had managed to make some money with her paintings, so you can imagine the harsh and varied expressions of loathing that lay in store for Alta Conseco and Maya Watson.

When I finally did climb out of the sludge at the bottom of the sewer pipe, most of the media reports I found weren't very good and were pretty much the same. They spent about an equal amount of space or time presenting the scant details of Alta's murder and rehashing Robert Tillman's death. The reports that came a few days later weren't much better. No, actually, they were worse. They shed little if any light on Alta's homicide. In fact, as the week wore on, reportage of her murder became more of a pretext for the papers and TV outlets to sensationalize Robert Tillman's unfortunate end and to further vilify Alta and her partner. There was an almost inexhaustible number of articles, opinion pieces, and rants by TV talking heads, many of them delighting in portraying the two EMTs as representative of New York City itself.

Over the last few years I'd noticed that all the goodwill the rest of the country had shown New York City since 9/11 had steadily eroded and Robert Tillman's death was like the last nail in the coffin. It was Kitty Genovese all over again. New York was that cold uncaring place, the place where neighbors hear the screams of a young woman being murdered and turn their heads, the place where EMTs basically tell a dying man to go fuck himself.

I shut the computer down. There wasn't anything else there for me to know.

I'd had a long day, a happy day, for the most part. Just as I'd been able to put some distance between Carmella and me earlier in the day, I'd done a good job of keeping thoughts of the cancer at arm's length during the party. I toasted Sarah and Paul. I watched them dance. I danced with Pam, with my sister Miriam, with Paul's mom, and with Sarah. Still, it didn't take much for my thoughts to shift back to my pending mortality. The level of my obsession with the disease really surprised me. During the few days since the diagnosis, I would sometimes look down to find myself rubbing my palm across my abdomen. It was as if I was trying to make a silent peace with the damned cancer or reach an accommodation with it. *Come on, we can get along, you and me. Gimme a few more years. Let me see some grandchildren. No, okay, that was greedy. How about a grandson?* Fuck me, this was going to be harder to deal with than I thought. I was an ex-cop, for chrissakes, a pragmatic SOB, but here I was trying to do a deal with a malignant lump growing inside my belly.

There was no way I was telling Sarah about it, not this close to the wedding. The wedding was simply a convenient excuse. I wasn't going to tell anyone until circumstance forced me to. After Katy, my first wife, was murdered as an indirect result of some half-truths and secrets I'd kept from her, I'd sworn off secret-keeping and lies for good. That lasted about five minutes. A long time ago, I used to tell myself and anyone else who would listen that I was an open book, that secrets were an anathema to me. Bullshit! Secret-keeping was as reflexive for me as squinting my eyes in the face of the sun. And the cancer wasn't the only secret I'd be keeping and the lies I told myself weren't going to be much of anything compared to the ones I'd already started telling.

"That was Carmella, wasn't it?" Pam had asked, her anger still evident as we both watched my ex-wife and ex-business partner disappear around the corner.

"You've seen her picture before, yeah."

"God, she is beautiful. What was she doing here?"

"She heard about the party and she wanted to congratulate me and wish Sarah all the best." *Lie number one.* As easy to tell as breathing. "She knew Sarah from the time she was a little girl and they always liked each other."

Pam was professionally skeptical. It came with the territory. She was a PI, a real PI, not a PI like me, a guy who more played at it when owning wine shops with his brother got too boring to bear. Pam was licensed in Vermont and operated out of an office in Brattleboro. Brattleboro suited her. The rent was relatively inexpensive and its location gave her easy access to most of New England and New York. She did the majority of her work in New England, but, if the money was right, took cases as far south as Jersey. We met while I was looking for Sashi Bluntstone and the story of how we wound up together is pretty complicated. Let's just say that since our initial relationship was based on secrets and lies—hers, not mine—I was a total sucker for her. Kindred spirits, you know. It helped that she saved me from being beaten to death by a vengeful ex-cop.

We'd been together for about two years now, if you could call the cha-cha we did being together. We'd both been down the aisle before and neither of us was hankering to take that stroll again. It was one thing for Sarah to sell her vet practice down here and move up to Vermont with Paul. They were young and just starting out. But Pam and I were set in our ways and weren't going to pull up roots and relocate so we might live unhappily ever after. We had what I suppose you might call an adult relationship. One weekend a month I'd visit her. One weekend a month she'd come down to Brooklyn. Twice a year we'd go on week-long trips together. We enjoyed each other's company and more than satisfied each other's needs while managing to avoid the minefield of married sex. I hadn't really thought about it until now, but married sex was sort of a peculiar mix of comfort and resentment. Between Sarah's wedding and my ticking clock, I imagined I'd be thinking about a lot of things I'd let slide until now.

Pam, as unconvinced by my lie as I had been by her smile, was already headed back home. She was working an insurance fraud case that she thought would keep her busy for the next couple of weeks. I had a case to work too, probably my last case, my last chance for redemption. As atheists go, I guess I was a dreadful disappointment. I unfolded the paper Carmella had given to me that morning and punched in her phone number.

FOUR

We met on the boardwalk in Coney Island near Nathan's. The sun was strong. The wind stronger and fragrant too. It smelled of salt from the sea, of sunscreen lotion, and of hot oil. It smelled so intensely of hot dogs and French fries that I imagined I could hear them sizzle and bubble.

"Why meet here?" I asked, turning to face the beach.

"I used to work the Six-O too, remember?"

"Yeah, but it's also the place where—"

"—that scumbag took me from my family and raped me when I was a little girl. You know, when I first found out this was where the department was assigning me after making detective, I almost said no, but you know how the job was back then. I wouldn't get no second chance. They woulda stuck me behind a desk at One PP and made me a fucking showpiece. When the department wanted to prove women and minorities were getting ahead, they'd have wheeled out the hot piece of Puerto Rican ass and her shiny gold shield for the press. And when they were done making their point, they'd have put me back on the shelf until the next time they needed to flash my shield and pussy for the cameras. No, Moe, that man who did those things to me when I was a girl, he took too much from me. I wasn't gonna let him take my career away from me too."

"Still . . ."

"I like it here because it reminds me of the best of us. I loved you everywhere, but I loved you here most of all, in this place. Coney

15

Island is your place, Moe. When you die, they should just bury you right here, under the boardwalk."

I bit my lip and nodded, my palm pressing against my abdomen.

"Was that your girlfriend yesterday, the one who was staring at me?"

"Girlfriend? At my age, it seems like such a silly word, doesn't it?"

"You got a better one?"

"I guess not. Pam's her name."

"She's very pretty," Carmella said.

"She said something similar about you, but that's not why we're here, right? I checked into Alta's murder."

"So you know about the other thing."

"About her and her partner not treating Tillman? Yeah, I know what you can know from the internet, which isn't much. Do you think the two things are connected?"

"You know I do. Any good detective can do simple math," she said. "Alta became a target the second those stories about Tillman's death surfaced."

"What do the cops think?"

"I don't know what they think. Nobody's talking."

"Not even to you?"

"Not even to me."

I was surprised at that. As a rule, cops are a chatty bunch, especially with other cops. Put a few beers and some Jameson in them and the yak factor goes way up. Add Carmella's obvious charms to that mix and the chat factor grows exponentially. While Carmella hadn't exactly been Miss Popularity with the brass, she did have a good rep with her peers—some of whom were still on the job in high places. And she'd taken a bullet in the line of duty, which earned her a lot of respect even from the hardass old-timers who still thought a woman's place was in the kitchen or the bedroom and who thought a Puerto Rican's place was in San Juan.

"Why do you think lips are so tight?" I asked.

"I don't know. That's what's so frustrating, Moe. It's like they just want all of it to go away. And it's not only the cops. The fire department, they won't even return my calls because I'm not listed as a relative. Shit, I can't even get the media sources I used to have to talk to me. Something's not right."

"Sorry, but what do you think I can do for you? I'm pretty much outta the game, Carm. I—"

"You called me Carm." Her smile was full and white, but the grief and guilt over her long-estranged sister weren't far beneath the surface. "It's good to hear you call me that again."

"Doesn't change anything."

"In terms of us or the case?"

"Both," I said, disappearing her smile. "Look, I've got Sarah's wedding in a few weeks and I've got a lot going on right now, a lot of aggravation."

"You do look kinda pale and too thin. Is everything okay?"

You mean other than the cancer? "Just stress. You know how Aaron can be about the wine stores. The bad economy is hurting."

"Give it a week, Moe, please. That's all I'm asking. I'll pay you whatever you want."

"Don't be stupid, Carm. I don't want your money, but like I said, I'm outta this, pretty much. I haven't even been able to find my license for going on three years now. What can I do that you can't?"

"I was a good detective and a better PI, but you are lucky. You've always been lucky."

I heard someone laughing and it took a second to realize it was me. "That's rich."

"Please . . . for me, for old times' sake."

"You know, Larry McDonald said that same thing about old times' sake to me once almost on this very spot a few days before he killed himself. I turned him down."

"As close as you and Chief McDonald were, you never shared with him what we shared, what we will always share. That kind of history don't go away, Moe, never."

"Okay, Carm, I'll look around, but I'm not gonna sugarcoat anything. If I find stuff out that the cops or the FDNY don't know, like maybe that Alta really did turn her back on the Tillman guy as he was dying, I won't keep it to myself. True, we have history and maybe I owe you, but I don't owe you that." I handed her my card. "Fax me everything you have so far to that number and I'll see what I can see."

"Thank you."

She stepped toward me, arms extended, and the temperature rose. Maybe it was just my temperature. It was an innocent gesture, a hug to cement the deal, but there was no such thing as an innocent gesture between Carmella and me. That was the thing with us, the chemistry. When we were partners in Prager & Melendez Investigations, Inc., we managed to keep it at bay. Once we crossed the line, going back wasn't an option. For years, I hated her for moving up to Toronto with Israel, for pulling the rug out from under me the way she had so soon after Katy's murder. It was especially painful because Sarah, who held me responsible for her mother's death, had stopped speaking to me. But now I saw that Carmella was probably right to move far away when we began falling apart. Between the hurt and chemistry we would have eaten each other alive and Israel would have paid the price. I stepped back.

"No, Carm, this is business. We were never very good at mixing up our history with our business . . . and there's Pam."

She let her arms down and put her back against the boardwalk rail so that she faced Nathan's and away from me. "You are right, Moe. I will go fax you those things."

Carmella took a few strides away without looking back. Then I called to her.

"Who told you about Sarah's party yesterday?"

"Your sister," she said without hesitation and without turning to face me.

"Always the troublemaker, my little sister."

"Don't be mad at her. You have always been her hero."

"I'm nobody's hero."

"About that, you could not be more wrong."

I watched Carmella go down the steps onto Stillwell Avenue and disappear into the crowd. I didn't linger too long after that. I had a case to work and the rest of my life, however much of it was left, to live.

FIVE

The package Carmella faxed me was chock full of facts and details, accusations and innuendos. After studying it, I realized she wasn't exactly telling me the whole truth about her lack of headway in Alta's case. She'd managed to get the ME's autopsy reports on Tillman and on Alta. She'd gotten witness statements from both the High Line Bistro where Tillman had died and from the Grotto where Alta was murdered. She had even obtained still shots of security camera footage—not terribly revealing out of context—from both locales. People were talking more than she let on, just not a lot, and none of what they had to say did much to enhance Alta Conseco's reputation.

As I got in my car, I couldn't help but think about why Carmella had really come to me after so many years and in spite of the rough time we'd had together as husband and wife. By moving up to Toronto, Carm had cut a huge chunk out of my life. She had been my business partner, my friend, and, eventually, my lover and wife. And then there was Israel. In the blink of an eye, she had given me a son and then just as quickly taken him away. There are few emotional investments a man can make in his life like the one he makes in a new son, whether that son carries his DNA or not. Israel had been the kind of gift few men receive at that stage in life. It's a funny thing about men; they can love their daughters beyond all reason—believe me, I know—but without a son there's a kind of a hole. It's not reasonable or fair or even right, but there it is. I think it has less to do with passing on the family name than with wanting to set things right, to repair the damage between a man's father and himself. Carmella had to know how much wrenching Israel out of my life had hurt. Still, she had come to me.

Was I lucky like she claimed I was? I guess so. Carmella knew that better than anyone. I can't explain it, but I had the habit of stumbling into solutions when the cops and/or other PIs were stumped and things had gotten desperate. Desperation was always the door through which I came because I didn't really know what the hell I was doing. I'd never had any formal training. My days as a cop were spent in uniform. Unlike Carm and most of my old buddies from the Six-O, I'd never gotten my gold shield. I'd earned it, just never got it. There was a time when getting that shield mattered more to me than anyone or anything. Not having it ate at me. It bothered me so that when the devil came to me in his many shapes and guises over the course of years, I'd been tempted to take the bargain. Tempted, but never taken. Now that I had the devil inside me, literally eating away at me, I couldn't believe a hunk of gold metal and blue enamel ever mattered to me in the least.

Lucky or not, I was never the detective Carmella was. The fact that she had gotten as much information as she had, although no one seemed in a very cooperative frame of mind, proved my point. No, something else was going on here. Something I just couldn't see, at least not yet. I had to be conscious of that. It's not always the things in your mirrors coming up fast that are the biggest threats, but the things in your blind spots. I'd add it to the list of things to watch out for.

Humans are connectors by nature. It's how our brains work. It's how we learn, I think. We see things that happen, judge their proximity, and connect them. And in linking things or incidents together, we can't help but see them sequentially, in terms of cause and effect. But humans are funny creatures because once we link things, once we put the cause and effect stamp on them, it's very difficult for us to undo that link. And even if you hadn't read the witness statements or seen the media reports, you might have connected Robert Tillman's death to Alta Conseco's murder. So it was easy to see why Carmella thought they were connected: Tillman is ignored and dies—*cause*—and Alta is murdered shortly thereafter—*effect*.

Problem is, humans sometimes put the cause and effect stamp on things that are completely unrelated. I had a psych professor in college who used the example of a little boy tapping a light pole with a stick. One time the kid taps the streetlamp and just as the stick makes contact with the pole, all the lights in the city go out. Mightn't the kid or someone watching the kid link the two things together and attribute the blackout to the boy's tapping the streetlight? They might, but they'd be wrong, dead wrong. The same danger existed here. I had to be careful not to fall into the trap that had already snared Carmella. I had to work backwards from Alta's murder, not forward from Tillman's death.

SIX

Located just past Shell Road where 86th Street breaks off at an angle from Avenue X, the Gelato Grotto was a Brooklyn institution, a place that was already there when I was born and would be there after I was dead—the odds on that having just recently improved. I'd eaten at the Grotto a hundred times over the years with friends, my brother and sister, high school dates, but not because I liked the pizza. The regular pizza never failed to disappoint. Their Sicilian was better, but nothing to get excited about. I was partial to Totonno's in Coney Island or Di Fara's on Avenue J. Still, it was Brooklyn pizza and, like Ferguson May, the late philosopher of the 60th Precinct, used to say, "Sex and Brooklyn pizza got a lot in common. Even when they're bad, they're good."

For me, I kept going back because of the gelato. The Grotto was the first Italian eatery of any kind I could remember that sold home-made gelato. I'm talking the early '60s here, when most Americans thought Spam kebobs with pineapple chunks and green bean casseroles were gourmet food and everyone called pasta spaghetti. No matter how disappointed I was by their pizza, the gelato was compensation enough. Another thing that set the Grotto apart was how it looked. Unlike the usual cramped Brooklyn pizzeria, the Grotto was an al fresco affair with plastic trees and plastic vines and outdoor tables with colored umbrellas on a concrete patio surrounded by curved stucco walls. It was kind of goofy and felt as much like a secluded grotto as falling down stairs felt like skydiving, but it was just so Brooklyn.

Sadly, Alta Conseco wasn't the first person to take her last gasping breaths within the stucco confines of the Grotto. The place had a history of violence stretching back many decades. I guess what made the place so popular also contributed to the violence. Whereas most pizza places are strictly local neighborhood affairs, the Grotto drew crowds from all over the borough. It was located close to the Marlboro Housing Projects and the rail yards. You had a lot of people mixing—Jews, Italians, Irish, African-Americans, Puerto Ricans, Mexicans, Russians, Chinese, Pakistanis, Mafia-types, bikers, cops—who didn't necessarily want to hold hands and sing campfire songs together. You add a little alcohol to that mix on a sweltering summer night and watch out.

I didn't figure to barge in, flash my old cop badge, and get the information I was looking for. The days when I could use my badge and have people think I was still on the job had long since come and gone. The only thing I could flash with any credibility these days was my AARP card. But sometimes you don't have to improvise a strategy. You just have to get lucky, and I did.

In 1977, the year I fucked up my knee and got put out to pasture by the NYPD, Nick Roussis was in his second year at the Six-O. Nick was a good guy, but the job wasn't for him. He quit to go into the family business. The Roussis family owned several ethnic restaurants throughout Brooklyn, Queens, and the Bronx. We'd run into each other over the years and Carmella and I had done a job for him, flushing out a guy in the main office whom the family suspected of embezzling funds. That was in the mid-'90s and I hadn't seen him since, but there he was—a few pounds heavier, hair thinner and grayer—chewing out the guy behind the clam bar at the Grotto.

"Tony, how many fuckin' times I gotta tell ya, wiggle the knife to open a slit and then cut around the clam? You don't do that, ya gonna slice t'rough yer freakin' palm. Okay?"

I waited for Nick to walk away from the raw bar before approaching him. He saw me coming and I saw the recognition in his eyes.

I held out my hand to him for a shake, but he used it to pull me close and hug the breath out of me. When he was done with that, he playfully shoved me aside.

"Moses fuckin' Prager! How are ya, ya old cop bastard? It's been what, five years?"

"Fifteen."

"Fifteen! Nah, get the fuck outta here."

"Fifteen."

"Jesus, time flies."

"Yeah, don't remind me. So how you doing, you old Greek prick?"

"Good, good. So ya came to see me, Moe?"

"Not at all. I'm still getting over the fact you're here. I knew your family owned some pizzerias, but I didn't know you owned this place."

"Yeah, sure. We bought in after you did that job for us and then about ten years ago, when the original owners got too old to handle it, we bought the whole shebang. We made a nice deal with them and everybody lived happily ever after."

"Business is good?" I asked.

"The economy is killin' some of our restaurants, but this place is recession-proof. People come from all over the map to eat at the Grotto."

"Glad to hear it, but what the hell are you working the floor for instead of sitting back at headquarters counting your money?"

"I'm no good in an office, Moe. I go into the office a few times a week, but I'm bored there. I need to get my hands dirty. Keeps me alive. So how's that hot-lookin' partner of yours?"

"Carmella? Christ, Nick, it *has* been a long time and it would take a week to explain all that's happened between then and now. I'm basically retired from the security business and I spend most of my time at the wine stores these days."

"C'mon, let me get you some lunch or somethin'. You look like you haven't eaten a good meal or been in the sun since December."

We sat a table in the shade. I had a slice of Sicilian—pretending to like it—and a beer. Nick had a salad and a dozen clams.

"Between you, me, and the wall," Nick said, "I always hated the pizza here, but, hey, it helped send a whole generation of Roussis family kids to college. So, now that lunch is done, ya wanna tell me what yer really doin' here? I know ya didn't come for the pizza."

"I'm doing someone a favor, looking into something."

Nick's jovial face turned stony cold. "What thing is that?"

"Alta Conseco's murder."

Nick's voice got downright icy. "I thought you were retired."

"I am. This is a favor and don't worry, neither me or the client are looking to hurt anybody. This isn't an insurance thing and I'm not working for a lawyer looking to sue you or the business. You have my word on that."

I offered him my right hand again and this time he shook it. Of course, the next words out of my mouth were a lie.

"I'm working for the Tillman family, the guy who—"

"I know. He's the guy that cold-hearted bitch and her partner left to die. Can you believe that shit? I can't help thinkin' what if that was my mom or one of my kids. If it was someone from Tillman's family that clipped her, I can't say I'd blame 'im."

"Nice."

"I'm just sayin' is all . . ."

"It's okay. Will you help me?" I changed gears.

"Anyway I can."

My instinct was right. If I'd told him the truth, he'd have closed his shell tighter than any clam he had on ice at the raw bar. In New York City, Alta Conseco, even in death, was as popular as Ebola.

"Were you here that night?"

"I was. Wasn't supposed to be, but my manager called in sick and I filled in," Nick said.

"Anything unusual about that night . . . I mean, before the murder?"

"Nah, nothing. Typical night. A little slow, if anything. Then all hell breaks loose." He stood up from the table and walked toward the entrance of the Grotto. I followed. "She collapsed right here, bleedin' like crazy. One of my guys called 911, but she bled out before he hung up the phone. The fuckin' bodies, man, that's what I couldn't take when we was on the job. Remember the smell when we'd find some old guy who'd been dead for a week in a hot apartment?" He mumbled something in Greek and crossed himself.

"She say anything before she died?"

"*Ouch!*" Nick laughed. "Sorry, I shouldn't make fun. I didn't know who she was then."

"Hers wasn't the first body to turn up here."

"Nope. She was the first since we bought the place, but there were others. I hate to say it, Moe, but the violence is one of the things that made this place a legend. We get a lot of people who come to sit at the table where Jimmy 'Dollar Menu' DePodesta took two in the head. Some of 'em even order what Jimmy was eatin' that night. There was that biker from the Druids who was beaten to death by the Suicide Kings and that black kid that got hit by the car and landed over there when the Ricans were chasing him outta the projects. If people wanna come here for those reasons and not the pizza, what can I say? It's sick, but it's business."

I just shook my head no, but he was right. "You don't have to tell me," I said. "My brother and I have been in business for almost thirty-two years now and we've had to do some stuff to keep afloat that I'm not so proud of. Business is a strange kind of beast: a predator, scavenger, and a prey animal all at once. To keep it going, you've got to use what works, even if you gotta hold your nose while you do it."

We spent about another half hour together. He let me talk to the staff who'd been there the night Alta was murdered. Not surprisingly, none of them heard or saw anything. They were busy. After all, Alta had died at the Grotto, but she wasn't stabbed there. Nick gave me the cards of the detectives who'd questioned him and burned me a disk of the surveillance video from that night. He sent me on my way with a pistachio gelato and a promise to get together soon. At least the gelato was tangible. The promise was something else altogether, something meant at the moment it was uttered, but something that would soon be forgotten. I'd made a thousand such unfulfilled promises in my lifetime without a second thought. The bill for them was about to come due.

SEVEN

Some things it's just better not to know. Like about mermaids, for instance. As a kid, I loved the notion of mermaids and of sirens singing suicide songs to ancient sailors. The images of beautiful winged or fish-tailed women luring men to their deaths were potent things in the head of a teenage boy. But somebody's always waiting to piss on your fantasies. I don't think I'll ever get over Mr. Blumenthal, my ninth-grade English teacher, pissing on mine. He delighted in explaining to the class that those svelte and seductive mermaids of myth were really just dugongs, sea cows, manatees. That, as he put it, a peculiar quirk of dugong and human female anatomy combined with the deprivation and desperation of men who had been too many years on the bounding main led to the stories of sea maidens and sirens. So it was with the image of blunt-nosed and blubbery sea cows that I was confronted when I had to walk a beat on Mermaid Avenue in Coney Island. And now, parked as I was in front of Brooklyn South Homicide on Mermaid Avenue, I was confronted with those images yet again. I hesitated outside the door, remembering that there were some things it was just better not to know.

The detective in charge of the Alta Conseco case was a hotshot named Jean Jacques Fuqua. Fuqua was a dark-skinned black man in his mid-thirties. He was six-two if an inch, with shoulders so broad it looked like the hanger was still inside his light pink shirt. He was handsome, with a mouth full of white teeth, a flat nose, and

31

dazzlingly bright eyes. He spoke fairly formal English with just a pinch of Port-au-Prince. I wasn't surprised. There was a huge Haitian community in Brooklyn and it was only a matter of time until Haitians, like every immigrant group before them, began moving up the ranks of the NYPD.

I hadn't been looking at a mirror when my oncologist gave me the bad news, but I imagine my expression wasn't too dissimilar from Fuqua's when I told him who I was and why I was there. There had been a time when I would have simply whipped out my old badge or my license—still lost in my condo somewhere—or mentioned all my friends who were now bosses in the department, but the shelf life on all of those options had expired. I was over sixty years old and flashing my tin or my PI license would have seemed pathetic, and I wasn't in the mood to get laughed at. Is anybody ever in the mood to get laughed at? And those friends of mine who had ascended the brass ladder were now either dead, disgraced, or retired. I had about as much pull in the NYPD as a three-legged draft horse.

"So, Mr. . . . Prager," he said, voice drifting off as he looked down at my card. "Someone has asked you to look into the Conseco homicide, but you will not say whom nor why. Well, *mon ami*, I don't know who you think you are, but that is not the way it works. You have some information for me, I will be quite overjoyed to listen, but this is not a two-way street."

"Two-way street, huh? Nice to see you've mastered the art of the cliché."

If I thought that was going to endear me to Fuqua, I was wrong.

"Here are a few old phrases you may be familiar with, Mr. Prager. Fuck you and farewell."

"Yeah, I've heard those once or twice."

"You understand them, *non?*"

"Yes."

"Then why do you continue standing here?"

"Because a little professional courtesy might be nice."

"Professional courtesy! You must have wandered into the wrong office. We do not process Medicare claims here." His mocking laugh was fingernails on the blackboard. "Shoo, Mr. Prager, before I lose my patience and respect for my elders."

As a last resort, I reached around my back for my badge, but the leather case never made it out of my pocket. Another detective walked over to Fuqua's desk. I recognized his face. I drew a blank on his name. I wasn't sure his presence was going to improve things with Fuqua, but I figured, what the hell, they couldn't get much worse.

"Moses Prager, isn't it?" He held his hand out to me and said, "Sherman, Detective Sherman. I worked the—"

"—Tierney homicide," I said, shaking his hand and finishing his sentence. "I thought I recognized you."

Sherman was shorter, paler, and thinner than Fuqua, but had a few years on him. Detective Sherman was all handshakes and smiles now. It wasn't that way when we'd met two years ago, when he, two other detectives, and an assistant district attorney took turns interviewing me for hours on end.

"You know who this guy is, Frenchie?" Sherman looked to Fuqua, who frowned at being called Frenchie. Sherman didn't care and he didn't wait for an answer. "Mr. Prager here is not only an ex-cop, but a certified USDA hero."

By the sour look on Fuqua's face, it was difficult to tell whether he was simply unimpressed or still getting over Sherman calling him Frenchie. Cops are asshole geniuses. They are brilliant at finding their fellow cops' buttons and then pushing them really, really hard. That much hadn't changed since I was a cop. On the job, you either get past your sore spots or life can be pretty fucking miserable. Almost everyone toughens to the constant button pushing, but I had my doubts about Fuqua. He looked like a proud son of a bitch who didn't give up on things very easily.

Sherman was undaunted. "A few years back—you were probably still in uniform, giving out parking tickets—this little girl artist got snatched. Her name was Sashi Bluntstone. You remember hearing about it?" Fuqua deigned to nod yes. "Anyways, we thought we had the guy who did it, some nut job named Tierney who lived over in Gerritsen Beach. Well, Prager didn't buy it and proved us wrong. He saved the girl and this department a lot of embarrassment, so maybe you wanna give the man a break instead of busting his balls."

Detective Fuqua didn't exactly give me a standing ovation, but he did begin tapping his keyboard. Over his shoulder, he said, "Thank you for the testimonial, Sherman." Then Fuqua stopped typing, turning around to face the other detective. "And Sherman, watch your mouth or we shall have some business together. Now you may leave us alone."

"Yeah, well, fuck you, Frenchie, and help the man." Sherman walked away, laughing. It was whistling in the graveyard. He would have been no match for Fuqua. I know I wouldn't have wanted to tangle with him even in my younger, fitter days.

"Frenchie Fuqua was a pretty good running back for the Pittsburgh Steelers in the '70s. He was just as famous for his style off the field as his play on the field," I said when Sherman was out of earshot. "You shouldn't let him see he gets to you like that."

"I shall take it under advisement. So, what is it you wish to know?"

"Everything, for starters."

That got a smile. He pulled a chair over next to his, motioning for me to sit. I hesitated, thinking once again about things it was better not to know.

EIGHT

As usual, I wasn't following my own rules. I'd been determined to keep Tillman's death discreet from Alta's murder, but there I was outside Maya Watson's condo door.

In the end, Fuqua was very cooperative, but he didn't actually have much to share. Nobody was talking because, as I suspected, there was nothing much to say. The statements taken by the cops at the Grotto, most of which I'd already seen, were from people who basically watched Alta die. One minute they were eating their pizza and the next minute a woman in blood-soaked clothing collapsed to the concrete. No one had witnessed the crime itself and none of the very few leads Fuqua had developed had come to anything. Most of what the detective had for me was all rather clinical and sterile. Alta, like all victims, had been reduced to a statistic, a batch of test results, a group of crime scene and autopsy photos. Only in the hearts and minds of those closest to them do victims remain themselves. And even then, not always or forever.

"Let us be honest, Mr. Prager, the night of the homicide was my only real opportunity. Now that everyone knows the identity of the victim, no one will come forward. Rightly or wrongly, people feel as if she has received what she had coming her," said the detective.

"I didn't know Haitians believed in karma."

"Haitians believe in pain and suffering. They are experiences we are very familiar with."

"Do you feel that Alta Conseco got what she had coming?"

"I am not the judge of such things. To me, all victims are equal in murder."

As ultimately cooperative as he was, Fuqua could not supply a sense of who Alta Conseco had been. There was nothing unexpected in that. A homicide detective handles dozens of cases in a year and even the most dedicated ones don't really know the victims. I guess maybe because I was a stumbler and didn't approach cases with a logical game plan, I needed a hook, a connection, a feel for Alta. The saddest part of all this was that I couldn't go to her sister to get it. For although Alta and Carmella shared genetics and a family resemblance, they had shared very little else for going on three decades. As soon as Carmella could legally change her name and leave her family behind, she did. Her paternal grandmother, her *abuela*, had been the only person who kept Carm tethered to her family, and her grandmother had died many years ago. In the years we spent together as friends, as business partners, as lovers, Carmella's self-imposed exile from her family was the one taboo subject between us.

So I was forced to turn to Maya Watson, Alta Conseco's partner on the job and in infamy. I drew some rather suspicious and unwelcoming stares from her neighbors who had no doubt grown weary and wary of strangers. Many of the TV news reports I'd watched on the net were remotes done right outside this condo. Several of those remotes featured hair-sprayed blondes in makeup masks and million-dollar mouths, giving over-rehearsed, falsely earnest spiels in front of rows of protesters. It had probably been a circus around here for weeks. The news vans, blondes, and protesters were gone, but I could still sense them. It was as if they had bruised the atmosphere and it would take time to recover and forget.

Maya Watson came to the door, but did not let me in, not at first. Who could blame her? I felt her eye on me as she spoke to me through the front door.

"Go away. I ain't got what you're looking for, mister." Her voice was somehow tentative and defiant all at once.

"How do you know what I want?"

"What you want is what everybody else wants and I can't give it. You don't move away from this here door, I'm dialing 911. You hear me?"

That was my opening, the one opportunity for my old badge to do me some good. By the time Maya Watson processed that I was twenty years too old to be what my badge claimed I was, I'd be inside her apartment.

"No need to dial," I said, holding my badge up to the peephole.

I listened to her undo the deadbolt and chain and waited for the door to pull back. It didn't take long, but when the door opened, it opened only slightly so that I had to enter sideways. Maya Watson was nowhere to be seen. The apartment was dimly lit and the shadows stank of stale coffee and cigarettes, lots of cigarettes. Maya Watson had been shielding herself with the door and closed it quickly behind me. Not surprisingly, the burning stub of a cigarette was stuck between her elegant brown fingers. Her hand shook just enough to be noticeable.

"Come in the kitchen," she said and led the way.

Her looks—a striking mixture of African and European features— both defined and defied the label African-American. She was pretty enough in the photos I'd seen of her, but she was more attractive in person. This in spite of the obvious toll the last few months had taken on her. In her thirties and taller than I expected, she was athletically slender and wore her tightly curled hair short to her head. Her medium brown skin was taut over mile-high cheekbones. She had a gently sloping nose and angular jawline. Her lips were full without being showy, but the stars of the show were her hazel green eyes. Yet, in spite of her natural beauty, she was practically aging before my eyes.

"You're no cop," she said, resigned to the fact that I was already in her house.

"Used to be along time ago, probably before you were born. Do you know who Carmella Melendez is?" I asked.

"Alta's little sister, but what's that got to do with me?"

"Probably nothing. Listen, this may not mean anything to you, but my name is Moe Prager. Carmella and me—"

"—were married and business partners once."

I was stunned. "How can you know that?"

"Carmella abandoned her family, but Alta never abandoned her. She told me she was very proud of her little sister and had followed her career as a detective and all. She had a scrapbook and everything. Don't look so surprised, Mr. Prager—"

"Moe. Please, call me Moe."

"Don't be so surprised, Moe. When you were a cop, didn't you and your partner ride a lot of miles stuck in a car together? What did you guys talk about?"

"Women mostly."

She laughed, her smile lighting up the room. Still, it seemed almost painful for her, like she was out of practice. "No, seriously, Moe."

"We told stories, talked about our families, talked sports, politics."

"Us too," she said. "Alta and I spent a lot of hours together talking."

"Alta told you a lot, but did she tell you why Carmella changed her name and broke away from her family?" I asked.

That wiped away any last traces of a smile from Maya Watson's face. The air went out of her as if I'd sucker punched her in the belly. She dropped the cigarette into an old cup of coffee and we listened to its death hiss. She lit another. Yeah, the last few months had taken a toll on her nerves. I repeated the question.

"That her mama was ashamed of her on account of her getting raped as a little girl, that their mama blamed her." Maya bowed her head. "Shame is a powerful thing, Moe, a powerful thing."

She was right about the power of shame. Problem was that these days, no one seemed capable of feeling it. That didn't seem to be one of Maya Watson's issues. Apparently, whatever had gone on with Tillman had stirred up a lot of shame in her. After a few more puffs on the cigarette, she looked up at me.

"But what are you doing here anyway? You didn't come here to talk about Carmella."

"In a way, I did. Carm was the one who asked me to look into Alta's murder."

"She's a little late to the game, don't you think? She might'a thought about doing something for Alta when she was alive. Like when her face was plastered all over the news. Alta could've used some support then."

"Maybe you're right, Maya. Carmella's wounds are old and deep, but I think she's feeling thirty years of guilt and loss all at once. I guess there's plenty of shame to go around these days."

"Carmella's shame won't do Alta no good now."

"Like I said, maybe you're right to be so hard on Carmella, but I had an old friend who survived Auschwitz. He had every right in the world to be angry and judgmental, but he was slow to judge and when he did judge, he never did it harshly. 'Look in the mirror,' he used to say, 'then judge.' Besides, I'm here, not Carmella, and I need your help."

She dropped the second cigarette into the coffee and gestured for me to sit at the table. When I sat, she sat.

"What do you need?" she asked.

"Whatever you can give me. I need a sense of who Alta was. What kind of men did she date? What did she love? What did she hate? That sort of thing."

Maya Watson didn't need any further prompting. She spoke for nearly forty minutes, stopping only to breathe and light up cigarettes. Alta was tough. She had to be. Female EMTs were now going through what women cops had gone through in the seventies and eighties. And minority women . . . forget about it. You had to be three times as good at your job just to tread water. Alta had taken Maya under her wing and had protected her from the worst parts of the job. Like Carmella, Alta had a temper, but was fierce and fiercely loyal. Alta would take a bullet for someone. She loved movies and detective novels and Indian food. But Alta was pretty secretive about who she dated. Eventually, Maya ran out of steam. Tears formed in the corners of her otherworldly eyes.

"What is it?" I asked, gently laying a hand on her shoulder.

"I couldn't go to her funeral and I've had to grieve Alta here, alone. I've been cooped up in this place for weeks with only my thoughts and my cigarettes. When I went back to work after the suspension, they put me on sick leave and told me I was bad for the morale of the department. I miss her. Can you understand how much I miss her?"

I thought of Sarah and noticed my hand on my abdomen. "I think I can. I really think I can."

"The cops won't find her killer, will they?" she asked, wiping away the tears with her thumb.

"I'm not so sure," I said. "The detective in charge of the investigation—"

"Fuqua?"

"Yes, Fuqua. He strikes me as a stubborn motherfu—as a stubborn man who doesn't give up on things so easily. Also strikes me as the kind of person who doesn't give a shit about what other people think."

"That's good?"

"In a detective, yeah. Carmella is like that."

"And you?"

"Me too, I guess."

"Did Alta have any enemies, spurned lovers, anyone you can think of who might have wanted her dead?"

Maya Watson broke into a jag of manic laughter so removed from joy that I was frightened for her. All this time alone was doing her a lot of harm.

"Enemies! You want to see some enemies?" She disappeared from the room and came back carrying two cardboard boxes stacked in her arms. She dropped them to the floor, sheets of paper spilling onto the tiles. "You talk about hate mail."

I picked up the sheets that had fallen out of the boxes and looked at the top one. The author had managed to use the words *nigger*, *spic*, and *cunts* in the first sentence. I stopped reading. I was quick on the uptake.

"Not exactly love sonnets, Moe. No one comparing me and Alta to a rose or a summer's day."

"You showed these to the police?"

"Every single one. This is nothing. These are just the ones off the net that I printed out. The newspeople and the crowds of people are gone from outside since Alta was killed, but these just keep coming in. I used to think potential was the greatest untapped thing in the world, but it isn't. It's hate. People got all kinds of hate in them."

"I know it. Do you mind if I take some of these?"

"Sure, go ahead."

The time had come, I thought, to broach the subject of Robert Tillman's death. "Do you think Alta's murder is connected to what happened with Tillman?"

"I can't talk about that."

"But—"

"I can't talk about it and I won't."

Her face got hard and determined. I wasn't going to get anywhere with her like this and didn't want to risk alienating her. She'd given me some sense of Alta, enough of one to start with, at least, but I might need Maya's insights again.

"Okay. Thanks."

"I don't know how much help I was," she said.

"I don't know either, but it's a start. Alta is real to me now and that's something."

Maya showed me to the door, the box of letters in my arms unexpectedly heavy. Whether that was a matter of physics or hate, I couldn't yet say.

NINE

I had intended to head back to my house or to one of the stores' offices to read through Maya Watson's hate mail, but I didn't feel like running into my brother Aaron. For all of his mishegas and obsession with the business, Aaron was an observant bastard and had recently commented on my weight loss and rather pale complexion. Besides, I had less and less patience for Aaron's craziness these days. We were both getting old and old men get cranky. An indirect blessing of Sarah's wedding was that I had three weeks off from work. No need, I thought, to risk having to lie to my big brother about the thing that was probably going to kill me. If he ever found out, he would just make me feel guilty for abandoning him and I already felt guilty enough for a thousand other things. And there was something else, something that stuck with me. Maya Watson had taken pains to mention how hard it had been for her and Alta at work.

I remembered how women cops were hazed and abused and basically tortured when I was on the job in the early seventies. It wasn't trial by fire. It was trial by inferno—all of it done with the winking approval of the brass. They were going to show those broads that police work was man's work. I remembered the stories Carmella told me about what she suffered through in uniform and then when she made detective. I'd witnessed some of it myself, how she was disrespected, disregarded, and treated, as she so indelicately put it, like pussy on the hoof. Most of the guys eventually came around,

if grudgingly, but some never did. A few of them took it person-
ally and made weeding women out of the job their own private
crusade. The more isolated these guys got, the more determined
they became. It took a long time for the NYPD to change, but it
changed. Walk into Times Square and look around. The people in
those dark blue uniforms with badges on their chests look freshly
minted from the UN. They're men and women. They're Asian and
Hispanic. They're African-American, Arab-American, and the chil-
dren of Russian immigrants. They're Irish, Italian, and Jewish kids
from the suburbs.

The FDNY was more like the Catholic Church. Change, when
it came at all, came slowly, very slowly. During my days as a cop,
the FDNY was almost entirely male, largely Irish, and if not quite
a private club, then something pretty close. I'm no sociologist, but
I think the pace of change had a lot to do with the way firehouses
were set up. They're small, close-knit units. Firemen live, eat, work,
and sleep together for days at a time. Guys in a precinct can be close,
but firemen are closer. Cops always talk about trusting other cops to
have their backs, but trust between firefighters is even more crucial,
because, let's face it, it's a more dangerous job. It was easy to understand how any foreign presence in a firehouse—most especially a
woman's—would be perceived as a threat.

As I adjusted my plans and my car's direction in kind, I realized
I was falling victim to the very thing I had vowed to avoid: linking
Alta's murder to Tillman's death. Whether it suited me or not, if
things were taking me in that direction, I had to follow. That's the
trouble with being a stumbler. I had no surefire methods to fall back
on. So I drove down through the trench of the Brooklyn-Queens
Expressway and up onto the Gowanus Expressway. *Expressway, my
ass!* In New York City, there's nothing express about expressways.

Finbarr McPhee's Brass Pole was a famous tavern in the shadow of the Verrazano Narrows Bridge in the Bay Ridge section of Brooklyn. The joint had built its rep on two things: the biggest selection of Irish bottled and tap beers in all of New York City and the biggest collection of firemen east of the Mississippi. Just as there were cop bars, there were firemen bars. Finbarr McPhee's—no one who knew better called it the Brass Pole—was top of the pops in this select group of public houses. Firemen came here to hang from all over the city and Long Island and they didn't come for the Guinness, Harp, Smithwick's, or Jameson Irish whiskey. They came to talk shop and swap war stories, sure, but mostly they came for the women.

That's right, the women. Rock stars have groupies, but folks in uniform have a fair amount of their own. Shit, I knew a few sanitation guys who swore they had groupies too. I think the one exception to the rule of uniform attraction was traffic enforcement agents—meter maids as we were once wont to call them in the unenlightened days before men hired on. Everybody hates meter maids, Paul McCartney and lovely Rita notwithstanding. Although I did once have a date who asked to see my gun, it took a long time for me to come to terms with the attraction to the uniform. It was only later, when I was off the job for many years, that I came to see what the groupies were all about. The revelation was that the attraction wasn't strictly about one thing.

Some of the women had the jones for the uniform or the perceived danger inherent in the job. They fetishized the trappings of the job: with cops it was the badge, the gun, the cap, the cuffs; with firemen it was the boots, the helmet, the axe. They got off on hearing the stories about life on the streets or responding to fires. But for some of the women, it was less about partying than pragmatism. It was about a solid future, a husband due fifty-two paychecks a year, medical benefits, and a killer pension. Because of their work schedule, firemen could work second jobs. Every fireman I ever knew held down a side gig or owned part of a business. Yeah, it was the end of the first decade of the twenty-first century and the world was barely recognizable to me anymore, but there were some things I hoped had remained constant. When I walked into Finbarr's and saw the ratio of women to men, I was happy to see that not every-thing in the world had changed.

It was still relatively early, but the place was packed. A lot of the men were in their twenties and thirties, but not all. There were plenty of older shaved heads and gray hairs too. There were even some relics as old or older than myself. *Imagine that.* Some guys can just never let go of the job and drinking with the kids who were still working helped keep them connected. Cop bars were like this too and just like in cop bars, the young guys steered well clear of the old-timers. The young guys were there to drink and hit on women, not to listen to stories about how the job used to be back in the day or what happened ten or twenty or thirty years ago. The ages of women also spanned a wide spectrum. They were mostly young, pretty, and eager. But there were plenty of emotional battle scars on the faces of the older men and women. Mixed in with the smells of stout and whiskey, perfume and cologne, were the darker grace notes of disappointment and regret.

There was something else too, something that hovered like a shroud over the flirtatious smiles and touches, over the beery laughter and the too-loud music pumping out of the CD jukebox. It was a shroud like the eight-hundred-pound gorilla in the room that everyone fought to ignore, but everyone knew was there just over your shoulder. It was the wall of honor listing the names of the men who had died in the line of duty. It was 9/11. And if you listened just closely enough, you could still hear the echoes of the Twin Towers collapsing and the screams of the firefighters who died that day. My mind flashed back to the Halloween Parades after AIDS had cut a deadly swath through the gay community. How the parades went on and everyone tried to be happy, but whatever happiness people mustered only seemed to make the sadness that much worse.

On the way over, I hoped I'd catch a break like I had with Nick Roussis at the Grotto. That there would be a friendly face at McPhee's, someone I knew from the job, the stores, or from having lived in Brooklyn my whole life. No such luck. There were a lot of familiar types, but not a soul I recognized. So I went for my next best option. I found the sourest, loneliest old-timer in the place and headed straight for him. He was over at the corner of the bar where it met the back wall. Everything about him, from his gray stubble to his untidy shirt and permanent sneer, screamed grumpy old prick. And if I needed any further proof, the empty barstool next to him was the only empty seat in the whole place.

"Fucking rap music," I groused, pulling in next to him. "I can't hear myself think. Whatever happened to real music like the Beatles or the Stones?" I made sure not to look at him and to seem like I was talking more to myself than to him.

I threw a fifty on the bar, caught the bartender's eye, pointed at the Guinness tap, held up one finger, and waited. Guinness takes a while to pour properly, so I had time to get my new friend going if the line about the music hadn't gotten his attention. Turned out I didn't need the extra time.

"Fuckin' A," he said. "It's not rap, it's crap." His voice was a boozy rasp: Bronx Irish with a heavy dose of Staten Island. "Used to play the bass in a band up in Pelham in the sixties. Man, we played the Beatles, the Four Seasons, even a little Motown. But, Jesus, this stuff! We used to get all the girls we could handle too."

I turned to face him and offered my hand. "Moe Prager."

He said his name was Flannery. He had a grip like a car crusher and breath like a distillery. I offered to buy him a drink and he didn't say no. I had the barman bring him a Jameson while I sipped at my stout. My oncologist had warned me against drinking, but fuck me if I was going to be a monk. I had months of surgery, radiation, and chemo ahead of me and I was still probably a goner. I wasn't going to be one of those poor schmucks who stopped living in order to die.

"What are you doing here, Prager? You don't look like one of us."

I knew what he meant. "Ex-cop, but some of my best buds were firemen and it's been a long time since I was in here." The former was a lie, but not the latter. I had been to McPhee's before, a long long time ago. I'd also been vague enough to let Flannery's imagination fill in the blanks.

"Cop, huh? Suppose it's okay since you sprung for the drink." He laughed at his own sense of humor and I pretended to.

"Yeah, I worked the Six-O in Coney Island with a firehouse right next door. We got on like lions and hyenas."

"That good, huh?"

I laughed again, only this time I meant it. Cops and firemen had this inbred rivalry that went back forever and persisted to the present. Who were the bravest? Whose underpayment was more egregious? Who did the city shaft more often? Who could piss farther? It was like that.

By his third drink on me, Flannery had told me a few hundred war stories—at least it seemed that way—and had begun grousing about how the world and the job had changed and, in his opinion, not for the better. I subtly egged him on, though he didn't really need any encouragement. Just when I was about to introduce the subject of Alta and Maya's alleged dereliction of duty, Flannery made a trip to the bathroom. The business at the bar slowed down momentarily and I waved the barman over. I had him bring another round.

"So what's my drinking mate's story?" I asked the bartender—a guy about my age—when he brought the drinks.

"Flannery? He's a pain in the balls, but make no mistake, the man's a hero."

"Him? Get the fuck outta here."

"I shit you not. Remember how bad things were in the ghettos in the early '70s?" he asked. "I was on the job then too, a ladder company in Brownsville. We used to get pelted with bricks and bottles on nearly every night run we made in them days. Trust me, it didn't fill me heart with love for those people. We were targets for their anger. Flannery, after getting hit in the head by a brick, made the best rescue anyone ever saw. It's fucking legendary. Singlehandedly saved five kids, their parents, and a cat from a kerosene heater blaze that lit up the building like tissue paper. Kept running in and out of a building he had no business going into in the first place. I know he can be a ornery bastard, but that bastard won the James Gordon Bennett Medal. That's the highest honor the department bestows and it ain't given out like Halloween candy. Just don't mention it or tell him I told you. He hates talking about it. Okay, here he comes."

Flannery sat back down beside me and made quick work of the Jameson. He nodded at the barman. "Big-mouthed son of a bitch bartender told you, didn't he? About the medal, I mean. Don't deny it. I seen that look on your face. I seen it plenty. *How can a broken-down drunk slob like Flannery be a hero?*"

"Don't get mad at him. I asked about you."

"Yeah, well, we'll get on fine, you and me, as long as we don't talk about that."

That was my opening.

"Fine. Then let's talk about something else."

"Like what?"

Finally, a song I knew came on. "Paradise By The Dashboard Light" played and most of the crowd in Finbarr's was singing along. I had to shout at Flannery to be heard.

"Like about the two EMTs that let that guy die in the city."

I guess I was a little too successful at being heard. Before Flannery could say a word, a heavy hand slammed down on my shoulder and it stayed there. The guy attached to the other end of it walked around in front of me. He was twenty-five with dark red hair, a healthy mustache, and light blue eyes shot with blood. He had the look of a man who'd been drinking for a few hours and was spoiling to flex his beer muscles.

"What are you, another fucking reporter here to stir up the shit?"

"No, I'm a man having a private conversation," I said, calm but serious. "Now if you don't mind, please get your hand off my shoulder."

"But I do mind, motherfucker!" He turned his attention on Flannery. "Don't talk to this asshole. He's looking to bury us."

Flannery didn't answer right away, but I was losing patience.

"Listen, I asked you politely to move your hand off my shoulder and got called a motherfucker for my trouble. Now I'm not asking, I'm telling you. Get your fucking hand off my shoulder."

"And if I don't?"

By now, the rest of the bar had stopped singing and focused their eyes on us. Not good. With an audience, there was no way for this guy to back down and save face. His friends started egging him on. *Kick the old guy's ass, Hickey. Come on, Hickey, fuck him up.* And so it went.

I may have been an old man in his eyes, but I stopped taking shit from morons like Hickey when I was eight years old. And there was this other thing: I was carrying. My old .38 was holstered in the small of my back and I could have it sticking under Hickey's chin in a second or two. I waited a beat to give him a chance to back off. He didn't avail himself of the opportunity. No surprise there. So I reached around under my jacket, but my hand never made halfway to my holster. Flannery had a hold of my wrist and when he had hold of something, it stayed held. I looked his way and he shook his head no. I nodded that I understood and he let go. Before I could exhale, Flannery was out of his seat and had his left hand around Hickey's throat.

"Listen, pup, what me and my friend choose to discuss is none of your fucking business. You ever interrupt me or lay a hand on a friend again and I'll make sure you get your medical pension in a hurry. Do you take my meaning, son?" He squeezed a little tighter as he asked. Hickey nodded that he understood. "Smart lad. Now my friend and I are leaving. I turn around and even sniff you behind us, I'll snap your arm off." He let go of Hickey.

I thanked the barman and left the change as a tip. Outside, I asked Flannery why he stopped me from teaching Hickey a lesson.

"Because we police our own," he said. "Now let's find a place to do some proper drinking."

And so we did.

TEN

Flannery knew a real neighborhood bar not two blocks from Finbarr McPhee's. The kind of place where they played Sinatra on the jukebox and the jukebox still played vinyl records. It was the kind of place that had a name, but you didn't need to know it because you knew where it was and what it was about. And what it was about was beers and shots of whiskey, a pool table, a dart board, and one old TV that hadn't worked in years. Nobody came here to hit on babes or to impress anyone at all. It was a bar for men to drink in and to be comfortable doing so.

The bartender knew Flannery, which didn't exactly shock me. I supposed most of the bartenders in Bay Ridge knew him. I gestured to a booth. Flannery wasn't having any. He preferred sitting at the bar and that was fine with me. I took out another fifty and ordered a Jameson and a Guinness. I think I'd managed two sips of my first Guinness at McPhee's and never got to the second. I meant to actually drink this pint. My drinking buddy had no trouble finishing his and made quick work of his whiskey. I figured that since he'd just saved my ass or saved me from making an ass of myself, I'd let him bring up the subject that had started all the trouble in the first place.

"You know why that pup got so agitated when you brought up the EMTs?" Flannery asked, his unfocused eyes aimed vaguely at the mirror behind the bar.

"I have some idea. They reflected badly on the department and all of that."

"That's part of it, but not nearly all. It's politics."

"What isn't?" I said, nodding for the barman to bring Flannery another.

"True enough, but this is ugly politics, internal politics. See, EMTs wear uniforms, but are civilian employees of the department. They're not firefighters like in other cities and they don't usually work out of the same houses that the men on the real job do. If an EMT wants to become a fireman, they gotta take a special test."

"I see. So even though these two women weren't on the job, the real firefighters get tainted by what they did. The public isn't big on making subtle distinctions."

"The media neither, but it's even more complicated than that, Moe." He looked around to make sure no one was in earshot. "Here's the deal. The department has never been the most welcoming place for certain kinds of people, if you catch my drift."

"I do."

"Going back to my days in the department, the blacks always sued over the test to get on the job, saying it discriminates against them. Even though I think that's all a crock of shit myself, when you look at the numbers. . . . And these days, the FDNY gets federal money too. So someone inside the union got the bright idea to get EMTs counted with the FDNY's numbers because a lot of the EMTs are women and minorities."

"Holy shit!"

"That's right, Moe. They wanna use the big minority numbers from the ranks of the EMTs to make the department's racial profile look better and more balanced for the feds and the courts, but they want them to remain civilian employees. Of course, the EMTs ain't exactly thrilled by this plan."

"There's a perverse kind of symmetry to that way of thinking. It unskews the curve, but without really changing anything."

"Bingo! When those two EMTs fucked up, they pissed everybody off. They really rocked the boat. It's a big-stakes game and everyone on all sides got a dog in the fight, so emotions are running high. People are edgy and like you found out back at McPhee's, just asking questions about it is risky business."

"Risky enough to get someone killed?"

Flannery didn't answer right away. I checked his eyes in the mirror. They were focused now, but seemed to be locked in on something in the distance, beyond my field of vision.

"Maybe," he said. "People don't think sometimes before they do shit. There's been a lot of grumbling. I think it's talk mostly, but let's face it, no one I know sent flowers or sympathy cards when that EMT got hers. Before you start pointing fingers, remember there are just as many EMTs as firemen pissed off at what those two did. Why do you care, anyhow? What's it to you?"

I figured I owed him the truth. "Alta Conseco, the EMT who was murdered, I was married to her little sister once. They were estranged for a long time and now I guess she feels sort of overwhelmed by guilt about all the time they lost."

"Guilt," he said, "a mighty curse to bear. I'll drink to that."

And drink he did, but he stopped talking. I finished my Guinness in silence and slid my card across the bar to Flannery.

"Leaving?"

"Yeah," I said, shaking his hand. "My stomach's killing me. Pleasure meeting you and thanks for saving my ass before."

"Forget it." When I turned to go, he called after me, waving my card between his fingers. "I hear anything, I'll call."

I nodded. As I walked to my car, I heard myself laughing. My stomach *was* killing me.

I didn't enjoy myself for very long because I got thumped in the ribs as I turned the corner to where my car was parked. The wind went out of me, my laughter transformed to gasping as I collapsed to the sidewalk. I suppose I might've tried to get up if I didn't get a kick in the back.

"Not so tough without your boyfriend to protect ya, are ya, old man?" It was Hickey.

I was preoccupied with trying to get my lungs restarted, so I didn't answer or reach for my .38. Breathing is easy to take for granted, but the rest of the machinery won't work without it. Funny, I thought about the tumor again, how it too was probably rooting for me to catch my breath. Nothing in this world likes getting cheated out of the chance to fulfill its destiny. It's pretty fucked up what you think about sometimes.

"Consider yourself warned, grandpa."

Grandpa. I couldn't help but wonder if I would ever hear that name spoken in love.

ELEVEN

I had two nasty bruises and a headache for my troubles. The hurt in my gut had diminished to the level I had grown accustomed to. The pain, which had so frightened me at first, was now just like background noise. Still, I couldn't sleep. The possible reasons were legion, so I didn't waste time considering them. What I did instead was read through a box full of hate mail. About halfway through, it occurred to me that people with hearts so full of hate must have no room in their brains for spelling or syntax. The drab sameness of the vulgarity and racism was mind-numbing. It was kind of like my pain; after a while it became noise. None of it made sense, really. Then again, when did reason ever have anything to do with racism or hate? It was a dumb question for a Jew to ask, even to himself. I imagined Mr. Roth showing me the number on his forearm and shaking his head at me in disapproval.

I pulled a few letters out of the pile. These were the ones that moved beyond simple expressions of hate or vague hopes for terrible fates to befall Alta and Maya and their families. They were the letters in which the writers made specific threats of violence, some alluding to stabbing and throat slitting. I wondered just how hard Detective Fuqua had worked at looking into the origin of these. As he said, many, if not most, New Yorkers felt as though Alta had gotten what she deserved. And no matter how determined Fuqua seemed, I doubted the NYPD was willing to spend the money and manpower it would take to investigate hundreds, maybe thousands of anonymous letters and emails. But things sent electronically weren't as anonymous as people thought. Sure, there were clever computer geeks and hackers who could bury their cyber-footprints, but I somehow doubted that people who could barely spell fuck or use it in a proper sentence were likely candidates for jobs at Intel, Cisco, or the NSA.

I called Brian Doyle's cell. Doyle was an ex-cop. When he was on the job, he had a nasty rep for taking shortcuts and dishing out uppercuts. He was a stubborn, impatient prick who liked using his knuckles more than his noggin, but what made him a bad cop helped make him a good PI. When Carm and I owned our security firm together, we took Brian on and made a damned fine investigator of him. Then in 2002, after Carm and I split and dissolved the partnership, Brian and our tech guy Devo opened up their own shop in lower Manhattan. They had helped me with the Sashi Bluntstone case and I was hoping they could help me again.

"What? It's three in the fucking morning," Brian answered with his usual Old World charm.

"You doing surveillance?"

"What the fuck else would I be doing answering my cell phone at three a.m.?"

"I don't know. Maybe you're just lonely."

"Loneliness was never my problem, Boss." Brian had never gotten out of the habit of calling me that. "So what can I do you for?"

"Can you meet me tomorrow? I got a job for you and Devo."

"Where and when?"

"Lunch at noon," I said. "You pick the place."

"O'Hearn's on Church Street. I'm in a corned beef and cabbage kinda mood."

"See you tomorrow."

Click.

I realized I hadn't called Pam or Sarah in a few days. I'd call Sarah in the morning. Although Pam was still a PI, she wasn't Brian Doyle's type of PI. She wasn't big on late-night surveillance, but she did kick the occasional ass. I wasn't going to risk waking her, not at this hour. So I looked out my front window at Sheepshead Bay and thought back to when I was a kid and crossing the Ocean Avenue footbridge over the bay to Manhattan Beach seemed like a walk into another world. I was thinking about that kind of walk a lot lately, a walk into another world.

TWELVE

Whereas Sarah was thrilled to hear from me and excited about the wedding, the edge to Pam's voice was about as subtle as a chainsaw. I didn't need to scratch too far below the surface to understand why. The edge was there when she first saw Carmella in my arms. Although Pam had done a good job of sheathing it during the party on Sunday, the edge was there again in our goodbyes that night. Funny how this woman, who never seemed threatened by anything or anyone, was so thrown off her game. It was worse now than on Sunday night because she'd been alone for a few days with time to think. That was the worst thing of all, time to think. Time to think is life's Petri dish. It's the medium in which a random twinge of anxiety morphs into debilitating self-doubt, where a passing regret grows into paralytic guilt. Since walking out of my oncologist's office, I'd become very familiar with the dangers of time to think. That's why Carmella's reappearance was saving me from eating myself alive before the cancer could. Problem was, until after the wedding, Pam couldn't know that the more immediate threat to the two years we'd spent together wasn't Carmella at all.

"Hey, how's the case going?" I asked, ignoring the edginess.

"Fine."

"Fine?"

"What do you want me to say? It's a case."

"Specificity, that's what I always loved about you."

"Loved?"

Shit! I'd been trying to walk on eggshells when it was actually a minefield I was walking through.

"Come on, Pam, cut it out."

"I'm sorry," she said, sounding like she meant it. "I'm just feeling off is all. Listen, I should be wrapping this job up by next Monday latest. You have off, right? Why not come up here a few days early and we can spend time drinking in bed? Besides, you've looked pretty stressed out lately and you haven't taken good care of yourself. Let me take care of you."

Talk about a minefield. Jesus! "As incredible as that sounds, I can't."

"Why not?"

"I'm working a case."

"A case? You haven't worked a case in two years and you're working one now, a few weeks before your daughter's wedding."

"That's about it, yeah."

"It's for *her*, isn't it? That's why she was there Sunday."

I decided that lying would only make things worse. "For Carmella? Yes, for her. It's complicated."

"No, it's not, Moe. It's not complicated at all."

"But it is."

"Then explain it to me."

"You know the EMT who let that guy die in the restaurant and then got stabbed to death in Brooklyn? Her name was Alta Conseco. She was Carmella's older sister."

"Christ! I never thought to put the names together."

Pam knew the whole story about Carmella and me, about how Carmella had changed her name from Marina Conseco, even about how Carmella had added the extra l in her new first name as a *fuck you* to her mother for the way she treated Carmella after being molested.

"So what are you supposed to do?" Pam asked.

"Like I said, it's complicated."

"So of all the cases in the world, you choose this one? You're going to spend the weeks before Sarah's wedding doing a favor for a woman who basically ran out on you and robbed a child from you? No, Moe, like I said, it's not complicated. It's just plain crazy."

"May well be."

"This Alta Conseco just let a man die, Moe."

"Allegedly."

"Bullshit. Everyone in the restaurant saw it happen. So what's the point here, Don Quixote? You going to resurrect a dead woman's reputation or are you looking for a little redemption because you still blame yourself for your first wife's murder?"

"A little bit of both, I guess."

"Well, call me when you get up here for the wedding. That's if you still want to take me instead of your great love."

"Now you're just being cruel, Pam."

"Am I? We'll see."

We would have to, because she was off the phone by the time I opened my mouth to say something.

. . .

O'Hearn's was one of many bars of its kind in New York City. It was Irish through and through and served a hearty, if not exactly gourmet, lunch for reasonable money. Most of the menu choices were laid out in aluminum pans recessed into two rows of steam tables, the steam bleaching out the color and flavor of nearly all the food. The vegetables in particular seemed most susceptible to the vagaries of over-warming. Somehow, my mother used to achieve the same results without resorting to steam. The best feature of lunch was the carving board. There was ham and corned beef every day, sometimes turkey and roast beef too. Since getting off the job in

1977, I'd only been to places like O'Hearn's twice: once with Francis Maloney Sr., my former father-in-law, and once with an ex-precinct mate of mine, Caveman Kenny Burton. In fact, I'd met Kenny here at O'Hearn's. They were both dead now: Francis a victim of old age and his own bile, Kenny a victim of a bullet. Jesus did a lot of dying for their sins. Neither was missed, certainly not by me.

Brian Doyle had a half-empty pint of Harp on the table when I walked in. He was a naturally lean and athletic man and hadn't put on an ounce since I met him. His hair was graying, but he still had the eyes of a kid. I bought us lunch before settling down to talk. I had some turkey and mashed potatoes and not much of either. Good to his word, he had corned beef and cabbage and boiled potatoes and another Harp. I'd always wondered how he could eat like that and stay slim. My guess was he had so much energy that he lost weight in his sleep.

"So what's the deal, Boss?"

I handed over a large yellow mailing envelope with copies of the hate mail that directly threatened violence. "I need you and Devo to trace these back to the senders."

Doyle took a look. His eyes got big, not from the harsh language or the racism—he'd be used to those—but from the names Alta Conseco and Maya Watson. I couldn't remember how much of the story he knew about the history between Carmella and me before we hired him, so I simply told Brian that Alta was Carm's sister.

"Still, Boss, this isn't a good idea."

"Don't worry, you guys won't be mentioned at all. I'm your client and that's that. Charge me whatever you have to charge me. No discounts."

"For swimming in this shit, you weren't gonna get one. But there's a problem I see already."

"What's that?"

He put one of the emails on the table and pointed at the addresses. "See here? There's only so much Devo can do with this. If we had access to the actual emails, Devo could probably do what you want."

"How's that?" I asked.

"Look, I'm not as IT-savvy as Devo by a long shot, but there are reveal codes you can use to unmask people trying to hide their email identities. So if you can get her to forward those emails to Devo . . ."

"I'll get them for you."

"How?"

"You let me worry about that, Brian."

"I almost wish you couldn't."

"Why?"

"You know I love you and Carmella. You guys saved my ass and taught me the ropes and everything, but this bitch Alta deserved what she got."

I thought about saying that no one deserved a violent death, but I didn't believe it, not for a second. I'd seen too much, lived through too much to think that there weren't some people, maybe only a very few, who warranted a violent end: Caveman Kenny Burton, for instance. Besides, I thought, when did deserving have anything to do with it?

"I owe it to Carm," I said, "and so do you. When you get the information I'm looking for, you can wash your hands of it."

He wasn't enthusiastic. "All right. Whatever."

"Another drink?"

"Nah, just let me know when you get what we need."

He stood to go, but I grabbed his arm.

"I think I'm dying, Brian." The words came out of my mouth involuntarily.

He sat back down. "What?"

"Stomach cancer."

"Jesus. Fuck!"

"Yeah, tell me about it."

"It's bad, huh?"

"It's not good."

"Why tell me? I was gonna do the job for you anyhow."

"It's not that, Brian. I would never manipulate a friend that way. Weird thing is, I wasn't going to say anything to anyone, but I think I would have exploded if I didn't tell somebody. I knew I could tell you. You can't say a word about it."

"Not to Devo?"

"I suppose you can tell him," I said. "But that's it."

"Okay, you got my word."

"Shit, Doyle, lighten up. I'm the one with the cancer. You look worse than me."

He stared at me for a long few seconds and said, "No, Boss, I don't."

After he left O'Hearn's, I watched him walk away down Church Street. I caught a reflection of myself in the window. He was right.

THIRTEEN

Maya Watson was less than thrilled about doing what I asked, saying that it seemed like getting dirty all over again. I thought that was sort of a strange thing to say, but I wasn't in her shoes. Reading the hate mail made me feel a lot of things—angry, shameful, disgusted, eventually bored—but not dirty. Then again, I was a third party and the hate and racism weren't directed at me. Who was I to judge? No matter, Maya said she'd take care of it as soon as she could.

In the meantime, I headed back to Bordeaux in Brooklyn to make sure the wine order for the wedding was ready for shipment up to Vermont. When Sarah and Paul first told me they were getting married in Vermont, I thought it was going to be a relaxed affair in a ski chalet or local bar somewhere. I nearly broke out in hives when they told me it was to be a black tie wedding at Paul's parents' country club. The last country club wedding I'd been to was in the early '80s, just after Katy's miscarriage. It was at that wedding that the seeds of Katy's murder were sown. It was impossible for us to know then that those seeds would take seventeen years to sprout and that when they did the world would fall in around us. It frightened me to think I had become my mother's son. Were we, like she believed, always just one breath short of disaster, one nightfall away from the sun's refusal to shine? Had she been right all along?

I was also kind of shocked that they had country clubs in Vermont or enough Jews and other ethnic groups to actually form them. What surprised me even more was that tuxedos weren't contraband. I mean, I enjoyed my time in Vermont. It was a lovely and serene place that made Brooklyn seem like an Earth colony on a distant planet in a far-flung galaxy, but it had its quirks. After only a few trips up there to visit Pam, I was convinced that it was against the law for men to trim their beards or to get a decent haircut. The state police clearly seized most shipments of women's makeup at the border and banned all fashion magazines from sale. Pam must have smuggled her clothes, jewelry, and makeup in under cover of darkness. The state bird was the Subaru Outback and you could get a thousand different varieties of granola or cheddar cheese at the local convenience store.

I thought about what Rico Tripoli, Paul's biological father, would have made of all this hoopla, of French wines and country clubs. Rico, like me, had grown up a poor schmuck in Brooklyn. In that Brooklyn, the Brooklyn of immigrant parents, sewer to sewer stickball games, and ring-a-levio, you didn't dream of country clubs or black tie weddings. Well, maybe Rico did, which is probably why his appetites destroyed him. That was the thing about Rico, he could never tell you exactly what he wanted, only that he wanted more of it than he already had. It was why he sold his soul several times over and so cheaply. The first time it was for his gold detective's shield. Then he sold that for cocaine gang money, and, eventually, for the cocaine itself. Funny thing is that when he wound up in prison, he somehow blamed me. I suppose I should forgive him for that. By then he had been so long without a soul that he had forgotten the meaning of love and friendship.

Bordeaux in Brooklyn on Montague Street was our second wine shop and the only one I really cared for at all. The wine business paid my bills, sent Sarah to college and helped buy her vet practice, yet even now, it meant very little to me. The business had been my brother's dream, not mine. All I did was invest some money and go along for the ride. I hadn't ever really invested, not emotionally. Over thirty years in the business and I didn't give a shit. And if I hadn't cared up to now, dying wasn't going to make me see the light. All I could see was the time I'd wasted, the things I hadn't done. When I was gone, all that would be remembered of me was that I had been a shopkeeper. Does anyone dream of being a shopkeeper? Does anyone dream of dying as one?

I'd done a lot of thinking lately about the *what ifs* in my life. What if I hadn't slipped on that piece of carbon paper in the squad room in 1977 and torn my knee to shreds? That was the *what if* that really haunted me. Of the many things that had befallen me, that one careless step changed my life more than any other single incident before or since. Owing to my wrecked knee, the NYPD forced me into early retirement. From that day forward I limped down the road previously not taken until that road had taken me. Where would I be? Who would I be? What would I be? See, it's like what I said about asking *why me?* Once you start, you can never stop asking. Signs that read *Watch Your Step* meant more to me than a simple warning.

The trucking company arrived soon after I finished checking the wine order. I watched it loaded into the semi's box, then watched it disappear down Montague Street into the wilds of Cadman Plaza and beyond. I thought about heading back into Manhattan—only a very short ride over the nearby Brooklyn Bridge—and over to the High Line Bistro. Since, in spite of my better instincts, it seemed I was buying into the connection between Robert Tillman's death and Alta Conseco's murder, I supposed it was time to look into that aspect of things. But no, I wasn't up for it today. I wasn't up for pretending, for lying to people who would invest their trust in me when I told them I was a cop or an insurance man or a PI employed by the lawyers representing the Tillman family.

I'm not one of those people who much believes in the truth as an imperative or an elixir. If anything, it had been my experience that the plain truth often made things worse, much worse. It sure as shit didn't set you free. But I'd come to think that there *was* a price to be paid for lies. Not a price come judgment day with God as the cosmic accountant, having kept the ledger of sins great and small. Nor am I saying there's any individual cost to the liar him- or herself. It's a common cost, a price we all pay. Each uncovered lie is a corrosive thing, eating away at whatever trust there is left that binds us together. Without trust, we have nothing, and I just wasn't in the mood to add to the weakening of those bonds, not today.

. . .

McPhee's wasn't exactly hopping in mid-afternoon. I don't know. I guess I went looking for trouble, half-hoping that asshole Hickey would be there and I could embarrass him in front of his friends or better yet, a woman. I also wanted to see Flannery again. I liked the guy for having the *cojones* to be honest with me when it would have been easier to just let it be. There was something else about him too. He had the sadness in him, the demons. Fuck if I knew that was why he drank. There are a thousand reasons for a man to drink and only some of them have to do with tamping down the demons. I was curious about why he didn't want to talk about his heroics and why he was so eager to drink to guilt. Guilt, now there was a subject I knew a little something about. Maybe I was looking for answers in him for the questions in me. Short of running into my attacker or seeing Flannery, I hoped the same barman was on duty. He seemed a chatty sort and I was in the mood to chat.

I didn't see either Flannery or the shithead who'd cold-cocked me, but the bartender was on. The crowd was sparse: no women, not even very many fireman that I could spot. Who would be in a bar at three in the afternoon, anyway? Finbarr McPhee's, for all of its firehouse cachet, was no different than any other bar at that time of day. It catered to the lonely and the losers, people lost in their drinks or the newspaper or their own thoughts.

I found the same seat I'd sat in the other night. The barman nodded hello, a smile on his face, but it was a salesman's smile, not one meant especially for me.

"What'll you have?"

"Same as the other night," I said to test him.

It took a second, but he remembered. The smile ran away from his face. "You, huh? Guinness, right?"

"Right, but I've changed my mind. Make it a Dewars rocks."

"Not gonna start a fight today, are you?" he asked, scooping ice into a rocks glass and reaching for the Dewars bottle.

"Not on the agenda, no. And for the record, I didn't start one the other night either. I was just talking to Flannery. What time does he usually come in?"

He put my drink up. "Not till about seven. He works his way down Fourth Avenue. He needs to drink a little before he drinks in here."

I took a sip. "Why's that?"

"Ask him."

"Don't go all quiet on me now," I said. "You were quick to volunteer that story about him being a hero the other night, but that wasn't the whole story, was it?"

"Nope. What's it to you, anyways?"

"I like the guy. He stuck his neck out for me. I'm curious about someone who would do that for a stranger."

The barman nodded his head at the Wall of Honor.

"Okay, you got my attention," I said. "What about it?"

"Walk over and take a look. See if you can find Brandon Fitzgerald Flannery Jr. I'll make sure no one steals your seat or your scotch."

I walked over to the wall and found the name listed amongst the three hundred and forty-three members of the FDNY lost on 9/11.

"Flannery's son?" I asked, retaking my seat.

"His youngest. His only son."

"I'd drink too if I lost my kid that way."

"That's not why he drinks. He drinks because he blames himself. The kid didn't want to follow in his old man's footsteps, but Flannery pushed him. And you can tell by how he handled things the other night that when Flannery pushes, he pushes hard. The Flannerys have been fighting fires in this city since they stepped off the boat. They go back to before 1898, to before the job was the job and before the city was the city. No son of Flannery's was going to turn his back on family tradition."

"That guilt's a lot to carry," I said.

"More than he can bear and that man can bear a lot."

"Thanks. I appreciate it."

"You didn't hear it from me," he said.

"Here what from whom?"

The barman liked that and asked if I wanted another scotch on the house.

"No, thanks," I said. "I'm not supposed to be drinking this one. But I'll tell you what you can do."

"What's that?"

"That fireman who started up with me the other night, Hickey, what's his story?"

"He's too young to have a story. Leave it alone. I don't need any trouble in here."

"Fair enough." I took a last sip at my Dewars and threw a ten on the bar for a tip.

Suddenly, I wasn't feeling very well and decided that what I needed more than anything was an afternoon nap. Sleep, I found as I got older, was a much better retreat than the bottle.

FOURTEEN

The High Line Bistro was over in the West Village on Little West 12th Street in an area known as the Meatpacking District. The Meatpacking District had for many decades been the hub of the city's commercial butchery. And, until the eighties, it had also been known for its many gay clubs. Some of the clubs were notorious for catering to the rough trade segment of the community. But the AIDS epidemic and the city's insatiable thirst for real estate development remade the Meatpacking District into a chic neighborhood of exclusive shops and designer chef restaurants. Rising above the cobblestone streets of the district, north into Chelsea, was the High Line Park or, as it was more commonly known, the High Line: a long-disused stretch of elevated railroad track that had been converted into an elevated park replete with plantings, artwork, and great vistas on the Hudson River and the Manhattan skyline.

The High Line Bistro was in an old warehouse. The walls were the original brick and the interior post and beam construction was also original equipment. That's where the quaintness came to an abrupt halt. The tables and chairs, made of train rails and ties, were more sculpture than furniture and each must have cost a small fortune. The walls were covered with historical photographs of the High Line when it was operational and trains were bringing meat to and from the butcheries. There were also original paintings of the High Line itself and of the views of the city it offered. The bar was simple and sturdy, no rails and ties here. But when I sat down on one of the barstools and looked at the wine list just to pass the time, I nearly swallowed my tongue. Their wine list was pretty extensive and absurdly expensive. A bottle of good old vine Zinfandel, which you could buy on sale at one of our stores for under thirty dollars, was listed at one hundred and forty bucks. At that price, I thought, the waiter should not only open the bottle and pour the wine, but hold the glass and pour it into your mouth for you. The lunch menu prices, while not quite as outrageous, were no bargain. I could only imagine what the prices on the dinner menu would be.

Something wasn't right. I had that prickle on the back of my neck thing going. What were two EMTs doing in a place like the High Line Bistro for lunch? They'd have had to take out a loan just to walk through the door. Not to judge, but I didn't see Alta or Maya Watson as two women who were going to take a quick lunch of frisee salad with lardon or Thai duck confit with tamarind and pomegranate drizzle, certainly not at these prices. But the media reports had been absolutely consistent about the fact that Alta and Maya had called into dispatch that they were taking their lunch break at this address. I looked around at the half-full restaurant. There were lots of tourists, business types in expensive lightweight suits, women in lovely summer dresses, and not a single person in uniform.

The bartender broke my concentration. She was the ultimate Manhattan stereotype: a beautiful early-twenty-something with rich dark skin, exotic features—vaguely Asian and Hispanic—speaking mildly accented English. She was thin as a blade of grass, but with some curves, and her makeup was flawless. A model or actress who, I guessed, hadn't come to New York to work behind a bar.

"Excuse me, sir," she said, "what may I get for you?"

I showed her my old badge and put it away before she could get a good look at it. Her youth worked in my favor because she would focus on the badge and what it represented, not on me or my age.

"A glass of sparkling water and lime and five minutes of your time."

She looked around the bar for any excuse to get away from me, but I was her sole customer.

"Look," I said, "what's your name?"

"Esme."

"Look, Esme, relax. Just get me the sparkling water and talk to me like I was any older man sitting at the bar hitting on you. I'm sure you're pretty used to it."

She smiled at that and what a smile: welcoming, sexy, shy, and warm all at once. I couldn't imagine a camera not loving her. She used the bar gun to fill a tall glass, clipped a lime wedge over the rim, and placed it in front of me.

"What do you do, Esme, I mean besides tend bar? Actress? Model?"

There was that smile again. "Some of both, but I am a senior at SVA, the School of Visual Arts."

"Really? What's your major?"

"Film," she said, seeming to be more relaxed.

I squeezed the lime, raised the glass to her, and sipped. "Thanks. Were you here in March when Robert Tillman died?"

She wasn't smiling anymore. She looked gut-punched, in fact. "Yes."

"Can you tell me what happened?"

"I can't tell you very much because I was behind the bar here. It all happened over there around the other side of the bar by the kitchen entrance," she said, her head looking down.

"Did you see the EMTs come in?"

"Yes, I noticed them right away."

"Why would you notice them? Hadn't they ever been in here for lunch before?"

Esme, still looking down. "No. We do not get many customers like them at the High Line."

I played dumb. "Why not?"

She held the menu out to me. "I make good money and I get a discount and even I cannot afford food here. And each meal is always cooked to order by Chef Liu. People do not come here for a fast lunch."

"But even if you didn't see what happened yourself, people who work here must have talked. What did you hear about what happened?"

"People talked, yes."

"Come on, Esme, don't make this like pulling teeth. Just tell me."

"The EMTs came in and everyone says they were having an argument."

"An argument. An argument about what?"

"No one said."

"Okay, so they were arguing. Where did they go after they came in?"

"Toward the restrooms," Esme said, again pointing around the bar to her right. "Then as they were passing the kitchen door, Chef Liu came out of the kitchen screaming for a doctor and for the hostess to call 911. The short EMT looked into the kitchen and saw Rob—him on the floor. The tall one, she ran into the bathroom and the other one told the chef to call 911, that they were off duty and couldn't help. When the tall one came out of the bathroom, they left."

"You said the short EMT looked into the kitchen. Which one was the short one?"

"The heavier, older woman. The one who was murdered."

"Alta Conseco?"

"If that is her name, yes, that one."

"You said she looked into the kitchen. Did she go into the kitchen or just look?" I asked.

"I did not see for myself."

"I know, Esme, but what did the others say?"

"She just looked at him through the open kitchen door."

"That's it? She didn't touch him or anything?"

"That is what I was told. She just left him to die on the dirty kitchen tiles."

Except for the argument between Alta and Maya, Esme's hearsay story pretty much fell into line with the witness statements. I took out a list of names I'd scrawled down before leaving the house. The names were of other restaurant employees who'd given statements to the police. I read the list of names to Esme. None of them were on duty. Most of them, she said, no longer worked there.

"It is Manhattan," she said, "no one works here for very long. We get parts or roles or gigs or even better jobs and leave. It is nice to work here, but it is no one's dream."

I asked Esme to introduce me to Chef Liu. I don't think I'd ever seen someone so happy to be rid of me. Esme's introduction saved me the trouble of having to scam the chef. If she said I was a cop, I was a cop. His story included more details about Tillman's collapse—"Robert was just walking to the grill with a pan of diced onions and fell to the floor"—but was otherwise consistent with Esme's. He said that Tillman, a prep cook, had only started working there the week prior to his death and that he was good at what he did. Robert hadn't been there long enough for the chef to really get to know him, but that his death and the controversy surrounding it was a shame nonetheless.

"Has his family been in touch?" I asked. "Any lawyers or investigators come in to take statements?"

"No one from Robert's family, no," said Chef Liu. "Only the police and fire departments."

Uh oh, I could see the chef taking a second look at me, wondering what I was doing there if the cops had already come and gone. I thanked him and left before he could put it together and inquire as to why I was asking questions he'd already answered many times. Questions. Now I had more of them than when I'd walked in.

FIFTEEN

When I got back to the car I noticed a message on my cell from a number I didn't recognize. I thought about ignoring it as I was too busy trying to figure out what the hell Alta and Maya had been doing at the High Line Bistro that day in March and what it was they were arguing about. I considered calling Maya to ask, but she had been so resistant to discussing anything about Tillman's death when I'd been at her condo, I couldn't imagine she'd be more cooperative over the phone. This was the thing I guess I loved and hated about investigations: their individual complexities. Only in retrospect is life a simple series of easily connected dots. Humans yearn for simple answers to complex questions, but it just ain't the way things work. Nothing involving human beings is simple. Nothing!

I checked the message and was caught totally by surprise by Nick Roussis' voice. He said it had been good to see me the other day and that he hadn't taken enough time in the last few years to focus on his friends. He wondered if we could get together for dinner that night or the next night. "Come on," he said, "I bet you haven't talked old times with someone from the Six-O for years. It'll be fun."

Obviously, Nicky had been out of the loop about what had gone on with our former precinct mates since he left the job. Larry McDonald had risen to chief of detectives before gassing himself in his car at the Fountain Avenue dump. Rico Tripoli had died years ago, but had never been the same after getting out of prison. Ferguson May died after being stabbed through the eye while responding to a domestic dispute. Caveman Kenny Burton was gunned down by another dirty cop right in front of me. Nope, somehow I didn't think this was the kind of thing Nicky "the Greek" Roussis wanted to chat about over dinner, but he was right, seeing him had been good for me. I knew I could use the distraction. I returned his call and left a message that I would probably be available and that he should give me a call back to make plans.

. . .

One fifty-one West 27th Street in Chelsea was off 7th Avenue and across the street from the Fashion Institute of Technology. There wasn't much to say for the building: a slim drab affair wedged between two other slim drab buildings on a block full of slim drab buildings. Funny thing about Manhattan was that there were blocks and blocks of such nondescript buildings lurking in the shadows of those iconic skyscrapers. Except in Chelsea, slim and drab cost an arm and a leg. Many are the paradoxes of New York real estate, but I wasn't here to solve them. I wasn't scouting locations for our next shop or looking for a new condo. I was here to talk to Henry Handwerker. According to the statements Carmella had gotten me, Henry Handwerker had been at the High Line Bistro that March day when Robert Tillman collapsed in the kitchen.

I rode the tiny elevator up to the tenth floor after bullshitting my way inside the building. The list of lies was growing longer by the second and when the elevator door opened up directly into Henry Handwerker's apartment, I was prepared to lie some more. There was an engraved sign on the wall that read:

HANDWERKER LITERARY AGENCY, INC.

I was greeted by a handsome if compact man with blue eyes, short gray hair, a bright friendly smile, and a welcoming handshake. He was about ten years my junior and was comfortably clad in a blue and yellow striped shirt, khaki slacks, and deck shoes. It was an outfit I might have worn, but it looked different on him. His shirt was crisply ironed, the rolled cuffs perfectly squared midway up his forearms, the creases in his slacks just so. His office/apartment reflected that same sort of style: comfortable, yet everything in it was neat and clean.

"I'm Henry Handwerker. What can I do for you, officer?"

"Retired," I said, putting my badge back where it belonged. "Sorry, but the badge sometimes saves a lot of time."

"Lying may be efficient, but it is unwelcome."

"I agree, but I didn't think I could get away with claiming I was the Chinese food delivery man."

"I see your point, still . . ."

"I'm an investigator working for the Tillman family."

Handwerker's whole body seemed to sag. "Oh."

"See, it would have been a little difficult explaining through the voice box downstairs."

"What is it you want to know?" he asked and then volunteered, "I have no desire to crucify those two women EMTs. There was clearly something troubling going on with them."

"Troubling. How?"

"They were pretty agitated," he said.

"They were arguing with each other?"

"Not exactly. It wasn't an argument, per se. It seemed they were both upset over something, but in different ways."

"I'm sorry, Mr. Handwerker, but I'm a bit confused here. Can you be a little bit more explicit?"

"One, the Hispanic woman—"

"Alta Conseco."

"Yes. She was angry, but with someone or something, not at her partner. You could see the fire in her. Her face was contorted and her gestures were violent and purposeful."

"And what about Maya Watson, the partner?"

"A beautiful woman," he said almost wistfully as he remembered her face.

"She is, I agree."

"She looked frightened, very frightened and hesitant, almost nauseous really. Maybe she was because she basically headed right for the restrooms. Her partner, Miss Conseco, she was making a straight line for the kitchen."

This was why you couldn't just read written statements and take them as being representative of what had actually happened. In his original statement to the police, Mr. Handwerker, probably somewhat stunned, hadn't described things in quite this way. He'd stated that the two EMTs were agitated, yes, but hadn't made the finer distinctions he was making for me now, nor had he mentioned that Alta and Maya were in fact headed to different places when they entered the bistro. I pointed that out to him.

"I was still out of sorts and a little bit in shock, I suppose, when I gave my statement," he said, confirming my impression. "It was all very tumultuous. Things happened so quickly."

"I understand. So, Miss Conseco was headed to the kitchen and Miss Watson to the restrooms?"

"Exactly."

"Could you hear any of their conversation?"

"Not really. I was seated facing the door, midway between the bar and the entrance. It was crowded and noisy in there. I could barely hear my client across the table, but there was a definite vibe between them."

"A vibe?"

"I can't explain it. It's just something I picked up on. That's all."

I could see he wasn't going to say more about that and I moved on. We talked through the sequence of events, with estimates of how much time elapsed between the two EMTs entering the restaurant and Chef Liu emerging from the kitchen, screaming for help.

"I wouldn't have wanted either of those women treating me," Handwerker said in conclusion. "You could see how totally out of it they were. If it had been anything else other than a stroke, that poor man would have been better served to wait until reinforcements arrived. Both women were shaking and the beautiful one was completely distraught."

I thanked him for his time and told him I might be back in touch.

"As I stated before, I don't wish to crucify those women."

"It's all right, Mr. Handwerker. I'm not certain the Tillman family will pursue this. Besides, one of the two EMTs is already dead."

"I heard. Terrible."

"Well," I said, "at least she can't be hurt by any of this."

"Maybe not her, but her family can suffer and there's the other woman."

"Of course. If you don't mind me saying, Mr. Handwerker, you're the first person I've run into in this whole investigation who's had an ounce of sympathy for the EMTs."

"Those other people weren't there that day. They didn't see the distress on those women's faces. Something was dreadfully wrong there."

I thanked him again and hopped back on the elevator. It was nice to know there were still some people in the world like Henry

Handwerker. If there was any redemption to be found in this universe, it lived in the hearts of people like him.

The trouble with eyewitnesses was that they could all see the same exact things, but see them differently. Such was the case with what happened at the High Line Bistro that day last March. By four-thirty in the afternoon, I'd interviewed four other witnesses beside Henry Handwerker who'd given statements to the police about the circumstances that day and the only thing they all agreed on was that the two EMTs refused to treat Tillman. Otherwise, it was difficult to tell that they had actually witnessed a common event. One woman didn't notice the two EMTs were agitated. "Agitated?" she said when I suggested it. "No, they seemed fine." Another, younger woman who was then working at an exclusive jewelry boutique on Gansevoort Street and was taking her lunch at the bistro said that both Alta and Maya were headed to the restrooms. "The kitchen? No. They were definitely walking toward the restrooms. I'd swear to it." She did say the two EMTs were bickering, but not about anything serious. "A girl thing," she said as if that explained it all.

The older of the two men I spoke with swore Alta and Maya came in separately and resisted any suggestion they were arguing. The younger man barely noticed Alta. "That tall EMT was so hot and, man, she was amazing in that uniform."

One of the problems with how the human brain functions is its need for a coherent narrative. It perceives events and then builds a story around them, it edits and embellishes, it ascribes motives when none are obvious. The mood, age, and sex of the witness can affect the perceptions of events and, to an even greater extent, the narrative woven out of those events. Although I had no palpable reason to accept Henry Handwerker's version of what had transpired, I chose to trust his version instead of the others. I don't know, maybe it was his sense of detail. Maybe it was his sense of style. Maybe it was that he displayed compassion. No matter, because there was one inescapable truth here: Alta and Maya had refused to treat a dying man and no amount of parsing or pretzel twisting of the facts was going to change that.

SIXTEEN

Nick was late, so I sipped at a glass of Brooklyn Lager and munched on olives at the bar. The Kythira Café on 5th Avenue in Park Slope, was, as Nick described it, the crown jewel of his family's business. The menu featured updated and upscale versions of classic Mediterranean dishes. The interior décor was dark and moody and about as far away from the stereotypical white and blue stucco walls as you could get. There were no Ouzo or retsina bottles, no Greek flags, no bad murals of whitewashed houses on cliffs above the blue Mediterranean, no travel posters of Mykonos, Crete, or the Parthenon.

The bartender, a scruffy young hipster, was about as Greek as me and as invested in his work as a member of a prison road crew. His generation's attitude toward their jobs was one of the things about the new world I had trouble getting adjusted to. I grew up believing in doing the best you could do at any job, even if you hated it. Aaron and I had several employees, including Klaus and Kosta, who had worked for us for over thirty years and prospered because of it. Now such dedication was considered old hat or worse, foolish. And when I thought about it, their attitude made sense. In today's economy, job security and company loyalty were bullshit. Maybe they always had been.

I checked my watch—7:23—and surveyed the restaurant. For the second time that day, I was the lone patron at a restaurant bar. A guy could get a complex. There were about thirty tables and about eighty seats in the Kythira. Currently, the majority of them were as in demand as the barstools. In most places, this many empty seats at dinnertime would be cause for hanging a "Going Out Of Business" sign in the window or for the owner to hang himself in the window, but Park Slope was an alien part of Brooklyn, very different from the neighborhoods I grew up in and lived in. The Kythira probably had a late-arriving crowd and things got going when a man my age was going to bed. What did I know about Park Slope, anyway? Park Slope was a satellite of Manhattan, populated mostly by people who were transplanted Brooklynites, not natives. Funny, when I was growing up, people seemed as desperate to get out of Brooklyn as East Berlin. Now there was no East Berlin and this part of Brooklyn was the hot place to live. Go figure.

"Always this busy?" I asked the bartender to kill some time and to make sure he wasn't actually in a coma.

"This time of night, yup."

"Things pick up later?"

He opened his mouth to answer, but I saw his focus shift to over my right shoulder. "Hey, Mr. Roussis," he said, giving a quick smile.

"Wyatt," Nick said, clamping a hand on my shoulder, "this gentleman's tab is comped. Have a bottle of '97 Opus One sent over to table three and tell the chef to come out to see me."

"Okay." Wyatt headed for the kitchen.

I chucked a five onto the bar.

"Generous," Nicky said.

"You can't take it with you."

"Wyatt's a good boy. Come on."

We sat at what I guessed was table three. I could see why the owner would want to sit here. It was the best vantage point in the place from which to watch the bar, the comings and goings from the kitchen, the waiter's station, the hostess' podium, and the rest of the dining room. What people don't understand about owning a business is that when you're there you can't ever relax. There's no such thing as being off duty when you're in-house. The chef came out to us, introduced himself, shook our hands. Nicky spoke to him in Greek and the chef went away.

"I hope you don't mind, but he does this thing with rib steak that I absolutely love. I ordered it for us. It's not very Greek, but we don't do strictly Greek here, anyways. That okay with you?"

"Fine. I hate that you're going to waste a bottle of Opus One on me. I haven't been feeling great lately and—"

"Don't worry, Moe. It won't go to waste. No one's spilling the Opus One down the drain or watering the plants with it."

Dinner, what I ate of it, was fantastic. We started out with a platter of dips and vegetable concoctions, only some of which I recognized, then salad, the marinated steak with lemon, garlic, and rosemary roasted potatoes, creamed spinach and feta tarts, and dessert of assorted pastries. I ate just enough of each to carry the wine. Nick was right about the wine, there would be no Opus One going to waste. I had way, way too much of it and by my third glass I didn't really care about the physical price I was going to pay for indulging. The food aside, it was a lot of fun to tell the old stories about the Six-O. Enough time had passed for me to forgive and forget the betrayals so, at least for one night, I let myself feel about the guys the way I felt about them then. It was okay for me to laugh about what a ladies man Rico had been and to shake my head at what a practical joker Larry McDonald could be. I even laughed about the time Kenny Burton laid out a fireman during a pickup basketball game we played in Coney Island. Maybe it was the wine or maybe it was the dying that set me free of the baggage and the pain. Probably both.

When we weren't talking old times, we talked about our families and business and where we'd come to in our lives. In a weak moment at the end of the meal and with my third glass of Grand Marnier in my hand, I told him the truth about why I'd come to the Gelato Grotto the other day. That I wasn't working for the Tillman family at all, but that Alta Conseco was Carmella's older sister and I felt obligated to look into things when she asked me to.

"I knew that story you told me at the Grotto was a crock a shit," Nick said, but not angrily. "I figured you'd tell me. You always was big on the truth."

I laughed. "Not as much as I used to be. Life has weaned me off it."

He didn't pursue it. "Look, I get why you told me what you did. You didn't figure I would help otherwise. And I understand your helping out. You and Carmella was once family and her sister was her sister even if she did a terrible thing. You can't abandon your family no matter what. That's what a family does, it stands together when things get bad. Am I right?"

"Exactly. I couldn't just say no to Carm."

"But you should watch your back, Moe. Not everybody's gonna be as understanding as me if they find out what you're really up to. Defending those EMTs is kinda like defending Osama Bin Laden in this city, you know what I mean?"

"Thanks. I'm being careful."

"So what you find out so far?"

I figured I owed it to him to tell him as much as I could. Here was a guy I hadn't seen in fifteen years and the first thing I did was lie to his face. Plus, he'd been really cooperative based on that lie. He'd given me the surveillance video and sent me to Fuqua.

"So you think it's somebody in the FDNY?" Nicky asked.

"I don't know what to think, but it's possible."

"Okay, I'll keep my eyes open. I hear things. People do a lotta loose talking in restaurants. You'd be surprised at the shit you hear when you're not even trying."

"Thanks, Nicky. I appreciate it. This was fun. Next time, dinner's on me."

We shook hands. "Let's do it soon, Moe."

"Soon. You have my word on that."

Dinner with Nick would have to be soon, I thought, or it probably wouldn't be at all.

SEVENTEEN

If I thought the cab ride with the windows rolled down was going to cut into the intensity of my alcohol buzz or take the edge off the searing pain in my gut, I was wrong. Wouldn't be the first time. The cabbie dropped me at the corner of Ashford Street and Atlantic Avenue. Carmella's grandmother's house was a few houses in off Atlantic. For many years, Carmella had lived in the upstairs apartment while her abuela lived on the first floor. She had willed the house to Carmella and I'd wrongly assumed that Carmella had sold the place after moving up to Toronto. When she'd sent me that packet of information, I'd been surprised to see she'd written down this address as where she was staying. I stood outside, looking up at the old place. Except for a coat of paint, the house hadn't changed much in the last twenty years. This was where I kissed Carmella for the first time, a pretty chaste kiss even as first kisses go. And shortly after that, this house is where I learned of Carmella's true identity.

I tasted the tears and felt the wetness on my cheeks before I fully realized I was crying. I didn't make a habit of crying and I wasn't usually a sad drunk, but nothing about my life was usual these days. I had a laundry list of things worth crying over, yet I knew these tears weren't about Carmella. I may have had a pocketful of unresolved feelings for her. So what? She was here now, she'd be gone tomorrow. Maybe I'd be gone tomorrow. Who could say? These tears were for absent friends, for Wit and Mr. Roth and yes, even for Rico. When you reach a certain stage in life, you do a lot of wondering about the people who've passed in and out of it. Soon enough, I realized, I'd be someone's absent friend. You add alcohol to thoughts like that and you get tears. Who, I wondered, would shed tears for me? It's an unhealthy thing to think about, but nothing I'd done recently was very healthy. I walked up onto the porch and rang the upstairs bell.

Even through the front door I could hear the steps creaking under Carm's feet. I remembered how those cranky old stairs complained the first time I walked them, as we both walked them, trying not to awaken her grandmother. We had stood in her little kitchen, talking quietly, drinking Coronas, flirting.

"I want you to like me," she'd whispered.

As I recall, I said something like, "What do you think I'm doing here?"

"No," she'd said, "I want you to *like* me, Moe, not just want me. I know how to make men want me. That's something I could do even before I knew how."

Then I'd leaned forward and put my lips very gently on hers. In a way, it was more a caress than a kiss, but it was still electric. She slid her lips off mine and nestled her body against me. She was the first "other woman" I'd kissed with intent and it was to be the full extent of my extramarital activity in the twenty years of marriage to Katy. Yet that kiss was nearly as exciting to me now as it had been then, almost as exciting as the first time I slept with Carmella after Katy and I split. I was thinking about that kiss when the door pulled back.

I felt weak because the figure standing in the little vestibule wasn't Carmella at all. He was dressed in Shrek pajama bottoms and a Toronto Raptors T-shirt. His blue eyes were bleary from too many video games and not enough sleep. He had his mother's skin tone and hair, but his face and blue eyes were his father's: not my eyes, not my face, his real father's—a hotshot lawyer named Dukelsky who'd had a short, torrid romance with Carm, but who couldn't afford the stain of a bastard son. It was one thing to see Israel in the pictures Carmella had given me. It was something else to be standing in front of him. I wanted desperately to scoop him up in my arms, to swallow him up with eight years worth of love and pain, but I didn't want to frighten him.

"Didn't your mom teach you not to just open the door for strangers?"

"You're not a stranger. Mom has pictures of you in our house. You're her friend Moe. I saw you through the top glass on the door when I was coming down the steps."

When he called me his mom's friend, it hurt much worse than my gut. "So your mom talks about me?" I said, trying to smile through the hurt.

"Sometimes. She smiles when she talks about you. You used to work together, right, when she was a detective?"

"That's right." I put out my hand out and we shook. "I knew you when you were a very little boy."

"I don't remember."

"That's okay." I winked. "I do. Where's your mom?"

"She's sleeping."

"Can I come in?"

He thought about that for a minute. "My mom's asleep," he said. "I don't think—"

"That's okay, Israel," Carmella called down from the top of the stairs. "Tell Moe to come in. And you, mister, get to bed. It's late."

"Mom!"

"C'mon, you, up here and to bed!"

"Good night, Israel, it was nice seeing you again," I said, voice cracking. I patted his shoulder. "Listen to your mom and go on."

"Good night," he said without much enthusiasm, then turned and ran up the stairs.

I followed slowly behind him, my grip firm on the handrail. My knees were shaky and not from the wine and Grand Marniers. At the top of the stairs, Carmella kissed Israel on his forehead, gave him a quick hug, and gave him a gentle shove. He didn't look back. I watched him disappear for the second time in my life.

Carm, dressed in a loose cotton T-shirt over faded and torn jeans, stared down at me. Her eyes were still a little cloudy with sleep. "Beer?" she asked, leading me into the kitchen.

"No, thanks. I remember getting into some mischief the last time we shared a beer in this kitchen."

"I remember that too." She stretched the sleep out of her muscles and yawned. "What are you doing here, Moe?"

"I'm a little drunk."

"I can see that."

"I didn't know you had him here with you."

"How could you know?"

"Were you going to tell me?" I asked, a sharp pain bending me over.

"Are you okay? Sit."

She pulled back a chair for me and I took it.

"I ate and drank too much. My stomach's been off lately. Sorry."

"Can I get you something?"

"No. I'm okay now," I lied. "So, were you going to tell me Israel was here with you?"

"I thought about it, but . . ."

"He's a good boy. Handsome too. Best features of his mom and dad. Do you ever talk to—"

Carmella shushed me, shaking her head no and putting her finger across her lips. I got the message and moved on.

"He does well in school?"

"Top of his class and a good hockey player too." She beamed like any proud mom.

"Hockey!" I snorted. "Mr. Roth would think it was funny that someone named for him would be a hockey player. He loved baseball."

"Moe, what are you doing here?"

"I'm not sure. I came to see you."

"No shit, really?"

"What did you know about your sister?"

Carm's body clenched. I'd asked her precisely the worst question. "Why?"

"Because if you were hoping that the witnesses had somehow gotten it wrong, that Alta hadn't ignored Tillman and that all the rest of it was some big misunderstanding . . . well, stop hoping. If there's one thing I know for sure about any of this, it's that Alta and her partner refused to help the guy. And to be totally brutal about it, it seems to me it was Alta's call. She was the one who made the decision not to treat the guy. What I can't understand is why."

"I don't know why, Moe. I did not know my sister except when we were little. You know my parents sent me back to Puerto Rico after . . . after the thing happened to me."

"Was she a good big sister when you were little?"

"What the hell does that have to do with anything now?" She was red with anger, but careful not to yell. She lowered her voice to a vicious whisper. "I did not ask you to be a psychologist for me. I asked you to—"

"People don't change, Carm. My brother Aaron is pretty much the same as he was when he was eight years old, and your buddy and my little sister Miriam has always been a troublemaker. So, was Alta a good big sister?"

Carmella bowed her head. "Yes. She was always protecting me like I was her own. She was a mother bear. I think when I was taken as a little girl, it hurt Alta more than anyone. She felt like she didn't do her job. Why don't you go to the partner, Maya Watson, to ask her about Alta?"

"I *will* ask her, but it won't get me anywhere. She was very cooperative until I brought up what happened with Tillman. Then she clammed up. I don't know why. You'd think she and Alta would have been desperate to explain their side of things, but instead they refused to say a word about it. That's only one of the things that doesn't make much sense about this case."

"What do you mean?"

"I went to the High Line Bistro. On an EMT's salary, you couldn't afford an appetizer and a bowl of chowder in that joint. Their least expensive wine was sixty bucks. Coffee is seven bucks a pop. It's not the kind of place people in uniforms go to. But Alta and Maya traveled over there from the other side of Manhattan for a quick lunch? I don't buy it. And under careful questioning, some of the witnesses said that Alta and Maya were arguing when they came in. About what? It's just weird, Carm. It doesn't feel right. I don't think they were there about lunch."

"Then what for?" she asked.

"That's the million dollar question. What the hell were they doing there?"

I think I had something else to say, but suddenly I was lightheaded. No, it was more than that. I was dizzy and my vision got hazy around the edges. My heart was beating its way out of my chest and up into my throat. My head, now impossibly heavy, fell back over the top of the chair. I could feel myself soaking through my shirt. I was nauseous as hell.

"Moe! Moe!" I heard someone calling my name, but from somewhere far far away. "Moe, are you all right? You look gray." I felt a hand touch my face, my neck. "You're clammy. I'm going to call 911."

"No! No. Get me to the bathroom," I slurred, holding my leaden arms out. "I'll be okay."

I was up, but not for long. My legs were deboned and demuscled. I remember feeling myself dropping. I don't remember landing. It must have been a hell of a fall.

EIGHTEEN

I stopped at my condo for another shower and a change of clothing before heading over to see Detective Jean Jacques Fuqua. Neither the shower nor the new clothing made me feel like a new man. I was past the age when feeling like a new man was possible. The best I could hope for was feeling like a retread and recently even that had become a pipe dream. I no longer got just tired. That ship done sailed. These days my exhaustion was profound as a Russian novel. Exhaustion for me was now a whole other state of being and last night had taken more out of me than I had to give. I wasn't sure if this new state of being was simply my body giving me a preview of what I'd feel like once chemo and radiation kicked in or if it was preparing me for death. Death, I thought, had all sorts of potential for unpleasantness, especially if I was wrong about all those many things I didn't believe in. What if the face of God was a sneering one and he was the type to say I told you so? What if he was just a universal hurt machine? Man, in either case, I was fucked.

Even last night as I lay on Carmella's bathroom floor, I knew I wasn't quite dead. I couldn't imagine the departed could taste their own vomit or feel as though their kishkas were being torn apart from the inside out. Nope. I was pretty sure that sort of unpleasantness was reserved for the living, but as poorly as I felt, it was much better than I had at the kitchen table. The nausea was gone and my vision was no longer blurred at the edges. My view of the base of the toilet was crystal clear. I was weak, but my arms were no longer leaden and my legs seemed like they might once again support my full weight. I hadn't been foolish enough to test them out. I was content to just lie there and enjoy the coolness of the tiles.

Eventually, I got around to showering and rinsing my mouth. There wasn't enough mouthwash left in Carm's medicine cabinet to fully rid me of that awful taste. There probably wasn't enough in all of East New York to do that. I was feeling much better when I spit the last of the mouthwash into the sink, but the exhaustion had set in. It was the exhaustion, along with some other less savory symptoms, that had forced me to go to my doctor in the first place. I looked at myself in the mirror. I'd been doing that a lot lately. I looked old. I noticed my hand on my abdomen and turned away. I wrapped two big bath towels around me, and asked Carmella if I could lie down on the couch and just shut my eyes for a few minutes. A few minutes turned into a long deep sleep of forgotten dreams.

When I opened my eyes, the sun was just sending the tips of its fingers over the east end of Long Island. The birds were in full throat—the birds in Brooklyn sing like any other birds, except maybe a little louder, in order to be heard. The apartment itself was quiet and I found my clothes on the chair next to the couch. Carm had washed my shirt, briefs, and socks. She'd pressed my suit and sprayed it with that stuff that was supposed to pull the stink out of fabric. It had worked well enough. In a book or movie, I would have tiptoed to look in on Israel. I just left. I'd had enough pain for the time being.

Catching a cab on Atlantic Avenue at that hour had turned out to be easier than I thought it might be. The cabbie dropped me off in front of the Kythira Café. I could scarcely believe my eyes: my car was still there and there was no parking ticket wedged under the wiper blade. It's something of a miracle to park your car on the street overnight in New York City without it getting towed or ticketed. I had a friend who worked in the city budget office who told me the city took in like five hundred million dollars a year from parking violations and towing fees. Nice, huh? Talk about predatory practices. Lions and crocodiles could take lessons from New York City meter maids.

Now more than the sun's fingertips hovered in the cloudless blue skies over the County of Kings and the pain in my gut was back at the level I'd grown accustomed to. But there was no getting around it, last night had scared the shit out of me. I was afraid: mouth-dry, hands-shaking afraid. I'd felt many things since walking out of my oncologist's office. Mostly anger. I suppose I accepted the diagnosis and filed the reality of it away somewhere. It was one thing to think about dying in the abstract, which is what I had been doing to hold it at bay. The holding my abdomen, the silent deals with the tumor, the waiting until after Sarah's wedding to begin treatment: it was a kind of denial. The fact was I hadn't faced it, not really. Last night changed that. There was going to be a lot of pain and suffering. Not all of it would be mine. I was glad Sarah had Paul and that she wouldn't be here to watch me suffer in close-up. I was thinking about Sarah when I parked the car on Mermaid.

Fuqua actually smiled at me when I walked over to his desk.

"You are a stubborn man, Moe Prager."

"I prefer persistent."

He gestured to an empty chair. "Sit. What may I do for you on this glorious day?"

"I'd like to see Alta Conseco's apartment or where her personal effects are stored."

"*Porquoi?* Why?"

"A feeling."

"A feeling? What sort of feeling?"

"Did you pay any attention to the witness statements from the High Line Bistro?" I asked.

"Of course. You are referring to the alleged argument?"

It was my turn to smile at him. "Exactly."

"It is my understanding from the detectives and the fire department investigators who interviewed both my victim and Maya Watson that they refused to discuss any aspect of that day other than to say they were there for lunch. And when I interviewed the Watson woman after my vic was killed, she once again refused to discuss the matter and denied there had been an argument. She stated only that she and Conseco were there for lunch."

"Bullshit!"

"I agree. Bullshit. But if Watson did not cooperate after her friend and partner was murdered, she will not cooperate now."

"Maybe not."

"There is that persistence again, Mr. Prager. How will you get the Watson woman to talk with you?"

"Good question."

"I am a detective. I am full of good questions."

"It doesn't add up," I said. "There's something obvious here that I can smell, but I just can't see."

He laughed. "Yes, a familiar feeling for me."

"With this case?"

"With many cases, but with this one, very much."

"That's why I want to see Alta's things. Maybe I will spot something."

"It is a stretch, *non*?"

"*Mais oui*," I said, using the full extent of my junior high school French. "I think stretches are all that's left to us, detective."

"Of course the items Miss Conseco had on her person when she was murdered, we are still holding as evidence."

"I understand."

"Here," he said, "let me write down her address for you."

. . .

Essex Street between Liberty and Glenmore Avenues was no more than six or seven blocks away from Carmella's house on Ashford Street. I had meant to ask Carmella about why she'd held onto her *abuela's* house for so many years and why the upstairs apartment still looked pretty much unchanged after two decades. I seemed to have forgotten several things I had gone there meaning to ask. Someone once said that men get older but they never grow up. How true, because when I really thought about it, I hadn't gone to Carmella's to ask about Alta or about the house or anything like that. No matter how I might rationalize it away and regardless of the date on my birth certificate, alcohol had reduced me to nothing more than a drunk and horny teenage boy desperate to sleep with his old girlfriend. Men never get over rejection. Seeing Israel again had pretty much put a damper on any of my plans for conquest. The fainting and the puking didn't much help.

Besides, in my heart I knew why Carmella hung on to the house. That house represented her last remaining connection to her family. Not the family she had voluntarily cut out of her life, the family that had so carelessly let a seven-year-old girl fall into the hands of a pedophile, the family that afterwards treated her as an object of shame and disgust, but the idealized family she'd created out of the dreams and memories of her life prior to Easter Sunday, 1972. I have often wondered how Carmella hadn't torn herself completely apart given the powerful and contradictory nature of her feelings toward her family. I don't think she ever stopped wanting to belong to them, but I know better than most there are walls that cannot be scaled and wounds so raw they never heal. As best as I could tell, Carmella had long ago come to terms with the abduction and days of abuse. She has never come to terms with how her family treated her in the aftermath.

The address on Essex Street was a two-story, red brick row house with a small brick stoop. The wrought iron handrails had been freshly painted in a thick coat of black, but not much else in the way of maintenance had been done to the place in years. The wood around the old single-paned windows was rotting away and the mortar between many of the front façade bricks was missing. What once had probably been a lovely wrought iron and glass front door with side panels and transom had long since been replaced by a simple steel door with a peephole as its major design feature. The new door wasn't pretty, but it was practical. As Brooklyn neighborhoods went, East New York was one of the roughest and in such places, safe always trumps aesthetics.

I read the names in the slots beneath all three doorbells. *A. Conseco* was the name on the little black and white plastic label in the slot for the top floor apartment, not that her name being there meant anything. New Yorkers aren't exactly anal about getting names right on doorbells and mailboxes. I'm not sure why we're like that. We just are. Maybe we have too much other shit to worry about to fret over the small stuff. And in East New York, there were probably a lot of people only too glad to have someone else's name on their bell or mailbox. I rang the top bell for the hell of it. No answer. I wasn't expecting one. The name in the slot under the main floor bell was T. Truax. I held my thumb down on it long and hard and I could hear it ringing through the front windows. Again, no answer. The name in the basement apartment slot was Rodriguez and I held that button down for quite some time as well. And just like the bell for Truax, I could hear it ringing inside the apartment. Same results too.

Depending upon your point of view, I was either batting zero or a thousand. Felt more like zero. Lacking x-ray vision or the will for risking a felony conviction for breaking and entering, I decided to go. I made it down three steps when I thought I heard something at my back. I took a quick peek over my left shoulder and saw the main floor curtains covering the windows closest to the stoop had been pulled slightly to one side. I felt eyes on me, but I didn't turn immediately around. Instead I took my time reaching street level and then made a lazy about-face. I tried to make myself seem as unthreatening and forlorn as possible. Much more easily accomplished these days than it had once been. I turned my lips down, shook my head, threw my hands up in exasperation, and made to go. The act must have played well for my audience because the front door opened and someone called out, "Hey, mister, you jus' hold on."

She was a stout black woman in a well-worn bathrobe and men's brown slippers, the kind my dad used to favor. She had a fussy hairdo with lots of elaborate twists and curls and it glistened in the midday sun. She didn't have to touch it for me to see that her hairdo was a source of great pride. She had a lovely, welcoming smile, but wary eyes taking my measure. The problem was I was at a loss. I'd been going through the motions, ringing the bells and all, but I was still preoccupied by the implications of what had happened to me last night and the fear of what lay ahead. I remembered Carmella first telling me about Alta's murder. I could see her mouthing the word Gravesend in my mind's eye. Gravesend, indeed.

"Hey, mister, you all right?" the woman on the stoop asked, breaking the trance.

"Fine," I said for lack of anything else.

The thing was, I'd been so preoccupied that I hadn't bothered thinking about what I would say if someone answered one of the bells. I knew I had to say something right then or lose her. What to say was the issue. I opened my mouth, but she spoke first.

"I seen you before," she said, the wary squint of her eyes evaporating. "Where I seen you at? On TV somewhere or the papers?" It wasn't really a question, not for me anyway. She closed her eyes tight and scrunched up her face as if she were trying to squeeze the memory out of her head. "Tha's it! I know where from. You the man that saved that little girl, the artist. Your face and hers was all over the news."

"Sashi Bluntstone," I said. "Very good."

She seemed pleased with the both of us. "C'mon up here . . ."

"Moe," I said, walking up the steps with my right hand extended, "Moe Prager."

"Thelma Truax. I own this place. Husband left it to me when he passed." Her hand was meaty, her handshake genteel. "I imagine you here about poor Alta, such a nice woman."

"Not many people in this city share your view of Alta, Mrs. Truax."

"It's the Lord's place to judge, Moe, not ours. Alta was never nothin' but sweet to me and mine. Times when we couldn't afford to go to the doctor, she'd see to my grandchildren. If it was serious, she would make arrangements with doctor friends of hers. So I hope the Lord shines his light of forgiveness on her."

"Then you believe the media reports about Alta?"

"Don't have to believe 'em," she said. "Alta tol' me her own self that they was true."

Thelma's words hit me like a tire iron. No matter that I'd already come to the same conclusion, that Alta had abandoned her principles and turned her back on her oath. I clung to the hope that I was wrong, that when I waded through everything there'd be some reasonable explanation for her actions or, more accurately, her inaction. Now I had independent confirmation that she had stood by and let Tillman die.

"When did she tell you that?"

"It's quiet on this street now, but right after it all came down, it was just a shame how them newspeople hounded Alta. There was news trucks all over the street, people be ringing her bell at all hours. She took shelter in my apartment sometimes in that first week. We tried to comfort her, but she wouldn't have none. She said she deserved what she got, that she had let that man die."

"Did you ask why?"

"She wouldn't never say and I figured wasn't none of my business really."

"You're a good woman for doing that for her, Thelma."

"You don't turn people away when they need you most, was how I was taught. But why you here, Moe?"

"I was taught like you, I guess. Someone's got to stand up for Alta."

She placed her hand on my shoulder. "Bless you."

"Don't go blessing me just yet. Do you think it would be possible for me to see Alta's apartment?"

"Not much to see. Just furniture mostly."

"The cops take most of her stuff?"

"Them too," she said.

"Them too? Who else?"

"Her sister. She come round 'bout two days ago with all sorts of papers and things to prove she had inherited Alta's belongings, but I knew it was Alta's sister the minute I seen her. She look like Alta, but more beautiful."

"Carmella?"

"That's the one. After the police took what they would, which wasn't much from what I could see, she come and take the rest. She said I could keep the furniture, if it would help me rent the place."

"Do you remember what Carmella took?" I asked.

"Not in my nature to look. Why? Is it important?"

"For Carmella, probably. For me, not so much. Thelma, can I ask why you haven't rented the apartment?"

"Haven't had a heart to, though Lord knows, I need the money. And, to be honest with you, I wanted to wait till people on the block kinda forget. Tough to rent with this so fresh on everybody's mind, you know?"

"I understand. Thank you for your help."

"I wasn't much help that I could see, but I was happy to do it for Alta's memory. People should know she wasn't always like that, like she was that day when the man died. We all do things we know we shouldn't. We all have regrets in our hearts."

"I know the truth of that," I said.

Thelma took my hand and stared right up into my eyes so intently I could not look away. "I believe you do, Moe. Yes, I believe you do."

NINETEEN

Okay, so now I was preoccupied with something else, but I wasn't clicking up my heels. Why the hell hadn't Carmella told me she had been to Alta's apartment and that she'd taken her sister's things? Was it important? It was hard to know. I mean, on the one hand I somehow doubted that Alta had the identity of her killer-to-be written in code in an envelope hidden in a photo album. On the other hand, a decorated ex-NYPD detective like Carmella knew that personal belongings could be very revealing and that if she had Alta's, I would want to see them. Having a sense of the victim can point you in the right direction or it can stop you from wasting time pursuing dead-end leads. Who knew what I might find: a love letter or hate mail, a name scrawled on a piece of scrap paper, a photograph, a phone number in a day planner? A detailed investigation into all of Alta Conseco's things might have come to nothing, but it was impossible to know that.

I pulled across the block from Carmella's house on Ashford Street, but before I could get out of the car, my cell buzzed in my pocket.

"Yeah?"

"Nice greeting." It was Brian Doyle.

"I'm not in a nice greeting kind of a mood."

"I didn't know cancer made you cranky too."

Shit, I'd forgotten telling Brian. I didn't regret telling him, not yet, anyway. I'd had to tell someone before I melted down or

113

exploded, but I wasn't thrilled by his being so fucking casual about it. Nor was his timing very good. I'd finally put it out of my mind for the first time in hours.

"I'm old, Brian. Everything makes me cranky."

"I just wanted to let you know that Devo did his magic and we traced down a lot of the names on those hate emails. We also did background checks on the senders."

"A lot of firemen I bet."

"Cancer make you cranky and clairvoyant or is that an age thing too, Boss?"

"Just logic," I said. "And since when do you know words like clairvoyant?

"Since I started reading Webster's on the crapper."

"Lovely image, Doyle. Lovely. About the firemen . . ."

"Lots of firemen and lots of them assholes. They break down into three basic categories: guys with less than five years on, union hard-ons, and headcases."

"It would break down the same way if the NYPD were involved. It was always the same bunch that got worked up over stuff in the papers."

"Yeah, I guess. Listen, I had the stuff messengered over to your condo. There's an invoice attached and—"

"Don't worry, Brian. I'll pay it before I drop dead."

"Phew! That's a relief." He was laughing.

I was laughing too. "Fuck you very much, Doyle. Thank Devo for me, okay?"

"No problem, Boss. Take care of yourself."

"I intend to."

That was that.

I got out of the car and strolled right up to the front door. I don't know how I knew it, but I knew things had changed since my drunken visit the night before. No one answered the bells or my insistent knocking. I stepped back away from the house and stared up at it as if by staring intensely enough I would somehow divine what had changed and why no one was home. That strategy was about as effective as foam darts against armor plating. The house wasn't giving up any secrets. Houses seldom do. I headed across the street to my car and tried Carmella's number on my cell. Nothing doing. It went right to voice mail. I turned back to the house one last time.

"No home," a voice came from behind me.

Turning, I spotted the old Puerto Rican gentleman sitting on a discount store beach chair in the midst of his postage stamp-sized garden. Under his bleached-out Mets cap, he had a wizened, age-spotted face and a tobacco-stained smile. He had lived on the block for forever and was old when I first came here twenty years ago.

"Carmella isn't home?" I asked.

"No home," he repeated, but didn't leave it there. "The boy . . ."

"Carmella and her son aren't home?"

He shook his head yes and added again, "No home."

"Did they say when they were coming back?"

He turned his palms up and shrugged his shoulders. "No English." But I could tell he had something else to say. He said it in Spanish, finishing with a hopeful smile.

I hated to disappoint him. "*Lo siento*, I'm sorry," I said.

He was undaunted. Standing, he put his arms down by his side, but not completely straight down, and made his hands into fists. He pantomimed carrying something.

"Luggage. They had luggage."

"*Que?*" he asked. What?

"Suitcases. They had suitcases," I said, imitating his posture.

"*Si*, suitcases." His smile was very broad now.

"*Gracias*," I said, having almost exhausted my entire Spanish vocabulary. That was the odd thing about Carmella, when we were together she avoided speaking Spanish if at all possible, so I hadn't picked much up. It had never hit me before, the extreme lengths to which Carm went to cut herself off from her family. Not only had she physically removed herself and changed her name, but she had made all sorts of symbolic breaks from them. I was conscious of them before, but it was more glaring now that we had been apart for so many years. When you're close to someone and entangled in their *mishegas*, their craziness, it's hard to see the full extent of the damage.

The old man sat back down, lit up a cigarette, and let the sun take him in its arms. Sitting on your stoop or on your lawn or in your front garden, watching the world go by was a very New York thing. We didn't understand backyards very well. You can't see much from your backyard. There's not much action in your backyard unless you consider charcoals turning white with heat action. All the action's out front. Even when Katy, Sarah, and I had the house in Sheepshead Bay, we grilled out front on the porch. I lingered a bit, admiring the old man, enjoying him enjoying the moment. I wondered if there would be any moments like this for me to enjoy, or would I spend the rest of my life in and out of the hospital?

I put that thought right out of my head because I was pissed at Carmella. What the hell was she up to, dragging me into this and then splitting? Why hadn't she told me she had Alta's personal things and why didn't she let me see them? I was working myself up into quite a nasty mood as I retreated to the front seat of my car, but it didn't last. I'd slapped the rearview mirror with the back of my hand in anger and when I went to readjust it, I recognized the hypocrite looking back at me. Who was I to rage at Carm for keeping secrets and hiding from the truth? For fuck's sake, I was the king of kept secrets and adept at slicing the truth into sheets so thin they were nearly two-dimensional. Carmella had her reasons. I would know them eventually, whether she wanted them known or not. That's why I wasn't about to give up on this case. That and what was waiting for me if I did.

I pulled away from the curb, waving to the old man as I went. He nodded goodbye, the sun's embrace too strong for him to wave.

TWENTY

The package from Brian Doyle was there on the welcome mat outside my condo door. I can't say that I was particularly excited to see the thick envelope. Basically, it meant I'd be spending the next few days doing grunt work—going from house to house, interviewing angry firemen who would be about as happy to see me as they would be about a bad case of the crabs. I was getting too old for this shit. No, not getting too old: too old. I noticed it when I was working the Sashi Bluntstone case. The going from door to door, the lying and the half-truths, the drama, took a toll on me.

There was a day when I was interviewing potential suspects in Sashi's abduction that I had to kick a field goal using an art professor's testicles as the football. He was a big man with a short fuse who tried pushing me around, but even in my sixties, I wasn't easily pushed. In Brooklyn, the rule is, someone pushes you, you don't just push back, you push back twice as hard. If that doesn't work, you go for the throat or, sometimes, you aim a little lower. In my neighborhood, you learned to never bring a knife to a gunfight. Bring an F-16. But my roughing up the art professor that day wasn't the half of it. Later that afternoon in Alphabet City, I went to talk to a woman art blogger whose screen name was Michelangelo or was it Leonardo? . . . I forget. She turned out to be a meth freak, turning five- and ten-buck tricks for rent and drug money. She had been no threat to Sashi. The only child she was a threat to was her own son, who I found dead cold and blue in his crib. I didn't think I would ever recover from that day. I'm not sure I have.

Now I would go inside, open up the envelope, and start that process all over again. I laughed at myself, pushing in the front door. I laughed because I remembered the romance being a PI once held for me, how I was so hungry to work cases when I first got my license, but romance fades. I knew that love faded. Anyone married for more than a few years knows that lesson. Sometimes it evaporates completely and so abruptly you question whether it was ever there to begin with, but love and romance are different animals. I remembered how desperate I'd been for my gold shield, how getting it had once been more important to me than the fate of the Western world. As I've said before, there were several times over the three decades following my forced retirement from the NYPD that the serpent in varied disguises had offered me that apple and I'd turned him away. Each time it was offered, my desperation faded just a little bit more, until my hunger for the apple completely disappeared and the serpent stopped asking. Poor Eve, I thought, if she'd only been slightly more patient.

The first thing I noticed was the invoice. Talk about sticker shock. Doyle wasn't kidding about charging me for the work. He seemed to have added an eminent death surcharge. He was going to soak me for all he could while I was still breathing. I didn't mind, really. He had swallowed the cost of plenty of favors he'd done for me in the past and I'd been around long enough to know the bill always comes due one way or the other. Always.

The size of the invoice was about the only surprise in the pile of paperwork. Just as I had predicted and just as Brian Doyle had said, most of the more violent hate mail was from members of New

York's Bravest: some retired, most not. And the background checks Doyle and Devo had done were very helpful. With these guys' ages, addresses, contact info, police records, if any, and the public record aspects of their service records there in front of me, I would be able to eliminate a lot of the legwork. I would be able to generate a list of more and less likely suspects without having to interview each and every one of these schmucks.

First thing I took into account was proximity. Although I supposed someone might have been following Alta Conseco around for weeks just waiting for the right moment to kill her, I didn't think it was likely. There was something about the violence of the attack, the sloppiness of it—Alta had, after all, managed to make it back to the Grotto before she died—that made it seem like a spur of the moment, impulsive attack. Someone who would have been carefully following her for weeks wouldn't have risked such public exposure and would have made sure she was dead before abandoning the body. I had no proof or experience to back it up. What the fuck did I know anyway? I hadn't been a homicide detective. It was just a hunch, but I'd done pretty well following my hunches. So I took out an old road map of New York City and drew concentric circles in inch-wide increments extending out from the Gelato Grotto and carefully plotted the addresses of the hate-mailers.

Just as I finished pressing the point of my red pencil to the map where the last potential suspect lived, a stray thought crossed my mind that quickly turned into something else: a question. What in the hell was Alta Conseco doing at the Grotto in the first place? She lived on the other side of Brooklyn, for chrissakes! Okay, so some people loved their pizza and the homemade gelato was outstanding, but why would Alta travel to the Grotto? Did she have a craving?

Did she go there to meet someone? If so, who? Like all good questions, the original suggested a hundred more.

I snapped my red pencil in two. My daughter was getting married soon and three days after that, some surgeon would be cutting out half of my kishkas. I didn't have time for a hundred more damned questions. I wasn't sure I had time for one.

TWENTY-ONE

Grunt Work 101.

I began the unpleasantries early, figuring to squeeze as much in as I could in one day. It was a useless approach, but it was something. After my pencil-snapping fit of pique and brief wallow in the woe-is-me shallows, I came up with a plan. Any of the hate-mailers who had a history of violence, either on the job or off, moved to the top of the suspect list. Any with a history of violence against women, went to the top of the first list. And any of the folks on that list who lived within walking or short-driving distance from the Grotto, went straight to the head of the class.

Anthony Marinello batted lead-off. He was a nasty piece of pie. He'd only had about four years on the job, but had been moved around from firehouse to firehouse in his brief and undistinguished career. He was now on desk duty in Queens. Just like with the NYPD, there were legitimate reasons for desk duty: injury, advancing age, frayed nerves, et cetera. There were less than legitimate reasons too. I suspected the latter was the case with Marinello. He was a real nut job, a big mouth who was hated by the people he served with. According to his reviews, he wasn't much of a fireman either, but he hadn't yet crossed the line far enough to get fired for cause. He probably had a rabbi—someone more senior on the job with some juice who looked out for him—maybe a family friend or relative. Both the NYPD and FDNY were big enough to eat some of their mistakes or bury them, as it were, behind a desk or in a supply room somewhere, where they collected their paychecks without doing much harm.

Anthony also had had a few run-ins with his destined-to-be ex-wife. The wife hadn't gotten to the order of protection stage quite yet, but she had filed for divorce. Given the number of times the cops had been called to the house, you didn't need to be a soothsayer to think Marinello's arrest was on the near horizon. There was something else Marinello had going for him: his address was on West 6th Street near Avenue U, only a hop, skip, and a jump from the Grotto. I walked up the concrete steps to the old brick two-family house and rang the bell.

I hadn't worked on the lies I would tell to whomever answered the door. I found that the lies always sounded best when I hadn't rehearsed them. They just seemed more convincing somehow if I heard them at the same time as the party I was telling them to. There was no answer at first, but I didn't get discouraged. Too late for that. I was already discouraged and besides, it was early. I rang the bell again and this time I heard stirring on the other side of the door.

"Hold your water!" was the shrill order from the woman inside the house.

What a quaint expression, that. Most men my age had a little trouble in that area and didn't like being reminded of it. Between her voice and choice of words, I already wasn't particularly fond of the woman on the other side of the door. Things went downhill from there.

"Yeah," she said, pulling the door back. "What?"

Dressed in a garish, red satin robe, she was as hard looking as her voice was shrill. An unlit cigarette dangled from the corner of her frowning mouth. She smelled like an ashtray rinsed out in vanilla bathroom spray. I carried various sorts of business cards with me: one of the tricks of the trade. From one interview to the next, I never knew who I was going to need to be. I had cards I'd collected from insurance salesmen, doctors, rabbis, transport executives, lawyers—lots of lawyers—collision shop owners, plumbers, and a hundred other professions. I kept it simple and the lies to a minimum by handing her one of my own old cards from Prager & Melendez Investigations, Inc.

"Mrs. Marinello?"

"Not for too much longer, I hope."

"Your lawyer sent me," I said, yawning with false disinterest.

Mrs. Marinello stared at the card and I at her. She was probably thirty, but looked forty: too much sun and too many Marlboros. She had been pretty once, probably in high school. Her body was still intact and she knew it, but even that seemed to have some sharp edges. Her blond hair didn't match her coloring and it had been teased and hair-sprayed to within an inch of its life.

"What did the lawyer send you for?" she asked, finally looking up at me.

"To discuss your husband."

"I been t'rough this with the other guy."

"I'm better than the other guy. That's why I'm here."

"Okay. What the fuck? You wanna come on in?"

I hesitated. "Is your husband on the premises?"

"That asshole? Nah, I kicked his ass outta here in March."

"Where has he been living since March?" I asked, pulling out a notepad and pen.

"With his cousin Vinny up in the Bronx by Fordham somewhere."

I tried recalling the dates on the reports Doyle and Devo had supplied me with. "But he's been back, yes?"

"Yeah, I had to call the cops on him in April. He's such a prick. Started ripping up my underthings and smacked me around a little."

"But you didn't have him arrested," I said.

"Nah, I'm protecting my investment in that motherfucka. When we make the settlement, I need him to be on the job. I want half of his pension. If I got him arrested and he got shitcanned, where would that leave me? What would I have to show for marrying the prick? He's stayin' on the job as long as I can help it and now that Vinny got him assigned to some dumbass desk, I figure I'm in good shape to hammer him. Vinny, now there's the guy I shoulda married. He's already got fifteen years on and a vinyl siding business that triples his department take-home."

"You got it all figured."

"Too bad about Vinny. I blew him the night I met him and Anthony, but he came almost before I got him in my mouth. Anthony, now that man can fuck. I shoulda known better than to listen to my pussy."

Charming. "I wouldn't know."

She gave me a look that would've killed me and anyone within a twenty-foot radius. "What's that supposed to mean?"

"Nothing. Sorry. So back to the matter at hand. . . . Do you know of any other time your husband has been back? Have you seen him driving by, spoken to any of his friends or family, have you spoken to anyone who might've indicated he's been back in the neighborhood?"

"You are better than the other guy," she said. "All he wanted to know was, was I fucking anyone else or did I know if Anthony was fucking somebody else."

"I was getting to that, but can you answer my—"

"No, he hasn't been back around that I know of. He knows I got him by the nuts and he don't wanna lose his job neither. He's been a good boy and stayed away."

"So you've had no indication at all—"

"Didn't you hear what I just said to you, mister? No, from what I can tell, he's staying up in the Bronx banging this little cooz he hooked up with."

"That doesn't bother you?" I asked.

"If it keeps him in line and away from me, I wouldn't care if he was fuckin' Vinny."

Lovely sentiment, I thought, but I supposed she had a point. And by mentioning Marinello's new girlfriend, she'd given me an opening to ask about Alta Conseco. I took out a copy of the email Anthony had sent to both Alta and Maya and handed it to the wife.

"What's this?" she snapped.

"It's a death threat your genius husband sent to those two EMTs who let that guy die a few months back and it's what's going to screw up your plans for half the pension if your husband doesn't watch himself. If we caught him sending hate mail like this, the FDNY can catch him at it too. So, do you think there was anything to this threat?"

"Nah, Anthony's basically a coward. Yeah, sure, he's slapped me around a little bit, but he's just a frightened little boy. He wouldn't have the balls on him to kill anyone. Besides, ain't it already too late? Ain't one of those bitches dead already?"

I bit the inside of my cheek and nodded yes. "The problem is if you want to keep him on the job so we all make out here, I need to know for certain he had nothing to do with the murder. You do realize that Alta Conseco was murdered over by the Grotto, not a five-minute walk from here."

Her brown, hungover eyes got big. "Anthony didn't have noth-ing to do with that!"

"How can you be sure?"

"I thought you was working for me," she said, the first traces of doubt about me seeping in.

I ignored the doubt. "Look, if you can help me eliminate Anthony as a suspect here, you can get your dream settlement, but if he's tied up in this in any—"

"Okay. I can prove it if I have to, but it's not gonna look good in court."

"Maybe it doesn't have to get to court," I said, reassuring as all hell.

"We were in the Dominican Republic when that bitch was killed."

"*We?*"

"Me and Anthony and another couple." Her leathery skin sort of changed color as she looked away from me. On her, it's what passed for blushing. "We swing. We used to, anyways, and there's this resort down there that caters to swingers. We bought the airline tickets like last year and they weren't refundable and we, um, we didn't want to, you know, miss the opportunity, if you get my meaning."

"Oh, I get it. You can prove this?"

"I got the fuckin' credit card bills, receipts, and doctor bills right inside."

"Doctor bills?"

"Me and Anthony both got some stomach thing down there. We was sick for a month after we got back. You wanna see the receipts?" she asked, turning to go. "Like I said, I got 'em right inside."

"No, that's okay. I don't think it will come up, but I just had to make sure. If I need the documentation, I can get back in touch with you, right?"

"Yeah."

"Okay, I think that about covers it."

I left, hurrying down the stairs. I could feel her eyes on me, but I didn't look back. I wanted to get as far away from her as fast as I could. It wasn't as if she were the most despicable person I'd ever met—not by a long shot. My former father-in-law Francis Maloney made her look like Rebecca of Sunnybrook Farm. Nor was her sense of ethics, as fucked up and convoluted as it was, the most self-serving. It was just that her focus was so narrow, her goals so small, so unimportant in the scheme of things, that I wanted to scream. Is this what she was born to dream of, I wondered? Was half of her husband's pension all she wanted out of life? By the time I reached the street, I wanted to turn around and run back up the stairs and shake her by the shoulders and tell her life was too short to want so little from it. I turned, but she had already gone, gone back inside with her tiny dreams to keep her company.

She'd done me a favor by eliminating Anthony Marinello as a suspect. Did I believe her about them being out of the country when Alta was murdered? Yeah, I believed her. It rang true. If the wife was lying, she was a better liar than me, and if she was lying, she deserved a lot of credit for coming up with an amazingly embarrassing alibi on the spur of the moment. Besides, her story was easy enough to check out. She had done me a favor because looking for the right suspect was like shopping for a house: unless there are very few on the market, you don't buy the first one you look at.

TWENTY-TWO

The guy at the next stop was no less a fuck-up than Anthony Marinello, just an older, more accomplished one. This time there was no wife for me to talk to. Patrick Scanlon had stubbornly clung to his career until the department basically told him to take a hike. He was a classic red-noser, a professional drinker with so many busted blood vessels in his face you could scan them like a barcode. He had skated by for nearly three decades until the FDNY really cracked down on drinking a few years ago. The last straw was a New Year's Eve brawl at a firehouse on Staten Island that involved whiskey, a folding chair to the chops, a broken jaw, and a tumble down a staircase. When the incident was thoroughly investigated, all sorts of bad things came out of it and the department put its foot down hard. Indiscretions that'd traditionally been tolerated or treated with wrist slaps were now fireable offenses. Guys like Scanlon either saw the writing on the wall or had it shown to them. I wouldn't have been shocked to learn that the desk Scanlon vacated when he put in his papers was taken over by Anthony Marinello.

Scanlon showed me down to his den in the basement. He was a hunter and a fisherman and had the trophies to prove it. He was a big man with a shock of white hair and gray stubble and a surly son of a bitch. No matter how I tried, it was difficult to get him to focus. That sort of worked for and against me. When I pointed out that his Cropsey Avenue address was only a short car ride to the Grotto, he looked at me like I was talking in tongues.

"I don't even like their fucking pizza," he said.

Well, I thought, Scanlon had at least one redemptive feature: he knew mediocre pizza when he tasted it.

He sobered up a little bit when I showed him my old badge and a copy of the rather disgusting email he had sent to Alta Conseco and Maya Watson only a week before Alta was murdered. He wasn't the type to challenge my badge even if I looked too old to be carrying it. When I pressed him about his threats, he didn't exactly ask for forgiveness.

"Fuck them two cunts," he said. "They stained us all by leaving that man to die like that. They're a fucking disgrace!"

I bit the inside of my cheek again. It was going to be a rough day for the inside of my cheek.

"Is that how you see women, as cunts? You seemed pretty sure about what you'd do to their anatomy if you ever got hold of them."

"How did you get a hold of that anyways?" he slurred. "I didn't put my name on it."

"You're proud of that, huh, hiding behind a phony name? If you had half a brain, you'd know there are ways to track emails."

"No need to get insulting."

"I'm sorry. Did I hurt your feelings? Why would I want to insult a coward who hides behind a fake name and threatens women and calls them cunts? Gee, I wonder."

"Okay, so I'm an asshole sometimes. It's the drink."

"First refuge of a coward, blaming everybody and everything but himself."

He seemed not to hear me. "Hey, I gotta piss. All right?"

"It's your house and your dick. Go ahead."

When he left the den, I took a closer look at the décor. I noticed three taxidermied fish on the walls and a framed photo of Scanlon with some hunting buddies standing over the carcass of deer. In another, he posed holding the limp body of a wild turkey by its neck. In yet another, his feet were surrounded by a stack of dead ducks and geese. On the wall to my right I noticed a locked gun rack with two shotguns and three bolt action rifles. There was a glass case with some wall-mounted handguns that weren't just there for show and next to that case was a wall display of hunting knives, machetes, bayonets, ceremonial knives, one with an ivory handle and a black swastika affixed to the hilt, a Confederate cavalry saber, and a samurai sword.

"What were we talking about?" he asked when he returned.

I ignored him. "Where's the knife that goes there?" I asked, pointing to a conspicuously empty spot on the wall.

He didn't like that question and I could see the gears turning. "No knife goes there. I, um, I haven't filled that spot yet."

He was completely unconvincing. "Don't bullshit me, Patrick. You can see the silhouette of it. You know that Alta Conseco was stabbed to death, right? So here's what I'm looking at: a death threat from you, a nasty drunk who lives five minutes away from the crime scene, a missing knife, and a very dead woman. Can you do the math? Because I can."

"I wouldn't'a killed that dyke."

"Dyke?"

"Yeah, yeah, she tried to hide it, but I heard shit."

"How the fuck would you hear shit?" I said. "You've been out of the department for a few years."

"What, you think because I got forced out, I don't hear things? You hang out at McPhee's, you hear plenty."

I shook my head. "That place again. What is it with you guys and that bar?"

"You know McPhee's?"

"I know it. But we're getting off the subject here. You haven't said one word that disputes my math, Scanlon. I still got the same problem."

He dipped his head like a little kid who'd been caught boosting a pack of gum at the local candy store. "I sold that knife months ago, way before that—before what's-her-name was murdered. I can prove it."

"Why didn't you just say that?"

"It wasn't my knife to sell. It belonged to one of my old hunting buddies. We had a falling out, but I kept it and then I sold it."

"Do you think I give a shit? I'm not from the stolen knife squad, for chrissakes!"

That was a dumb thing to say because now Scanlon was taking his first good look at me. I hadn't quite told him before who I was and what the exact nature of my business was. The old badge had worked well enough and I had let his drunken mind fill in the blanks. Now fear was sobering him up pretty fast. I had to get his mind off me and back on the subject.

"Okay, so you sold that knife, but you got lots more here and probably dozens more I don't see." I picked up the Nazi knife with the fancy handle. It was probably some bonus gift to an SS man for killing the largest number of my relatives in a single month. "What about this one?" I asked, twirling it in my hand and then dropping it.

He cringed. "Hey, cut that out. That's worth a lotta—"

"Or this one?" I knocked a hunting knife to the floor.

"Cut it out. Cut it out! Those are worth—"

I knocked another one to the floor. That did it. He came at me, swinging wildly, blindly and missing by a mile. I sidestepped, leaving my right leg out for him to stagger over. He tripped, sprawling into a leather recliner and then to the floor. He rolled over, but didn't get up for a second run at me. He probably wanted to, but the thing of it was I was now showing him some hardware of my own. I had my old .38 out and pointed straight at his belly.

"That's enough of that, shithead. I couldn't miss you from here even if I was blindfolded."

He held his hands up, palms out in surrender. "I swear I didn't do nothing to her. I was mad, sure. We was all mad at them, but I didn't kill nobody."

"Not like you haven't hit a woman before," I said. "You were arrested a few months ago for—"

"It wasn't like that. She hit me first. We had a fender bender on Bay Parkway and the bitch gets out of the car and slaps me in the face. I grabbed her wrists and then some passersby grabbed me and called 911. It was all fucked up. The charges were dropped. You can check it out. I done some shitty things in my life, but I ain't never hit a woman."

"Okay, get up." I put my gun away. "I'm leaving now. If I were you—god forbid—I would try real hard to find someone who could alibi you for the night Alta Conseco was murdered. Someone other than a relative."

"I didn't touch that dyke, I swear."

I let myself out. Problem was, I believed the prick. I had nothing to back it up beyond the sense that he was telling me the truth. He was a bad liar and it was my experience that it was hard for people to fake being bad at something. Scanlon was just a bag of leaves: all puffed up, but ultimately weak and full of hot air and decay. I suppose he'd be worth taking a second look at and I would call Fuqua to let him know what I'd found. What bothered me more was him calling Alta a dyke. I mean, that's what guys on the job do. If a woman doesn't swoon at the sight of them or keeps to herself or doesn't wear enough makeup to suit them, she gets labeled as gay. It happened when I was on the cops and it hadn't changed. I didn't care one way or the other but if it was true that Alta was gay, it added yet another ingredient to the mix that might complicate things more than they already seemed to be. With every step, the slippery slope got steeper and more slippery.

TWENTY-THREE

The address was on Havemeyer Street in the Williamsburg section of Brooklyn. Before evolving into hipster central, Williamsburg had once been a German, Italian, and Jewish immigrant stronghold. By the late sixties and early seventies, White Flight had emptied the neighborhood of its more traditional residents and that void was filled by the oddest of ethnic odd couples: Puerto Ricans and Hasidic Jews. Even as the area was transforming into its present incarnation as hipster heaven, the Puerto Ricans and Hasidim stayed on, if in somewhat smaller numbers than during the last two decades before the new millennium.

The uneasiness hit me before I got to Jorge Delgado's street. I'm not sure why that was. Probably had to do with the dubious pleasure of starting my morning rounds with Mrs. Anthony Marinello and Patrick Scanlon, but maybe not. My unease intensified as I pulled into the spot across from Delgado's address and it grew stronger still as I got out of my car. It was, I thought, an omen. I'm not one for omens except when I am. I mean, you don't believe in God, it's tough to believe in omens. Fuck that! Logical consistency only counts if you care about what other people think and my oncologist had given me license not to care.

Although his hate mail to Alta and Maya was just as scathing and cruel as the others, Jorge Delgado was a distinct creature, unlike Marinello, Scanlon, and the other douche bags on my list. He had been part of the FDNY for nearly twenty years. Delgado was highly decorated and very well-respected, if not exactly beloved. His fury at Alta and Maya—Alta in particular—came from a different place than almost all of the other hate-mailers. Not only was he good at his job, but his was a strong minority voice in the union and Delgado was a leading member of a Puerto Rican fraternal organization. He had fought long hard struggles for equality and fair representation of women and minorities on the job. Although he did, apparently, sometimes let his temper get the better of him. There were reports of the occasional shoving match and shout-down with fellow firefighters who stood on the opposite side of the issues.

Entering the building, I held the front door open for a big guy on the way out. It didn't hit me immediately, but the man who nodded his appreciation as he passed was wearing a blue FDNY T-shirt. After 9/11, half the men in New York City were wearing T-shirts just like his. They'd been sold to raise money for the families of the dead. I had a few myself. Those shirts, like my old PI license, hadn't seen much action in the last several years and had been consigned to the bottom of a drawer somewhere. The man who walked by me was black, which didn't necessarily mean he wasn't Puerto Rican, but he was about ten years too young to have been Delgado.

"Excuse me," I called to him.

He stopped and about-faced. "What's up?"

"The Delgados?" I asked, hoping the question in my voice would suffice.

He nodded, his rugged face drooping in sadness. "You here to pay respects too, huh?"

"No, I'm sorry, I hadn't heard, but I'm glad I ran into you," I said, furiously working out my cover story in my head. "I had an appointment with Jorge to discuss retirement investments. God, it would have been awful to walk in on his grieving family. What happened?"

"Traffic accident about three weeks ago. Georgie was walking to his car after a shift and this little girl was crossing the street. He saw a car blowing through a stop sign, so Georgie ran for the kid. Knocked her out of the way, but he took it full on. Wound up nearly a hundred feet away. He was totally fucked. Brain dead. The family finally gave up and pulled the plug a few days ago."

"Christ! That was him?" I said, pretending to have known about the accident. Since my family tragedy in 2000 and 9/11 the following year, I'd stopped reading the papers or listening to the news. Reading the paper had once been a part of my everyday routine and one of the great pleasures in my life. Not anymore.

"Yeah, that was Georgie: the bravest of the brave."

I lied. "The first time I spoke to him, he was still pretty upset over those two EMTs who stood by and let that man in the restaurant die. He sounded really angry."

"That shit drove Georgie nuts. Said they had set back the cause by twenty years. Man, I tell you what, there was times I thought he was mad enough to kill those EMTs if he got the chance. I've seen him pretty crazy mad, but never mad like he was 'bout those two. He only just stopped talking about it."

"You can't be serious, not about him hurting those women. He seemed like such a nice man."

"True that. He was a great guy, a brother. Kept my ass alive more times than I'd like to say, but Georgie had a temper on him, a bad temper. It was his Achilles heel. You know what I'm saying? When the man got a bug up his bee-hind about something, it was hard to calm him down. Don't matter much now, does it?"

"I guess not," I said, shrugging my shoulders. "I do work with some other firefighters. One of them told me that EMT that got murdered was . . . that she was a . . . you know . . ."

"Gay?"

"I guess that's the better way to say it."

The man's previously sad and caring expression turned suddenly cold. "So what if she was? She fucked up, but even that don't mean she should've been cut up like that."

"You're right," I said. "I'm sorry. That came out wrong."

"Forget it."

He turned and walked to his Honda Accord parked down the street. I watched him drive away. It's an amazing thing, what people will tell absolute strangers. They'll tell you things they wouldn't tell their best friends or their priests. Investigators count on that impulse. I was kind of disappointed that I'd upset him because he was clearly grieving for Delgado, but one of the things about doing PI work is that you're never going to win any popularity contests. Whether you tell the truth or lie through your teeth, you're not usually saying things people want to hear. I thought about finding Delgado's apartment, but decided there were some situations that were off limits no matter how just your cause. I wasn't going to intrude on the Delgados' grief. What I needed to know, they probably couldn't tell me. Even if they could, I wasn't going to ask, not today.

I'd never met Jorge Delgado. I'd never even seen a picture of him. To me he was a man who wrote a threatening email and, until I knew more, simply the sum of the parts of a limited background check and the brief testimonial of a grieving firefighter. Still, I could not ignore the feeling in my belly. Hunches worked both ways and I had to trust them equally. If I had been willing to believe that a complete scumbag like Patrick Scanlon was telling me the truth based solely on my sense of him, then I had to believe the gnawing in my gut about Jorge Delgado. I wasn't prepared to be judge, jury, and executioner—I was already too late for that last part—but I couldn't deny that bells had gone off in my head during my conversation with the firefighter with whom I'd just crossed paths.

Back in the front seat of my car, I called Brian Doyle. He answered on the second ring.

"Yeah, Boss, what's goin' on?"

"I sent your check yesterday as soon as I got the package."

"Thanks, but that's not why you called, is it?"

"Nope."

"Then why?"

"Jorge Delgado. He's one of the firefighters you guys did a preliminary background check on. I want you—"

"Delgado," he interrupted. "Why does that name sound—"

"—familiar? He's that hero fireman that got killed saving a little girl's life," I said, suddenly an expert on the subject.

"Right. Right! What about him?"

"I need you and Devo to do the full Monty on him. The works."

"He's dead, Boss."

"You have a flare for the self-evident, Brian. Anybody ever tell you that?" I didn't wait for his answer. "Yes, he's dead. Doesn't matter. Do what you have to as soon as you can."

"Even if it means rubbing some people the wrong way?"

"Especially that. And I know it's gonna cost me, but I can't take it with me, can I?"

I could hear him thinking of how to respond. Brian was a loud thinker at the best of times and this wasn't one of those. Brian was a doer. I let him off the hook. "Look, forget I said that. Just do it. It's important to me."

"Sure thing, I'll get somebody right—"

"Not somebody, Doyle. You. I want you for this, please."

"You know, Boss, you're more of a pain in my ass now than when you really were my boss, you know that?"

"Yeah, but the pay's better."

I left it at that and clicked off.

I sat and stared up at Delgado's building. On the second floor, I saw a chubby-faced little girl staring blankly out her front window. She reminded me of another little girl I'd met once a long time ago. That little girl's mom, a nickel and dime crack whore, had been beaten to death in a dreadful SRO hotel called the Mistral Arms. The last time I saw that girl, on the day her mom was murdered, she was sitting in a wobbly chair with a one-eyed cat in her lap. She fed him from a tin can. She had the same blank expression on her face as the girl across the way. Maybe I was reading too much into her expression, maybe that wasn't Delgado's daughter at all. Maybe, but I knew in my gut it was his kid.

TWENTY-FOUR

I undressed and showered. The shower wasn't so much to rinse away the sweat and grime, but to wash off the remnants of the people with whom I'd shared the day. It's no wonder that good cops sometimes turn to the darkness. When you spend more time with the worst people imaginable than with your family, it rubs off on you. You can't go down into the sewer and not come up smelling like shit yourself. If I could have scrubbed out the linings of my lungs, I would have. I remembered talking with Mr. Roth about the camps, about how he said the worst part of it all was the breathing.

"Yes, there was smoke," he said, "lots of smoke and the stink of burning flesh and hair, but it wasn't all smoke. There was ashes too, Mr. Moe, ashes of the dead falling like snow. You could not help but breathe it in. You would wonder sometimes, who it was you were breathing in. It was better not to dwell on it. If you would dwell on such things, it was all a man could do not to rip his own chest open or to throw himself onto the electrified fence. It was better to think of the small things like surviving."

Only a man like Mr. Roth, a man who came out the other end of Auschwitz, could call surviving a small thing. But I don't suppose all the scholarship and study by those who didn't live through it could make sense of it. I never judged things Mr. Roth told me about his experiences in the camps. Who was I to judge, after all? And some truths can't be argued.

I had seen three more hate-mailing scumbags that day, but my heart wasn't in it. My lies were unconvincing and I barely listened to the answers to my questions. There was just something about Jorge Delgado that sang to me. He lit me up like a neon Christmas tree and I couldn't say why exactly. Maybe it was that he wasn't simply another run-of-the-mill misogynist or misanthrope. He wasn't the typical griper or whiner. He didn't feel sorry for himself or wronged by the world. He wasn't a narcissist. No, he was something much more dangerous: a believer, a believer with a bad temper. But it wasn't Delgado I was thinking about when I got out of the shower.

Still damp, I stood naked, staring at myself in the mirror and saw for the first time what I had become. I *was* thin and pale. I could see something in my future, brief as it might be, that I could never have imagined: frailty, my arms and legs as easy to snap as dried twigs. For the first time in my life I felt old. I didn't want to think about the implications of old, especially if this was as old as I would ever get. I found self-pity especially unattractive. It's what I hated about the people I'd spent my day with, but there I was, feeling cheated somehow. I turned away. As my Bubbeh used to tell me, "It is one thing to say *oy vey*—oh, woe—and something else to say *oy vey iz mir*—oh, woe is me."

The phone interrupted my sad reverie. In a moot gesture, I wrapped the towel around my waist and rushed to answer. I wouldn't have cared if it was a phone scammer calling. I just needed to speak to someone, anyone to help pull me out of the hole I'd been digging for myself.

"Hey, Moe." It was Nick Roussis.

"Nick! Glad you called." And I was. "What's up?"

"Like I said I would the other night, I been keepin' my eyes and ears open."

I was confused. "Huh?"

"About the murder, you know? I said I would listen and I also sent out some feelers."

"Then I take it you heard something."

"You always was pretty smart that way, Moe. There's no gettin' anything by you."

"I didn't know Greeks were big on sarcasm."

"Sure, it's like democracy, we invented it."

"Okay, Socrates, what did you hear?"

"You busy tonight?"

"I guess I am now," I said.

"Come by the Grotto around eight. There's somebody I think you should talk to."

"Okay, as long as you don't make me eat that shitty pizza."

"Moe, you don't show up, I'll have pies delivered to your house for a week."

"Now that's a threat that scares me. I'll be there at eight. Thanks, Nicky."

"See you then."

I hung up and was pretty curious about who it was Nicky wanted me to talk to. Sometimes I thought I would live as long as I was still curious. I bet a lot of cats had that same thought as they breathed their dying breaths.

TWENTY-FIVE

The Grotto was standing room only. I had been here before on many such late spring nights when I was a kid. Back then, in ancient times, before shopping malls, iPhones, or texting, it was a place to meet friends or girls or to go on tentative first dates. A lot, maybe too much, about the world had changed to suit me, but there was something comforting in seeing the faces I saw there that night. Kids might dress differently than they did when I was young, but all the technology in the world couldn't beat the awkwardness and hormone-fueled behavior out of them. Girls still whispered in each other's ears and giggled. Boys still strutted about trying to get noticed.

I thought of Pam and ached, not because I missed her, but because I didn't. I hadn't really thought about her in days. Carmella had done that to me. That was her particular brand of magic, or her curse. She had done it to me the first time I saw her in the lobby of the Six-O precinct over twenty years ago. The immediacy of attraction wasn't mutual. I think the first thing Carmella ever said to me was, "Yo, you got a problem?" Which was followed with some crack about her not needing some middle-aged guy stalking her. Not exactly the start of a beautiful friendship. I was married to Katy then, happily so, though the first hairline cracks between us were beginning to show.

Carmella was the classic bad drug, my bad drug: once she came back to town, she blotted out the rest of the picture and all I could see was her. My reaction to her was chemical, reflexive. Even though

I was pissed off at her for withholding Alta's personal effects from me and for skipping out without an explanation, I couldn't wait to see her again. My anger heightened the electricity between us; it always had. It was potent, this dance we did, unhealthy, but powerful. I guess, it's why Carmella left me to go to Toronto in the first place. And now my being sick brought it to a whole new level. How could Pam compete with that? Suddenly, I wasn't quite as wistful about the kids on their first dates. I kept my eyes straight ahead and walked to the door at the Grotto marked "Employees Only."

Nick Roussis was sitting at his desk, his back facing the door. He didn't seem to be conscious of me standing behind him because something on the computer screen had his complete attention. Just about the time I opened my mouth to say something, he slammed his fist down on the keyboard, sending keys flying off in all directions.

"What did that computer ever do to you?"

"Oh, Moe, Jesus! You startled me," Nick said, trying to compose himself. "I'm sorry. I didn't hear you come in. This," he said, tossing the ruined keyboard in the trash," is just about business. My suppliers are making me crazy. You own a business. You know how it is."

Yes and no. I knew what it was like to have suppliers give me a hard time, but it never got me mad enough to take it out on the hardware. Then again, I'd never invested enough of myself in the wine business to lose it like that. I never cared about it like my brother Aaron cared about it, the way Nick cared about his restaurants.

"What, are the suppliers shorting you on your orders? Not giving you full value on your credits?" I asked.

"That should be the worst of it. Forget it. C'mon, the guy I want you to meet is—"

"Nicky, pick up line two," a disembodied voice filled the room. "It's your brother, Gus. He says it's important."

A angry look washed across Nick's face, not dissimilar to the one he had after making short work of his keyboard. "Fuck!" He picked up the phone. "What?" He listened, his face hardening. Then he barked something out in Greek—a curse, no doubt. You don't have to understand a language to understand its swear words. A long stream of Greek followed and it wasn't love poetry either. Nick smacked his palm down on the corner of the desk. He listened for a couple of seconds and screamed into the phone before slamming it back into its cradle. I may not have been a keyboard smasher, but I certainly understood arguments between brothers.

"Not having a good night, huh?"

Nick was distracted. "What?"

"Having a bad night?"

"Yeah, let's get outta here before the roof collapses. The guy I want you to talk to is waiting for us at a restaurant in Bay Ridge. C'mon out the back way. I'll drive."

We stepped through the near empty kitchen, out the rear door of the pizzeria, down the loading dock steps, and onto West 10th Street.

"My car's over here." He pressed a button on his key and the tail-lights on a gray BMW 525 winked at us.

"Nice ride," I said, sliding into the front passenger seat.

"Gotta have some perks for all this fuckin' aggravation, no?"

"You'll get no argument from me, Nick."

When Nick turned right onto 86th Street, neither he nor I had much of a stomach to look as we passed by the Grotto.

. . .

An old school Italian restaurant, D'Alto's was an endangered species. Smelling of backyard red wine, garlic bread, Parmigiano cheese, and oregano, dimly lit with Chianti bottle candlestick holders covered in generations of melted wax, full of tables dressed in red and white checkered linens, the place reminded me very much of Cara Mia and a hundred other red sauce restaurants that had vanished from the Brooklyn landscape over the last decade. These kinds of places weren't hip, weren't Food Channel enough. Nothing that came out of the kitchen required a degree from the Culinary Institute of America. But I loved places like D'Alto's because it smelled and tasted like my childhood, like eggplant and veal smothered in red sauce and covered in mozzarella cheese, like Brooklyn was supposed to taste.

An old man approached us with menus.

"We're with him," Nick said, pointing at a man seated at a table in the darkest corner of the restaurant. "Bring us three glasses of red to start, okay?"

The old man nodded yes. In a place like D'Alto's, the wine list was very short: red or white. Period. Sometimes, it wasn't even that extensive. Mostly, it was just red and then it was homemade either in someone's basement or backyard. You drank it from water glasses and if it wasn't fit to drink straight, you squeezed in some lemon and threw in a couple of ice cubes to cut it.

When we got to the dark table, the lone figure fairly popped up out of his seat. Except for some acne scars, he was a good-looking guy, maybe six-three, two hundred and sixty pounds, early thirties, with a huge upper body, a real prison build. Lots of empty time to fill up with push-ups and pull-ups and free weights. He had a head of neatly kept black hair, dark brown eyes, and a strong chin. He had a confused nose that couldn't decide which way to go, but it added a nice bit of character to him.

"Joey Fortuna, this is Moe Prager, the guy I want you to talk to," Nick said. "Moe, Joey Fortuna."

We shook hands. Fortuna's handshake and prison tats on his arms reinforced my guess about his workout routine.

"Joey here was once a firefighter, one of New York's Bravest," Nick continued.

"No wine for me," Fortuna said, waving his glass away when the old man delivered the red wine and a basket of crusty bread. "Just some sparkling water and lime."

I snickered. Nicky did too and told the old man to leave the third glass on the table, that he'd drink it.

"What's so funny?" Joey wanted to know.

"Should you tell him, Moe, or should I?"

"Be my guest, Nicky."

"Kid, in a place like D'Alto's, you're gonna get tap water with lemon. These old Guineas don't know from sparkling water."

The kid tried to laugh with us, but it sounded hollow. He was on edge. Whether that was because he didn't like getting ragged on or because of what he'd been brought here to talk about, I couldn't say. What was obvious was that he wasn't having himself a grand old time.

Nick and I sampled the red wine. Definitely homemade, but not bad, no ice or lemon required. I put down my glass.

"You said Joey *was* a firefighter or didn't I hear that right?" I asked.

"No, Moe, that's right. Past tense," Nick said.

Joey spoke up, "I got caught—"

"—selling steroids, right?" I finished his sentence.

"Fuck, man, how'd'ya know?"

"Acne scars, prison build, tats. You still juicing?"

"No way," he lied. "I swore that shit off. I'm on parole. If they ever heard I was—"

"Calm down, kid. Calm down," Nick said, patting Joey's huge shoulder. "No one here's interested in that kind of thing. No one wants anybody to get jammed up. Just tell Moe what you told me."

The kid opened his mouth just as the old man came back to take our order. Nick did the honors.

"Cold antipasto plate, eggplant parm, veal parm, a big dish of ziti with red sauce. And him," he said, pointing at Joey, "he'll have two grilled chicken breasts with a salad. Oil and vinegar on the side. That okay with you, kid?"

"Lean protein and leafy greens. Just what I was gonna order."

The old man shook his head in silent disgust. *Grilled! No breading! No red sauce! Sacrilege!* He was still shaking his head as he walked away.

"Okay, kid, tell the man," Nick cued Fortuna. "Tell Moe what you've been doin' to make ends meet."

Fortuna bowed his head and muttered, "Collections." Then louder, "I been doing collections."

"Not traditional collections, I take it. You've been working for someone who puts money on the street," I said.

"That's right. I sorta convince guys that are slow payers to speed up their delivery, if you know what I mean."

Nick spoke for both of us. "Yeah, kid, we know. We were cops once."

"Who you muscling for, Joey?" I asked.

The kid went green and Nick came to his rescue.

"Moe, let's just say he works for friends of mine and leave it at that, okay?"

"Fine. Business must be booming in this shitty economy," I said. "People are desperate to get loans wherever they can, but then when they have to pay the principal back with the vig on top . . . You must be doing a lot of convincing these days."

"Fuck, yeah. Busy all the time. I'm making out pretty good."

"This is all very interesting, but what's this got to do with—"

"He's coming to that, Moe. Relax. Go ahead, Joey, tell him."

"A few months ago, a guy comes to me that I used to work with in a firehouse in the Bronx. He says he heard I was looking to pick up extra cash since I got out of the joint. Sure, I says. Why would I turn down extra cash, right? So he says he got a friend that wants to talk to me about a job, but when I ask him what kinda job, he don't answer. All he says is that it ain't about collections and I should talk with this other guy and he'll fill me in. He gives me a phone number for this other guy and—" Joey stopped abruptly, nodding toward the waiter headed our way.

"Cold antipasto platter," said the old man as he laid the dish at the center of the table. "Enjoy."

Nick forked some Genoa salami, provolone cheese, and a roasted pepper, ripped off a hunk of bread and made a little folded sandwich. He washed it down with wine and finally noticed Fortuna's silence. "You like a jukebox, kid, or what? I gotta put a quarter in you every time I wanna get sound out? Tell the fuckin' story already or we'll still be here when they open up tomorrow morning."

By the sour expression on Joey's face, it was evident he didn't appreciate Nick's sarcasm or his ordering him around, but my guess was that Joey wasn't here out of the goodness of his heart and he was either doing someone a favor or being paid handsomely—maybe by Nick, maybe not—to be here and tell me his story.

"So I called the guy and he says he's asked around about me and that he heard I could be trusted because I didn't give up the names of the guys I was dealing 'roids with and I did the full bid inside instead of rolling over on my partners. So he asks me if I'd be interested in picking up some extra 'scarole for a job. I asked how much and for what. Before he tells me, he asks if I get squeamish about hurtin' women. I told him I didn't get off on it or nothin', but if a bitch borrowed money and didn't pay back on time, she got treated like the rest of 'em. Their fingers and arms break jus' like everybody else's."

"Is this going somewhere?" I asked, sipping on the wine.

"Let the man talk and you'll see," Nick chided.

"The guy says he'll pay me five large to t'row a scare into this bitch, that I can hurt her all I want and that if she died, he wouldn't shed no tears over it. He said just to make sure it was slow and that it hurt. I told him I wasn't gonna kill nobody and that if I was, five large wasn't large enough. He said ten was the best he could do, but that if he had some more time, he might be able to come up with another five. I said that I still wasn't interested in killin' nobody, especially a woman, but that five grand would buy him a lot of hurt. He said he'd send me half the money and information about where I could find the woman."

With a sense of where this was going, I speeded up the process. "He sent you the money?"

"Twenty-five hundred in used twenties and this," he said, sliding a folded piece of paper across the table to me.

Tucked inside the paper was a grainy newspaper headshot of Alta Conseco. Alta's address and phone numbers were printed on the paper. Even knowing what was coming, I felt my eyes get big when I saw the photo.

"Did you kill her?"

"No, man. What are you, fuckin' crazy? You think I'd come in here and tell you this shit if I—"

"Calm down, Joey," I said. "I'm not stupid and I don't think you are either, but I had to ask. So, what happened after you got this package?"

"I recognized the bitch. I mean, the guy even sent me a newspaper picture, right? I read the papers and I listen to the news. No way I was gettin' mixed up in this shit. It's one thing to put some hurt on some loser nobody ever heard of. It's somethin' else to do somebody who's got reporters following them around. I kept callin' that number until the guy answered. I told him I wasn't interested and asked him where I should send the money back to."

"What happened when you told him you weren't interested?"

"Man, he went like freakin' batshit on me. Cursin' at me in Spanish, callin' me faggot and cunt and—"

I interrupted him. "Spanish?"

"Yeah, you learn those curse words pretty fast inside. He told me he'd kill me if I ever said a word to anybody and he sounded like he meant it. What a fuckin' temper on that guy. He went off, man. He gave me a PO box to send the money to, but I told him I was keepin' the paper to make sure he stayed away from me. I'm tellin' you, he was crazy, that guy."

"You never got his name?"

"Are you kiddin' me? That was the whole point of workin' over the phone."

"Did he have an accent?"

"Only when he was screamin' at me and cursin'."

"But this friend of yours," I said, "the one you used to work with in the Bronx, he knows the—"

Joey shot out of his chair. "I'm not goin' there. Forget it. If I didn't give up no names or roll over on anybody to save myself jail time, I ain't gonna give you no names. The only reason I'm here now is because my boss told me I had to talk to Nicky, but that's it. I told you what I had to tell you. What you do with it ain't none of my business." He grabbed the paper and newspaper photo and shoved them in his pocket.

"Okay," I said. "Okay. Let me ask you a few more questions and then we're done."

Joey sat, but looked ready to bolt at any time.

"The guy you used to work with in the Bronx, the one who hooked you up, I don't want to know his name, but he doesn't work in the Bronx anymore, does he? He works in Queens, right?"

Joey didn't run, but kept silent. That was answer enough for me.

"And this unnamed guy, he's Puerto Rican, right?"

That did it. Joey stood up and bent over the table, looming right above me. "Look, I was here because I was told to talk to Nicky, but I don't know you and I don't like you. You jam me up with any of this and I'll do to you what that guy wanted me to do to the bitch. You hear me, old man?" He reached for my collar, then stopped. I guess he didn't like how my .38 felt against his ribs.

"I may be old, but my finger still works pretty good. All the steroids and HGH in the world won't do you much good from point-blank range, asshole, so step back and get the fuck outta here. I don't give a shit about you, but I owe Nicky, so you're safe."

He didn't need to be told twice and was gone. I ate very little of the meal, good as it was, nor did I hear much of the background music over the sound of Jorge Delgado singing to me from the grave.

TWENTY-SIX

It wasn't time to go to Detective Fuqua, not yet, anyway. So far I had some interesting, even compelling circumstantial evidence that pointed to Jorge Delgado, but nothing that would stick—as if anything would really stick to a dead man. Besides, I had a problem with things that came together too quickly and nested so seamlessly. People's lives weren't like model airplanes. They didn't come with glue or parts that fit perfectly together according to the instruction sheet. They were sloppy, messy things full of competing impulses, conflicting emotions, and unresolved feelings. It had been my experience that unresolved feelings were like that undigested food people carried around in their gut: it festered and grew into the things that eventually ruined us, turned us ugly, and sometimes killed us. Unresolved feelings, I thought, were probably at the root of more pain and destruction than any other single cause in the history of humankind.

Twice before I had worked cases where the parts seemed to fit perfectly together, but the model came out wrong, all wrong. The first time was in the early eighties when Moira Heaton, a state senator's intern, disappeared from her boss's office on Thanksgiving Eve. After some digging, I thought I had her killer nailed. The other time was when I was looking for Sashi Bluntstone. The kidnapper and alleged murderer was practically served up on a silver platter like John the Baptist's head. In both cases all the evidence—circumstantial and substantive—pointed one way and in both instances the evidence was wrong. I had been manipulated into taking what I had at face value. The prime suspects turned out to be false positives. So, no, I didn't trust seamlessness and it didn't escape my notice that on the same day I stumbled across Delgado as a suspect, I got that call from Nick. It doesn't get more seamless than that. This time I wanted to be sure to dot all the i's and cross all the t's before I shouted that the sky was falling.

It was a piece of cake finding out who the fireman was who had acted as the middleman between Delgado and Joey Fortuna. No need for me to go to Doyle and Devo for that. Fortuna had all but told me the guy was Puerto Rican and it wasn't much of a leap to guess he had worked out of the same firehouse as Delgado. A few little lies and a few fifty dollar bills later and I had a name: Nestor Feliz. I waited outside the firehouse until Feliz's shift ended and approached him as he opened his car door.

"Nestor Feliz?" I asked in that same antiseptic voice I used as a cop. It got people's attention and it fucked with their equilibrium. He looked up, scared. Nestor had a guilty conscience about something. I held up my leather case that contained my old badge, but didn't open it. Then I lied a bit about what was inside the leather case. "If I show you my gold shield, this will be an official conversation. If I don't, we can have a nice little unofficial chat at a local bar and leave it at that."

He stalled for time. "What's this about?"

"Nestor, I can feel my fingers about ready to show you my shield."

"Okay. There's an Irish pub on Austin Street off Queens Boulevard."

"I'll follow you there."

Parking was easier to find than usual in Forest Hills. Irony was, the pub Feliz had chosen was only a few blocks away from the 112th Precinct and I had little doubt that half the people in the bar with us were real cops, not retired old farts playing pretend. We found a quiet table in a corner. I bought Nestor a Bud and I had a Dewars. The alcohol was meant to prove this was all very unofficial.

"So, Nestor, let's get something straight. I'm not looking to hurt you, but if you bullshit me once, I'm gonna come down on your head like a tornado."

"What's this about?" he repeated.

"Jorge Delgado."

Nestor went from looking worried to angry. "He's dead."

"No shit! I know that. C'mon."

"Georgie was a great fireman, a hero. Let him be. I don't know what you want from me."

"Okay, fair enough. I'm gonna give you another name and if you say to me, 'She's dead,' I'm gonna cuff you and march you down the street to the One-One-Two and book you. You ready? You understand?"

"Go ahead, yeah."

"Alta Conseco."

Now he went from looking angry to nauseous, which, in a way, was all the answer I needed. "I didn't have nothing to do with that shit."

I had to be careful here, because as much as I detested scum like Joey Fortuna, I couldn't betray the deal Nick Roussis had made in order to get him to talk to me. It wasn't important to me to know how Nick got word about Joey or with whom he had made the deal. You do business in New York City, you have dealings with all sorts of unsavory types. Ridiculous taxes and exorbitant fees weren't the only reasons prices in the city were high. There were all sorts of invisible taxes and hidden fees too. Part of every dollar you spent on trucking or carting refuse or construction went into some gang-ster's pocket and it wasn't just the Mafia, the Irish, the Chinese, the Columbians, or the Russians anymore. Organized crime was a growth industry and everyone from the Indians to the Israelis to the Dominicans to the Haitians to the Vietnamese were looking for their taste. Don't think for a second that Aaron and I were somehow above it. We weren't. We knew where the money went and that's why I couldn't hurt Nicky.

"My bullshit-o-meter is starting to click away here, Nestor. Word on the street is that you were a middleman between a hitter and Jorge Delgado. I don't have the hitter's name, not just yet, but if I start digging around out there, I'll find it and I'll find him. He's not gonna go down by himself, not for murder one."

"Georgie was pissed at those two EMTs. When he got that way, there was no calming him down. I tried, I swear. I tried, but he just got madder. I made a few phone calls, that's all. One guy took the job, but when the guy found out who Georgie wanted him to hurt, he backed out. When Georgie told me he offered the guy money to kill her, I told Georgie I was out of it. I mean, we was all mad at the two EMTs, especially us Puerto Ricans, but I didn't want to kill nobody."

"But how about Georgie? After you told him you didn't want to be part of it anymore, did he let it go?"

"It wasn't Georgie's way to let things go. He was a stubborn man."

"What happened when he found out Alta Conseco had been murdered?"

"I don't know."

"What do you mean, you don't know, Nestor? There goes my bullshit-o-meter again."

"I mean I don't know because Georgie took that week off."

"Did he go away on vacation?"

"No."

"No?"

"No, he said he stayed home and did work around the apartment."

"And when he came back to the job, how was he?" I asked.

"I don't know. He was himself."

"Was he still angry? Did he say anything, anything at all about Alta Conseco's homicide?" I held up my hand. "Listen, Nestor, don't even try to con me here. If you're lying to me about this, I'll know it, so think hard before you answer."

Feliz bowed his head and mumbled something I only caught part of. I told him to repeat it loudly enough for me to hear.

"He said, 'One down, one to go.'"

TWENTY-SEVEN

My cell phone rang as I approached Maya Watson's condo. I let it go to voicemail. I had taken the thing with Delgado as far as I could take it until I got word from Brian Doyle. Even with Feliz's confirmation of what Joey Fortuna had told me the previous evening, I still didn't have enough to go to Fuqua. As good as Delgado looked on paper, the paper itself was as thin and fragile as a tissue. All I had was a dead hero fireman who had been angry enough to have hired someone to hurt Alta Conseco, but just because he'd tried to hire a hitter once didn't mean he'd tried it again or that he had killed Alta himself. Delgado's "One down, one to go," comment to Nestor Feliz about Alta's murder wasn't exactly damning evidence. Most of the city probably thought karmic justice had been served when they read the headlines the morning after Alta's murder.

Regardless of my good fortune—if that's what it was—in stumbling across Jorge Delgado, I needed not to fall in love with him as a suspect. I had to block out his love song to me from the great beyond. A healthy dose of skepticism is always a good thing and if you love a suspect too much, it's impossible to remain skeptical. I knew that better than most. I wanted to run Delgado's name past Maya Watson. I guess I could have called and asked or called to warn her I was coming, but I wanted to see her face, to judge her reactions. And even if her reaction supported my belief in Delgado as the most likely suspect, there were still things about the case that bugged the shit out of me. I didn't buy for a second that, on their salaries, Maya and Alta had gone to the High Line Bistro to grab lunch. And if they weren't there for lunch, what the fuck were they doing there? What were they arguing about when they got there? And the ultimate question still remained: Why, in spite of their training and spotless performance evaluations, had they stood by and let Robert Tillman go untreated? What good would it do Carm, I wondered, if I could wrap up her sister's murderer in a tidy package with a silken bow, but not explain why her sister had simply let a man die? Someone had those answers and I meant to get them.

The bruise in the atmosphere around Maya Watson's condo development had healed a little more since my earlier visit. Kids were outside playing and none of her neighbors gave me the evil eye as I approached Maya's door. This time, when she opened up to let me in, there was a hint of a smile on her face. Her hand wasn't shaking and there was no cigarette burning between her fingers. The place still reeked of them, but her windows were open and the living room drapes were pulled back to let the sun stream in. The drapes danced to the tune of the ceiling fan and the shadows danced with them. But it was all part and parcel of a false promise, a lie with a brief shelf life that Maya was telling herself, an attempt to wish herself back to Kansas from the dark depths of her personal Oz. It was as if she were telling herself it was all going to be better now, but I could see it wasn't. The lies we tell ourselves are always the worst lies of all.

Some of the sunlight from the living room managed to bend its way into the kitchen, but only enough to show me just how false hope could sometimes be. The kitchen was still an utter mess: a platoon of unwashed coffee cups stuffed with half-smoked cigarettes covered the entire table. Bulging plastic garbage bags were stacked in a pyramid at the side of her refrigerator and the sink was piled above countertop level with dirty dishes. Worst of all, that hint of a smile on Maya's face had so thoroughly vanished that I questioned whether it had actually been there at all.

"Okay, this is bullshit!" I said, grabbing two of the garbage bags. "Where are you supposed to throw the trash out around here?"

Stunned, she said, "There's cans around back."

"Go take a shower and get dressed while I clean up in here."

Maya opened her mouth to object. *What was I doing there and who was I to order her around in her own house?* Instead, she did as I asked. People have an amazing talent for self-preservation and she understood in her bones how desperately she needed to get out of her self-imposed prison. All the sunlight and fresh air in the world weren't going to make that place anything but a prison cell until she walked outside and faced the world.

The trash was gone and most of the dishes were done by the time she reappeared. For the first time I saw how tall Maya really was. The weight of the controversy and the grief over Alta had literally compressed her. With makeup covering some of the stress lines, I could see what a complete knockout she was. And even in a simple gray, v-necked tee, jeans, and low heels, her athleticism showed through. She moved with the grace and ease of a cat. The best part was that hint of a smile had returned.

"Go open the rest of the windows and turn on every fan you've got, while I finish the dishes. Then we'll get out of here."

She'd come this far with me and I guess she didn't see the point in arguing with me now. She turned and left the kitchen.

"Come on, we're going for a ride," I said after I finished drying my puckered hands, putting her hand in the crook of my elbow. "How do you feel about hot dogs and french fries?"

She didn't answer, not with words, but with a smile.

The hardest part for her was the stroll from her front door to my car. Maya dug her fingers into my arm as we walked. She kept her eyes straight ahead for fear she might crumble at a disapproving glance or worse, that she might run back to her solitary confinement. We didn't talk much along the way and I was glad of that. We both were. The two of us knew, I suspect, that I wasn't a boy scout and that although my heart did ache at her dilemma, I had motives beyond doing my good deed for the day. We had made a silent bargain: she would let me get her out of her dungeon and I could ask for something in return, but that was for later. Now she just wanted to enjoy her freedom.

Carmella had said it, Coney Island was where I was my most comfortable. It was the place where I most belonged in this world and the world most belonged to me and when we stepped out of my car and up onto the boardwalk, it seemed the right place to have brought Maya Watson. She took deep breaths of the salted air, her first free breaths in months. The breeze was light and cool off the water, cutting against the intensity and warmth of the sun. Sea gulls complained noisily at water's edge, fighting over some scraps of discarded food or the last bits of rotting flesh sticking in the overturned shell of a horseshoe crab. Maya was leaning over the guardrail, her eyes peering so far into the distance she might have seen Galway Bay.

"Lunch?"

"Not yet, Moe, please."

"Fine."

I let her look to Ireland a little longer before asking my questions. When I finally asked, she seemed almost relieved.

"Have you ever heard of Jorge Delgado?" I was staring at her profile.

"That hothead? Yeah, I heard of him. He had a hard-on for Alta even before all this shit come down. Why you wanna know about him?"

I didn't answer her question, not directly. "Funny thing, Maya, when I was checking into who might've murdered Alta, a few people called her a dyke."

She looked gut-punched. "Guys are assholes like that. You know how it is. You were on the job. A woman don't get wet for some man who's hot for her and he starts that bullshit, the rumors."

"I didn't say they were guys."

That really unnerved her, but she soldiered on. "Don't matter who said it."

"Did you hear about Delgado getting killed in a car accident saving a little girl?" I asked, purposely trying to confuse her. I was basically interrogating her. She knew it and I knew it. And there were two methods that worked best for me: silence and confusion. Silence—giving her time to fill in the void—hadn't worked on the almost hour-long car ride here, so I went with the other bullet in my gun.

"Couldn't help but hear it. Why you wanna know about Delgado? Why do you keep asking me about him?"

"In a second. First, why don't you tell me about the hard-on Delgado had for Alta even before all this shit came down?"

Maya Watson went stiff as a board. "Take me home. This was a mistake. I shouldn't'a come here with you. Take me home."

"No."

"Did you just say no?"

"That's about it. You wanna run away, I'm not gonna help. There's several subway lines right over there at the Stillwell Avenue Terminal," I said, pointing in the opposite direction from the water. "It's only a block away. You need money for a Metro card?"

"Fuck y'all!"

"No, Maya, I'm not fucked. You're the one who's fucked and you'll be fucked until you talk to somebody about what really happened that day at the High Line Bistro."

It really was amazing how liberating cancer could be. In the face of a possible death sentence, I didn't much care about Maya Watson's opinion of me. Cracks were starting to show in her castle walls.

She hesitated, then said, "I can't talk about it. I told you that."

"Are you gay too?"

That really shook the castle walls. She turned to go, stopped, tears streaming down her face. "Leave me alone. Why can't everybody just leave me alone?"

"You are alone. I've never seen someone more alone in my life. That's how I found you, eating yourself alive in that filthy apartment. You wanna go back there or do you want to live again?"

She didn't answer, but she didn't leave either.

"Was Alta a lesbian?"

"Yes," she said, walking back to lean on the rail for support. "But I wasn't her type. She liked military types, younger chicks, white girls mostly. That's what she said anyway."

"Did people on the job know she was gay?"

"No. I mean, not for sure. People suspected. She never hit on anybody at work, but people hear things. They see stuff. One woman I trained with saw Alta in Chelsea with another woman."

"Is that what Delgado's beef with Alta was about?"

"Yes, it was. He had this crazy Puerto Rican pride thing and you know how Latin men can be, all macho and shit. If Alta was African-American or white or Chinese, he wouldn't'a even given her a second thought, but because she was Puerto Rican . . . let's say he tried to make her time at work as hard as it could be. He had a lot of friends in the department, people with sway, and he fucked with her. He had his friends mess with her schedule and shit. But why are you always bringing Delgado up?"

I hadn't planned on telling Maya yet, but I had her talking and I didn't want to risk losing her now.

"I spoke to a guy last night who was offered five thousand dollars by Jorge Delgado to hurt Alta. And by hurt, I don't mean her feelings. He wanted him to break bones and, if he was so inclined, to kill her."

Maya's face went blank, then icy cold. I was surprised the tears didn't freeze right on her cheeks. "Why you talking to me and not the police?"

"Because the guy I spoke to turned the job down and I can't prove anything yet. Besides, Delgado is a hero, a dead hero. The time's not exactly right to go making charges against him, not if I want to be taken seriously."

"Alta was a hero too," she screamed in my face.

"I'm afraid the rest of the universe doesn't quite see her that way."

"Well, fuck them and fuck you."

"If I'm wrong, if they're all wrong, explain it to me. Tell me what happened that day with Tillman. If there's an explanation, people will understand."

I felt like I almost had her. She leaned into me, but she just couldn't cross that line she had drawn for herself. I hammered away at her.

"What is it you're afraid to let people know? Are you gay too? Were you and Alta lovers? Is that the big secret? Christ, Maya, it's the twenty-first century. Would it be worse for people to know you're a lesbian than for them to think you cold-bloodedly let a man drop dead?"

"I'm not gay," she said, calm as could be. "If I was, I would be proud of it, not ashamed."

"Then what is it? What's the big secret? What don't I understand? What are you so ashamed of?"

"Which way is the subway?"

"That way," I said. "Right over there: down the boardwalk, along Stillwell to Surf."

Maya pushed off the rail and started across the wooden planks toward the steps to the street. I kept pace.

"Come on, Maya, what is it? What can be so terrible that you can't even bear to think about it? Tell me."

She ignored me and kept on walking. She didn't run, she didn't even walk very fast. Finally, at the corner of Stillwell and Surf Avenues, across the street from the subway terminal, Maya stopped and faced me again.

"You know, Moe, I think you're a good man and that your heart really is in the right place, but you ain't asking the right questions about the right person. There's somebody involved in this whole mess that nobody wants to see for who he was, not really. Think about that and stop hounding me. Leave me be."

By the time my mind snapped back to the moment, Maya Watson was across the street and disappearing through the entrance of the Stillwell Avenue terminal.

TWENTY-EIGHT

I was confused. Wasn't the first time, wouldn't be the last. Who the fuck was Maya Watson talking about? No one in this entire mess was innocent. I suppose she might have been talking about Jorge Delgado, but that couldn't be right. Any fool could see I was already taking a hard look at Delgado and Maya Watson was no fool. Maybe I wasn't looking hard enough at him to suit her or maybe she didn't like the fact that Delgado—guilty of Alta's murder or not—had been beatified in the press. I mean, getting killed while saving the life of a little girl is a kind of permanent baptism. One good act, your last act, and all your sins get washed away. It's like getting dunked in the cleansing waters and never needing to come up for air. Is that what Maya was referring to? I don't know, there was something obvious I wasn't getting. Wouldn't be the first time for that either.

My cell phone vibrated and chimed in my pocket to remind me I had a voicemail message. I got off the crowded, noisy street and retreated to my car to listen. The car still smelled of Maya Watson's vaguely sweet perfume. The message was from Detective Fuqua, but I would have recognized his voice even if he hadn't given his name. He left his cell number and told me it was important to call him back as soon as possible.

"Mr. Prager, it hurts my feelings when you do not pick up my phone calls," he said. "And it makes me suspicious as well."

"You sound like a jealous wife, Detective."

"I suppose."

"Sorry, but I was busy making arrangements," I lied. "My daughter is getting married in a few weeks."

"Really? *Fantastique! Mazel tov.* You must be on *schpilkes*, on pins and needles, yes?"

His French I might have expected, but his Yiddish caught me off guard. "Your Yiddish is good, Detective Fuqua. Are there many Haitian Jews?"

"I worked in community relations in the Seven-One. Big Caribbean and Hasidic populations in the neighborhood. I got along very well with the Hasidim. They have great respect for the police."

"For the law, Detective Fuqua, not the police. Those are two very different things. Jews are naturally suspicious of agents of the state. Long history of persecution at the hands of those agents, don't you know?"

"Have you ever heard of the Tonton Macoute, Mr. Prager?"

"Papa Doc's own private little terror squad."

"Just so. No one need lecture a Haitian on distrust of the police."

"Fair enough. So you and the Hasidim made nice. That explains your Yiddish, but it doesn't explain how you knew I was Jewish."

"Oh, but Mr. Prager, I know many things about you that you might not suspect. We should discuss them over lunch."

"Maybe tomorrow."

"That seems like such a waste of time, *non*? Why wait until tomorrow when you are sitting in your car on Stillwell Avenue at this moment?"

My skin prickled and I felt a solitary bead of sweat roll along my ribs. "How the fuck do you know where I am?"

"Such language, Mr. Prager. As I said, I know many things about you. I am sitting at a table on the other side of Nathan's with too much food for me to eat myself. Come join me. I do not enjoy dining alone." He clicked off.

As I walked the two hundred yards from where my car was parked to where Fuqua was sitting, I didn't waste my time looking for the cops who'd been assigned to follow me. In the big crowds around Nathan's Famous Hot Dogs on a sunny June day, I could have been there for hours and never found them. When I was on the job, cops pretty much sucked at this sort of thing because they were almost all white males who might as well have had COP stamped across their foreheads. But since 9/11 and since the ranks of the department had opened up to women and every ethnic group you could imagine, things had changed.

"Mr. Prager, come sit," Detective Fuqua said, standing to greet me with his right hand extended. I shook it with no enthusiasm and sat across from him. "It is a glorious day, is it not?"

"Weather-wise, yeah. Perfect. I love days like this in Coney Island."

"Yes, perfect for a stroll with a beautiful woman like Maya Watson."

"Get to the point, Detective."

"Was Miss Watson any more forthcoming than she had been? Did she say anything helpful?"

I stifled a laugh.

Fuqua was confused. "Something is funny?"

"In a way. All I managed to do was to piss her off enough to take the train back to Queens."

"That is unfortunate. Please, I forget my manners, take a hot dog."

"I'm suddenly not very hungry," I said.

"Some fries, then, at least. I adore Nathan's fries. They are most unique in flavor."

"I hear it's because they use some corn oil in the deep fryer, but who knows?"

"Indeed, who knows? It is the flavor which matters."

The aroma of the steam and oil coming off the fries was almost enough to make actually tasting them superfluous. Almost. I took a thick, ridge-cut fry, dipped it in ketchup, and bit into it. *Ummm.* The crisp brown and salted skin crunched and the moist, soft potato melted in my mouth. If there were things I would miss when I was dead, Nathan's fries would be one of them. If I knew I was going to have a last meal, they would be on the menu.

"Would you like me to purchase beers so that we might drink to the wedding of your daughter?"

"No, thanks."

"A pity."

"So, Detective, can we get to the point of this?"

"Jorge Delgado," he said, before biting into a hot dog.

"What about him?"

He finished chewing. "Let the man rest in peace, Mr. Prager."

"He's gonna rest in peace regardless of what I do. He's dead."

"But there is his family, his memory to consider."

"No, not if he killed a woman in cold blood."

"That may be, but you have been stirring the hive. And even very peaceful bees will sting when they are sufficiently agitated."

"Just tell me what you've got to tell me, okay."

"*Bon.* Good. Let me then speak plainly so that you might understand. Jorge Delgado did not murder Alta Conseco."

"And you know this how?"

He laughed. "Because I have received indisputable word of this from on high."

"You and God been chatting lately, have you?"

"No, this comes from an even higher authority, Mr. Prager."

I understood, of course. "The brass."

Fuqua shrugged his shoulders. "I could not say."

"Too bad they didn't use the overtime money they wasted having me followed around to actually help you find Alta Conseco's killer."

"Yes, too bad. As sad as that may be, Mr. Prager, I have already looked into Delgado as a suspect."

"And . . ."

"Nothing."

"In other words, the city needs a hero and Jorge Delgado's been elected. The brass has been told, probably by the mayor, that no one is going to ruin the coronation. Not me, not anyone. And they told you to tell me."

"For what it is worth, Mr. Prager, I sincerely do not think Delgado murdered her."

"Is this your voice I'm hearing or is it the word of the brass gods?"

"My own. Delgado's name came across my desk almost immediately. He apparently made no secret of his distaste for Miss Conseco. And while his alibi for that evening would not hold up in court, there is no proof he was anywhere near the Gelato Grotto when Alta Conseco was killed. There is not a single piece of forensic evidence linking him to the crime. I have showed his photograph in an array to everyone who gave a statement that evening. Not one of them identified him as a person they saw on the night in question. Not one of the employees identified him. I canvassed West 10th Street on my own time. Nothing. I even had an informal meeting with Mr. Delgado not unlike the one the two of us are sharing at this moment."

"Funny how none of this turned up in those notes you shared with me," I said.

"Not funny. Purposeful. The minute I heard about Delgado's heroics, I made a separate file for safekeeping. I have my ambitions, and ambitions are best served with ammunition to back them up."

"You'll go far, Detective Fuqua, but be careful. I had an ambitious friend just like you once."

"What happened to him?"

"He got too close to the sun and his wings melted."

"I will keep that in mind."

"Do that. Did you know Delgado tried to hire someone to hurt Alta?"

"And did this gentleman take the job?" Fuqua asked.

"No."

"Would you be willing to produce him for questioning on the subject?"

"I don't think I'd be willing nor would he to volunteer what he knows."

"In that case, Mr. Prager, I would urge you to let this go, please. There can be nothing good gained. No matter who the murderer of Miss Conseco might be, the fact remains that she and Miss Watson stood by and let a man die."

"All right," I said, "you've done your job. I consider myself thoroughly warned. I will let the Delgado thing go for now. I don't need any shit before my kid's wedding, but I'm not gonna stop looking into Alta's murder. That I won't do."

"That is only fair, I think." He stood to go, leaving a table full of mostly uneaten food.

"Detective," I called after him. "I'm curious. What happened to your refrain about all victims being equal in murder?"

"The tune I have just sung to you was not my own composition. My own song is unchanged."

"That's right, you have ambitions."

"I am not ashamed of that."

"Neither was my friend. He wore ambition like a badge of honor. Problem was, he forgot about the other badge he carried, the one that really mattered."

Fuqua winced. That stung. Good. *Fuck him.*

TWENTY-NINE

I'd been warned off cases before and, in the scheme of things, Fuqua had carried it off pretty well. He'd been fairly direct without getting all heavy-handed or nasty about it. There had been no direct threats to me or to the people close to me. He hadn't gotten clichéd by listing the myriad ways the city or state could hurt my business. He didn't try to bullshit me about it being his bright idea to make me get in line. In fact, I don't think he enjoyed doing it at all. But he had the curse of ambition same as Larry McDonald. He saw big things for himself and didn't think clean living was going to get him there. The fuck of it was, he was right. Larry Mac hadn't climbed so high on the ladder by being a good cop—which he was, mostly. I believed Fuqua believed what he said about Delgado not being the murderer. Now maybe I was willing to believe it too.

That's the thing about perspective. It had been what, two days since Delgado appeared on my radar screen? And in that short time, his initial appeal had lost much of its luster. Not all of it, most of it. That aria he had been singing to me, while not a faint whisper, was not exactly a siren's song either. Did any of what Fuqua told me totally eliminate Delgado as a suspect? No, the late Mr. Delgado still had his charms. He'd hated Alta Conseco even before the incident at the High Line. He'd been angry enough to hire someone to maim if not kill her. And in spite of the fact that I trusted that Fuqua was telling me the truth, I was too familiar with the allure of ambition to trust him too much. If he could prove to the brass he had put me off Delgado, at least temporarily, there was probably a big reward—a bump up in grade or a plum assignment—coming his way. Apparently, a lot of powerful people had gone all in on making Delgado the next saint of New York. It wouldn't do to have your new martyr found with a woman's blood under his fingernails. Mostly I was clinging to Delgado's possible guilt because I didn't know where else to go.

Clinging to him as a suspect didn't mean I wouldn't keep my word to Fuqua. I wasn't going to pursue Delgado until I got the all-clear from the detective. I meant what I said to him, that I didn't need any shit before Sarah's wedding. Anyway, by the time Delgado's temporary sainthood had lapsed and his rep was primed for a bit of tarnishing, I might already be dead. If not dead, then certainly in treatment: losing my hair, my lunch, and my pride. I'd witnessed people go through surgery, radiation, and chemo. A doctor once told me that the kind of regimen I was in for was a kind of slow motion murder. That they sort of hoped the cancer would die before the rest of the patient, but that it didn't always work out that way. Happy happy. Joy joy.

For now I needed to think and, more importantly, I needed a drink. I was depressed by the notion of having to go back to my list of hate-mailers. Christ, the thought of doing more grunt work, of spinning more tales out of lies, half-truths, and false threats was making me ill. I didn't think I had the energy to go once more into the breach, not for this, maybe not for anything. And I couldn't get Maya Watson's parting words out of my head. That was a bad thing because it meant I wouldn't get anywhere with it. I almost never made progress on a problem until I forgot about it. That was another good reason to have a drink. I backed out of my spot, away from the parking meter. I didn't see that I was being followed, but just because I was looking for them now didn't mean I'd spot the cops tailing me.

I didn't figure on finding Flannery in McPhee's, so I went to that other neighborhood place, the one with the name that I never knew. And there on a lonely barstool was the great man himself in all his guilt and glory. He didn't turn, but saw me at the door in the mirror behind the bar. He tilted his head and slapped the barstool to his left.

"Dewar's rocks," I said to the barman as I nestled in beside Flannery.

He still did not turn my way, looking instead at my face in the mirror. "Rough day?"

"Rough month, but, yeah, today in particular."

The bartender put up my drink and started a tab without asking. "Any progress in the case?"

Shrugged my shoulders. "I thought so, but I've been warned off for the time being."

He was confused. "Warned off?"

I explained about Delgado, but did it very quietly so that not even someone right next to Flannery would be able to hear. Flannery shook his head and laughed. It was the kind of laugh that had more to do with disgust than good humor.

"Great fireman," Flannery said, "but a total prick, old Jorge. He tries to hire a leg-breaker to hurt a woman, then jumps before a speeding car to save a child. Go figure. Moe, I swear, I sometimes wonder if there is a God."

"I don't, not anymore. I was never much of a believer to begin with and with what I've seen . . ."

"The wife was a true believer. Madge went to mass every day and the rosary was like a sixth finger on her hand. I used to think she believed enough for all of us. Then, when she passed, I knew the lie of that. You can't believe for somebody else. They bury your faith with you."

"Then I guess my coffin will be light as a feather. No faith to bury with me."

"There's always the guilt to add the weight of absent faith. With the guilty cross I bear they'll need a forklift to lower me down."

"Maybe we can split the cost of the rental."

He waved his hand at me. "Ah, listen to the two of us bellyaching about the weight of our guilt. Only two types of creatures without the weight of guilt on them: the newly born and the forgotten dead."

Why did he have to use the word bellyaching? I hadn't even finished two thirds of my drink and I was already feeling the fire burning in my gut. I asked for a glass of ice water.

"Are you okay, Moe?" Flannery asked, looking directly at me for the first time since I walked in.

"No, Flannery, I'm pretty far away from okay." I gulped the water down and turned to the barman. "Get my friend here another."

He nodded. I left enough on the bar to cover more than two more Jamesons and a nice tip.

"I need to rest," I said, shaking Flannery's hand.

"You know, Moe, there's something I meant to talk to you about."

"What's that?"

"I hear there's some guy fanning the flames over at McPhee's," he said. "You've pissed off a lot of folks poking around the way you have."

"I have a talent for pissing people off."

"Best to watch your back carefully for now."

"For today, at least, I've got New York's Finest doing that for me."

"What?"

"Never mind and thanks for the heads up. Take good care."

Out on the street, I nearly keeled over from the pain in my belly, but the pain didn't last. It was only a tease, a calling card to say, "Welcome to the rest of your life."

THIRTY

I fell asleep with the sun still hanging lazy in the late afternoon sky and my shoes on my feet. When I awoke the memory of the sun was gone, washed away by the raindrops drumming against my bedroom window. I'd lately fallen in love with naps, though I usually managed to get my shoes off before passing out. For some reason I slept better in the late afternoon these days than at night. At my age, you're confident you'll wake up from a nap, but the same couldn't be said of a night's sleep.

I stripped off my clothes and showered, making sure not to stand and stare at my sorry-assed self in the mirror when I was done. I threw on a robe and stood looking out my front window at the storm roiling the oily sheen atop the black waters of Sheepshead Bay. Tethered to their docks, dormant fishing boats bobbed and listed. Spring storms in Brooklyn, even at their most fierce, were just so much bluster. The howling wind that carried bits of paper and plastic along the sidewalks and bent the few trees along Emmons Avenue blew warm and with little bite. I found my hand on my abdomen again and my mind filled with all the wrong kind of thoughts.

I did not fear death so much as the dying and I didn't suppose I was alone in that. When I was a cop, I never gave much thought to getting killed on the job. It wasn't healthy to think about such things, especially back in those bad old days when people called us pigs with impunity and we were targets for every radical group with a pistol or a pipe bomb. I don't think kids could even conceive of how dangerous it was for us then. No, I never really worried about it, but I did have my private dread. I didn't want to die in the cold in the rain. Just imagining the feel of an icy cold sidewalk against my cheek as a freezing rain soaked through my clothing made me nauseous. Even a hospital bed—and I detested the idea of dying in a hospital bed—would be preferable. Like Israel Roth before me, I did not want to be cold. I did not fear being alone so much. We are all alone in death. I accepted that, but I did not want to be cold and wet.

I turned away from the window and suddenly Flannery's voice rang in my ears. Something he had said earlier in the day came back to me. Not the stuff about pissing people off. That came with the territory. It was something else. *Only two types of creatures without the weight of guilt on them: the newly born and the forgotten dead.* I'm not sure why it hadn't registered at the bar—probably because my gut was already starting to hurt—and I wasn't sure I understood why it popped into my head just then or why it should matter. Sure, I was thinking about death and dying, but I was pretty certain that wasn't why Flannery's words had suddenly come back to me. Then, with my next breath, I swore I could smell Maya Watson's perfume in the air. Christ, I really detested sweet perfume. I'd driven to Bay Ridge with my windows down trying to get the smell of it out of my car. And now it was like I was summoning it up. I was at a loss. As undeniably attractive as Maya was, I wasn't particularly attracted to her. Besides, in spite of the sympathy I felt for her situation, I don't think I'd ever get past what had happened at the High Line Bistro.

That's when I knew. Maya Watson's parting words came rushing into my head. *There's somebody in this whole mess who nobody wants to see for who he was, not really.* She hadn't been talking about Jorge Delgado at all. No, Maya Watson had to be talking about Robert Tillman, the victim at the High Line Bistro, one of Flannery's forgotten dead. It seemed so obvious to me now, I wanted to kick myself. Of course he was the one person in this whole ugly mess that hadn't received much scrutiny at all. Even if it was his being stricken that started the chain of events that led to Alta Conseco's murder, why would anyone focus on some poor schmuck who happened to drop dead of an aneurism in a restaurant kitchen?

Let's say a stray dog runs out into traffic, gets killed by a bus, and starts a chain reaction that leads to a fatal car crash. In some sense, although the dog was the catalyst for everything that followed, he's the least important element. He's just another dead dog that happened to be at the wrong place at the wrong time. Well, Robert Tillman had been treated like that stray dog: a man in the wrong place at the wrong time. The irony was that if he had been murdered, the cops would have gone over every inch of his life, searching for the killer's possible motive. But he hadn't been murdered and, from what I could see, there was no connection between Robert Tillman, Alta Conseco, and Maya Watson beyond the unfortunate coincidence of proximity and unfortunate timing.

I dialed Maya Watson's phone number. It rang a few times before going to voicemail. I didn't really blame her for not answering her phone these days. She had no doubt changed her numbers more than once since March, but privacy, which had always been a cruel myth, was now nearly unattainable. No one knows that better than a private investigator. Before everyone used the internet like an anatomical appendage, we used to be able to find out pretty much everything about anyone. True, it used to take a little longer and it depended a little more on bribery, threat, and charm than on hacking, but the results were similar. I left a message, apologizing for what had transpired earlier and asking if we could get together to talk. I left my numbers and hung up.

I sat down at my computer and Googled Robert Tillman. If there was a connection between Tillman and the two EMTs, this was the place to start.

THIRTY-ONE

The High Line Bistro seemed like the logical second step after the Internet. Frankly, going back to the High Line was more like step 1-b. According to Google, there were a lot of Robert Tillmans in the world and most of them had accomplished a good deal more than landing a job as a prep cook at an overpriced Manhattan eatery. Even after I had made my search specific enough to get information on the Robert Tillman I was looking for, there wasn't much to find worth looking at. In a world where every other putz on the street managed to achieve some diluted form of internet celebrity with a video of himself doing something creative or creatively stupid, Robert Tillman had managed to remain as anonymous and unheralded as a store brand soft drink. In fact, there wasn't a single entry on him that predated his death.

The bartender recognized me immediately and smiled. Then, when she remembered why she recognized me, that lovely smile slid right off her face. It's funny how people's expressions so betray them. I knew a detective once, a guy named Micky Dingle, who used to watch TV with the sound off. He insisted it was good practice for learning how to read body language and facial expressions and it was hard to argue with his results. Dingle was a legendary interviewer—*interviewer*, that's cop speak for interrogator—and had a knack for getting suspects to confess to their crimes, large and small. These days they would say Micky was attuned to unconscious physical cues and nonverbal communication. The FBI probably taught

187

classes in it by showing videos of baboons doing threat behavior and dolphins recognizing themselves in mirrors.

I sat in the same barstool I'd occupied the last time I was here. There were actually a few other people at the bar this time around, so the bartender wasn't pinned and wriggling in front of me like she had been during my previous visit. But we both knew she couldn't avoid me forever.

"Sparkling water with a lime?" she asked.

"Good memory. Yeah, to start, sparkling water is fine. It's Esme, right?"

"Esme, yes."

"I'd also like a glass of Zin and a minute of your time."

"The water is with my compliments. The Zinfandel you pay for, but my time is my own. And please do not bother showing me your badge again. It took me a little while to figure it out, but you are old enough to be my grandfather."

"You know how to hurt a man's pride, don't you? No, I'm not a cop, but I used to play one on TV."

She didn't laugh. "I do not understand."

"Bad joke, never mind. I used to be a cop and I use my old badge sometimes as kind of a shortcut is all. I am a licensed private investigator, though. And no, I guess you don't have to talk to me, though I don't know why you wouldn't want to."

"No one enjoys being lied to. It makes them feel foolish," she said, pouring my Zinfandel.

"That wasn't my intention, making you feel foolish, I mean. I'm very sorry if I did."

The wine was so deeply red it was nearly black. I sipped: full-bodied, peppery with a hint of cherries. Pretty impressive stuff for wine by the glass, but at fifteen bucks a glass, the price was impressive too.

"What do you really want of me?"

"The truth?"

"That would be a change."

"The first time I was just poking around on behalf of a client. It was more like fact finding than anything else."

She got inexplicably agitated. "A client? What client?" Catching the semi-desperation in her voice, she calmed herself down. "Forgive me. I am not myself today."

"That's privileged information, Esme. I wouldn't be a very good investigator if I was willing to come right out and tell you."

She didn't like that answer and moved away from me for the moment, but she was soon right back in front of me. "Please tell me," she said, not-too subtly running the tip of her tongue over her red lips. "I would really like to know."

"If I were thirty years younger and you looked at me like that, I might just tell you."

"Please."

"Sorry."

Her lovely face turned to stone, her body clenching tight. "Is your client a woman?"

It was an odd question. I suppose I could have just said no and been done with it, but her reaction was so incredibly visceral I couldn't let it go. "What's wrong? What if it was a woman?"

"*Is* it a woman?" she practically growled.

"I told you, I can't say."

"Please leave." It might have sounded like a request, but it wasn't.

"Miss, can I get another Black Label, please," asked a man at the end of the bar in a thousand dollars worth of casual clothing, jiggling the ice in his freshly scotchless glass.

Esme did not turn her head. She did not move her legs. She did not answer him. "Please leave, now."

I took another sip of Zin. "But I haven't finished my wine."

With that, Esme's right arm shot forward, toppling my untouched glass of sparkling water into my lap, soaking my pants and jacket. "I am terribly sorry, sir," she said, not looking or sounding the least bit sorry. "Please accept the wine as an apology. You will find towels in the men's room."

When I came out of the men's room, Esme was gone. I asked after her.

"She quit," said the hostess, glaring at me. "I don't know what you said to upset her, but she was beside herself when she left."

I threw her a curve. "Can I speak to Chef Liu, please?"

The hostess didn't like that. "Why, sir, if you don't mind me asking?"

"Because I want to see if I can get him to quit too."

Ten minutes later I was in a hot, cramped little office off the kitchen with Chef Liu. He remembered me as well and was still buying into me as a cop. He was polite, if a bit confused about what I'd done to make his bartender quit. I explained that my asking about Robert Tillman's death had really seemed to upset Esme. That only confused him further.

"I don't understand," he said. "Esme did not see what happened. She did not even see Robert's body. Why should she be so upset?"

Why indeed? "I can't say. The last time I was here, you said Mr. Tillman had only been working here for a brief time and that he had skills in the kitchen."

"A week, yes. He was a fine prep cook."

"What does a prep cook do exactly?"

"It is a silly name, really. A prep cook does very little cooking. He does all the dicing and slicing of raw ingredients. Any cooking he would do would be limited to maybe skimming stocks, reheating sauces, things of that nature. It is hard, tedious work."

"Did you like him? Did the kitchen staff like him?"

"I never thought about it. I am running a restaurant, not a social club. I was pleased to have a good prep cook who spoke good English. Most prep cooks these days are Hispanic and my Spanish is terrible."

"Can I look at his job application, do you think?"

Chef Liu screwed up his face. "Why are the police so interested in Robert? The man died of an aneurism."

"We're just making sure we didn't miss anything before."

He liked that answer about as much as Esme had liked my answers. "I don't understand."

"I'm just following my orders, Chef Liu. Gimme a break, okay?"

"Okay, but there is no job application. It's all word of mouth here. Somebody knows someone else. Like that."

"Who brought Robert Tillman to your attention?"

"Tino."

"Tino?"

"Tino Escobar. He's no longer here. And no, I don't know where he went. Now, if you don't mind, I have—"

"One last question, then I'm outta here. Do you remember the restaurant Robert worked at before he came here. I mean, you didn't just hire him on Tino's word, right?"

"Kid Charlemagne's on 2nd Avenue and 7th."

Chef Liu gestured that we were leaving and he shut off the office lights in case I was thinking of another question.

Back on the street, I punched in Maya Watson's number. Voicemail again. I was apparently at the top of her shit list. This time, I didn't bother leaving a message.

The phone vibrated in my hand. Assuming it was Maya Watson calling me right back, I didn't check the number and picked up.

"Hey, Moe." It wasn't Maya Watson, but Nick Roussis. "How'd that intel I got you on Delgado work out?"

"Yeah, Nicky, I meant to thank you for that. First real lead in the case."

"Not a problem. So did he do it? Did Delgado kill that EMT?"

"Maybe."

"Maybe? What's that supposed to mean?"

"It means maybe. Some evidence points his way and some doesn't. Besides, I'm looking into other possibilities too."

He sounded disappointed. "Whatever you say, but let me know how it works out, okay?"

"You got it, Nicky. And thanks again. I won't forget your going out of your way for me."

Frankly, I was with Nick. I was disappointed too, but nothing is ever easy or uncomplicated. Nothing, at least where I'm concerned.

THIRTY-TWO

Man, Robert Tillman had really gotten under Esme's skin. The problem was that it wasn't particularly obvious why or how he'd done it. Chef Liu hadn't shed much light on the subject and given that I'd already cost him his day bartender, I somehow didn't think the time was right to start questioning any of his other employees. My initial inclination was to rush right over to Kid Charlemagne's, but I decided that would be a mistake. I wanted to find out a little bit more about Tillman before I went stumbling around the way I was prone to do.

As I got to my car, it hit me for the first time that no one had mentioned Robert Tillman's family filing a lawsuit. That seemed very peculiar in a city where litigation was everyone's second favorite sport and where there were as many lawyers as cockroaches. Don't get me wrong, those same lawyers and their evil big brothers, the insurance companies, kept Prager & Melendez Investigations, Inc. in the black until the day we closed our doors. The thing was, the case was such a total slam dunk; *I* could have tried it and won or gotten a huge settlement. With a guaranteed multimillion dollar judgment just sitting out there for the taking, I couldn't understand how some enterprising lawyer hadn't hooked up with a greedy member of the Tillman clan. I aimed my car toward the Brooklyn Bridge because there was someone I knew on the other side of the bridge who might be able to clarify things for me.

I walked through the lobby of 40 Court Street for the first time in many years. This building had been the longtime home of Prager

& Melendez Investigations, Inc. It was also home to most of the major criminal law and personal injury firms in Brooklyn. Given that Brooklyn Borough Hall and the courts were across the street, Brooklyn Law School was a few blocks away, and the Brooklyn House of Detention was a short walk away on Atlantic Avenue, it was all very convenient or, if you were more cynically minded, very incestuous. To my way of thinking, it was both.

The firm of Pettibone, Kinder, Hart, and Wang were Brooklyn's kings of torts and they had been Prager & Melendez's most lucrative account. They worked big money cases: major product liability, aircraft disasters, class actions. Cheesy TV ads weren't their style. They didn't beg for clients. Clients begged for them. They were the type of hired guns that insurance companies either loved or loathed depending upon which table they were paid to sit at. If anyone could explain to me how a case as ripe as Tillman's was still unpicked on the vine, Harper Pettibone Jr. could do it.

Harper was about my age, but still had an athletic build. He had been a club champion squash player and had obviously kept at it. Squash. No one in Coney Island played fucking squash. Then again, no one in Coney Island had a name like Harper Pettibone Jr. I used to bust his chops about his upbringing all the time. I think maybe that's why we got along. I wasn't big on kneeling to kiss anybody's ring and he liked that about me. He also liked that we did good work for him without padding our invoices.

"Moses Prager!" He put his arm around my shoulder when he stepped out of his office. "God, you look awful," he said with a laugh in his voice, but his soft blue eyes weren't smiling. "How are you, my friend?" Harper didn't wait for an answer. "Come in. Come in." He looked at his watch and turned to his secretary. "No calls for fifteen minutes, please."

Fifteen minutes. I'd hate to see how much time he gave people he didn't like.

We moved into his office. It was much the same as it had been the last time I saw it. Very classic. Very old school. One wall of floor-to-ceiling bookcases, walnut paneling, a brown leather sofa, two green leather wing chairs, a big-assed desk, and a properly stuffy portrait of his late father and his partners.

"You're a blended scotch man, if I remember correctly," he said as he fiddled at the little dry bar in a cabinet to the right of his desk. "Sit."

I settled into a chair across from his desk. "Nothing for me, thanks."

Harper twisted his lips in disappointment. "Well, I never did enjoy drinking alone." He closed the cabinet and sat behind his desk. "What can I do for you, Moe?"

I began to remind him about the circumstances of Robert Tillman's death, but I didn't get very far. Harper was well familiar with the case and with Alta Conseco's subsequent homicide.

"But what's all this to do with you?" he asked.

"Alta Conseco, the EMT who was murdered, she was Carmella's older sister."

Harper shook his head. "How awful."

"The cops haven't gotten very far with finding her killer and Carm asked me to try my luck with it."

"But you two are—"

"—divorced. Yeah, I know. There was too much history there for me to say no."

"I understand that. I do indeed. But how can I help?"

"Harper, if I told you that no one in Robert Tillman's family has filed suit, what would you say?"

"I would say his relatives are either very foolish or very dead because the case is a walk in the park, basically unlosable. My secretary could try the case. And we're talking about a multimillion dollar judgment, but the city would never let it go to trial. They would settle this one as quietly and as quickly as possible and be done with it. But you are a shrewd enough man to have known that before you walked through my door and if all you wanted was confirmation, you would have called. So, what is it I can do for you, really?"

"Can you find out if any of your brethren have tried reaching out to the family?"

I could see he was thinking about giving me his lecture on ethics, but decided against it. He knew better than to waste the time. Even the biggest firms did some form of ambulance chasing, only they tended to think of it as working through referrals. Carmella and I had made a nice chunk of change referring cases their way. Of course, we never felt like we were steering people in the wrong direction. It was in our best interests to think that, I suppose. Like most rationalizations, it helps you sleep at night.

Harper stood, holding out his hand. My time was up. "For you, I will have some people ask around."

We shook and I gave him my card. "Thanks, Harper."

"You're welcome, sir." He walked me to the door of his office. "Are you sure you are feeling quite well, Moe?"

"Fine. Just a little stressed. Sarah's getting married up in Vermont soon and you know how it is."

"I do. My congratulations to them and to you. I will be in touch."

With that I was out of his office, nodding goodbye to his secretary, and back out in the hallway. I was tempted to go look at our old offices, to see who had taken them over, but I rode the elevator down to the lobby. Too much of my life was anchored in the past. I guess that's true of anyone over fifty. I felt it was especially true for me. I couldn't afford to waste any of the time I had left looking back.

THIRTY-THREE

I woke up late the next day, close to noon, with no brilliant insights or fresh ideas. I'd spent a frustrating evening with my computer and the ghost of Robert Tillman. Several more computer searches had netted zilch. I couldn't even manage to find a picture of the guy, which, in this day and age, was really saying something. In fact, it was saying something, and rather loudly too. I just couldn't decipher what was being said or what it meant, not yet.

After some coffee and yogurt, I tried Maya Watson's number one more time. Nothing doing. If I wanted to talk to her again, it was going to mean a trip back out to Queens. I wasn't up for that. Before I confronted her, I needed more than amorphous suspicions. Besides, I was weary of her playing the role of the wronged party. Robert Tillman—slippery and anonymous as he was proving to be—was the wronged party here, not Maya, not Alta. I had to remember that. I couldn't let my sympathy for Maya's plight or my understanding Carm's estrangement blind me. I thought about calling Carmella, but decided I was still pissed off at her on several counts, not the least of which was her hiding Alta's personal effects from me. And though I had tried to bury the old pain, seeing Israel brought it all back. No, she was going to have to come to me and not halfway, either.

The house phone rang.

"I'm done with my case." It was Pam. "Come on up here for a few days."

I almost said no. I didn't. I didn't say yes, but I didn't say no. I took a long breath and remembered being at 40 Court Street and how I didn't go look at the old offices. I thought about why I hadn't looked. I thought about being mad at Carmella and about how she was my living past and not the happiest part of it. I thought about the case and how it was often better not to work things to death, that cases, like good red wine, sometimes needed to breathe. That there were things in the world that couldn't be willed or forced to happen. I thought about the tumor in my stomach. I thought about how good Pam had been for me, how good we'd been for each other. Okay, I thought, so there was no drama between us the way there would always be drama with Carm. So what?

"I'll be up there late tonight, okay? There's some stuff I need to handle down here first."

"You're coming?"

"Did I give the wrong answer?"

"It's just that—are you done with what you were working on?"

"No," I said. "Whatever I leave behind for two days, will be here when I get back. Anyway, I'll be able to check on the wedding arrangements and see Sarah when I'm up there."

"I know it's crazy, but when I saw you holding Carmella in your arms, I thought I was losing you."

You probably are, but not to Carmella. "Don't be silly. I'll see you tonight."

"Bye."

"Pam," I stopped her from hanging up, "don't wear too much to bed."

I felt the smile on my face before I realized I was happy at the idea of being with her. It might not have been mad love between us, but whatever it was, was good and I didn't want to piss it away the way I had so many other good things before it.

As soon as I put the phone down, it rang again.

"Good afternoon, Moses. Harper Pettibone here."

"Hey, Harper. This is unexpectedly quick."

"Well, you seemed anxious to learn whatever you could and it so happened I played squash this morning with Deputy Mayor Rosenberg."

"Who won?" I asked, but not to be polite. Harper didn't like to lose, so he made sure not to.

"Still busting my chops. You haven't changed, Moe, have you?"

"More than you could know."

"He gave me a few good games, did the deputy mayor, but in the end . . ."

"I'm hoping you didn't call to talk squash."

"I managed to work the circumstances of Robert Tillman's unfortunate demise into our locker room chat."

"I bet that gave him *agita*."

"On the contrary, Moe, Max Rosenberg looked like the cat who'd eaten the proverbial canary, cage and all. When I pressed him on it, he said, and I quote, 'It's futile fishing for that particular payday, old man. Not only is it unbecoming of you, but that's one wrongful death suit this city will never have to worry about.'"

"That's crazy, Harper. How can he be so sure?"

"*That* he wasn't willing to discuss, but he wasn't whistling through the graveyard. I can assure you of that. I play cards with the deputy mayor as well and he isn't much of a poker player. He couldn't bluff his way out of a paper sack."

"Would you care to speculate?"

"I never care to speculate, but I will. Either someone's already gotten to the relatives and paid them off to go quietly into that good night or the city is holding a trump card. My guess is it's the latter."

"How's that?" I asked.

"You can never be sure you've gotten to all the relatives who might have a claim. It's like that whack-a-mole game. Just when you pay one relative off and get a signed waiver, another one pops up. No, the city's holding some ammunition in abeyance and for the deputy mayor to speak with such bravado, it must be pretty potent stuff."

"Thanks, Harper. I really appreciate it."

"I'll keep checking with my other sources. Rosenberg was so annoyingly smug, I'm tempted to go find one of Tillman's relatives myself."

"If you hear anything else, I'll be reachable by cell. I'm going up to Vermont for a few days."

"Enjoy yourself. You looked like you could use the rest."

He was right.

This time, something else rang when I hung up the phone. It was the building intercom.

"Hello."

"Yeah, boss, it's me, Brian."

"Doyle! What are you doing here?"

"We need to talk and not over the phone."

"Come on up." I buzzed him in.

Brian Doyle didn't look quite the same as he had when I'd seen him at O'Hearns—the difference being his blackened right eye and the nasty, finger-shaped bruises on his neck. And seeing him, I knew why he was here.

"Have a run-in with the Jorge Delgado Fan Club? Took more than one fireman to do that to you," I said. "How many?"

"Three."

"Where?"

"Outside a bar by Delgado's old firehouse."

"How'd the three of them fare?"

"Two of 'em are at the dentist today, the other one's getting his nose reset."

"Glad to hear you haven't lost your touch, Brian."

He smiled at that, but the smile quickly vanished. "I'm off the case, Boss. Emotions are running way too high on this one. Those guys were spoiling for the fight even before I walked in there. Someone's been in those guys' ears whipping 'em up. It was like they were waiting for me or anyone to walk in there and start asking questions."

"Sorry, Brian. I owe you for this."

"No, you don't."

"If you say so."

"Boss, I never tell you what to do, but leave this thing alone for now. I know you can usually handle yourself, but if you had walked into that bar . . . Listen, they're burying the guy tomorrow. In a few weeks, who knows, maybe you can start asking some questions again. For now, it's too dangerous. You should enjoy yourself. Enjoy Sarah's wedding. You shouldn't be doing this stuff."

I held out my hand to him. "Thanks, Brian."

He ignored my hand and hugged me instead. "Thanks for everything, Boss."

"I'm not dying yet, you asshole," I said, playfully pushing him away.

He winked with his good eye. "Just figured I'd get it out of the way now . . . just in case."

"Fuck you, Doyle."

"Yeah, I love you too. Take care of yourself."

With that, Brian was gone. As I walked around the house, packing for my trip, his words, though only half-serious, rang in my head. ". . . just in case." We both knew in case of what.

THIRTY-FOUR

I headed west along the Belt Parkway, toward Manhattan, and into the setting sun. I had made this drive so many times in my life that but for the other cars on the road, I could do it blindfolded. I knew every bump, rut, and pothole, every twist and turn. Sometimes I liked to think this was all so familiar to me that I could name the individual blades of grass at the roadside and knew which rivets were the rusty ones on the east-facing façade of the Verrazano Bridge. That's the thing, though, isn't it? You never know anything or anyone as well as you think you do, least of all yourself. It is the great folly of humanity, the search for self-knowledge and significance. It's why we're all so fucking miserable. Oh, I thought, to be an ant or a cat or almost anything else that doesn't lose sleep over dying. Does an ant ever ask itself where do I come from, where am I going, or what does it mean?

I knew some stuff about myself. I knew I'd never been very good at just letting go, even for a little while. That's why I decided to stop at Kid Charlemagne's on my way up to Vermont. Although the East Village wasn't necessarily on the way to Vermont, it wasn't exactly not on the way either. Let's just say there's no direct route from Sheepshead Bay to Brattleboro, so it was going to take me five or six hours no matter how I chose to go. I'd thrown my duffel bag in the trunk, conveniently neglecting to pack the bottles of red wine I usually brought up to Pam's with me. I'd have to tell her about my condition soon enough, but I wanted to do it on my terms. Pam

203

was a damn good PI and I think she was already a little suspicious of my health. I didn't want a repeat of what had happened to me the other night at Carmella's.

Rush hour was at an end and the traffic was pretty thin as I headed around the bend from Bath Beach to Bay Ridge, the Verrazano Bridge looming up before me. It was hard for me to remember when I was a kid and the bridge wasn't there, when you used to have to ferry across from Brooklyn to Staten Island and the lost world of New Jersey beyond. The bridge opened to traffic in '64, like Shea Stadium and the World's Fair. Now, with the fair long closed and Shea turned into a parking lot for Citi Field, only the bridge remained.

I don't know what it was that drew my attention to the old '75 Buick Electra in the right-hand lane. Maybe it was its darkly tinted windows or the fact that the sun's glare off its windshield made it impossible for me to see the driver's face. Maybe it was the sparseness of the traffic and the fact that the Buick seemed to be hanging back and to my right, but keeping its distance constant. I shook my head at my paranoia. I think if Brian Doyle hadn't shown up on my doorstep with that black eye and sounding the retreat, I would never have noticed the Buick at all. So to test out my paranoia, I floored the gas pedal and shot under the bridge. When I looked in my passenger side mirror, the Buick was gone. Problem was, I looked in the wrong mirror.

Bang! The tail of my car jerked and fishtailed, but I held it steady. There was the Electra again, this time in my sideview and only a foot or two off my left fender. Before I could react, it closed in, ramming the left side of my back bumper. This time the hit was much harder, but he'd lost the element of surprise. Surprise or no surprise, it took all my police training and years of driving savvy to keep my car steady. I couldn't be sure whether the guy driving the Buick was a pro just trying to scare me—mission accomplished—or if he was an amateur trying to kill me who didn't know what the fuck he was doing. I'd have to worry about that later, because amateur or not, a few more hits like the last one and I wouldn't be able to keep my car on the road. It was time to play offense.

I put my foot to the floor again and my car zoomed forward. I knew the Buick probably had a huge old V8 under its hood and that it would quickly catch up. I was counting on it. While the Electra was built for straight line speed, weighed as much as an Abrams tank, and was great for ramming smaller cars off the road, it maneuvered like an ocean liner. I saw the Buick coming up fast as we both approached the point where the Belt Parkway curves right and up onto the Gowanus Expressway. I had one chance and it was now. Just when the Electra got within a car's length of me, I stepped hard on my brakes and yanked my steering wheel hard left.

Bang! I caught him pretty close to where I was aiming, the rear passenger tire. I'm not sure how close exactly, but close enough. The old Buick spun out in front of me and flipped over as I passed. I counted it flipping over twice more in my rearview mirror before it came to rest against a guardrail. It didn't burst into flames. Cars don't do that as frequently as in the movies, but I couldn't imagine the driver would walk out of that wreck unscathed. I exhaled for the first time in minutes. I shouldn't have.

My left front tire exploded. That much, I remember.

When I came to, a cop was gently shaking my shoulder and I noticed my car, which had been in the left lane and facing Manhattan when my tire blew, was now up against the opposite guardrail and facing traffic. My side airbags had deployed. I also noticed that I had a hell of a headache and that my neck hurt like a son of a bitch. There were flashing lights everywhere I looked and the wailing sound of a siren in the distance.

"Did I hit anybody else?" I mumbled, trying to work the pain out of my neck.

"Nah. You slid across all the lanes, but everyone avoided you. You all right? There's some EMTs on the way."

"I'm okay. A little sore."

He asked for my name, asked me the day and date, asked if I'd been drinking, held some fingers up in front of my eyes, and did some eye tracking thing with a pen. When he was done, I made to get out of the car.

"Wow, pal, you better wait there till the paramedics clear you."

I stayed put. "I used to be on the job," I said to the cop. "Used to work the Six-O."

"Long time ago, huh?"

"Long time, yeah."

"What happened?" he asked.

"Front left tire blew and I lost it. Busy night?"

"You know it. Must be a full moon coming tonight. There's a car flipped over on the Belt about a mile back."

"Anybody hurt?"

"If there was, they didn't hang around. It was a stolen car. Amazing."

"How's that?"

"It was an old beat-up piece of shit. Who the fuck's gonna steal something like that?"

Somebody who wants to run another car off the road. "Listen, Rafferty," I said, reading his name badge. "Do me a favor and take some pictures of my car. I was supposed to go up to Vermont and visit my girlfriend tonight. I need some proof." I handed him my cell phone. "She's the jealous type."

"Sure, for a brother, no problem." He took the pictures and handed the phone back to me. "Okay, the EMTs are here."

206

THIRTY-FIVE

Pam believed the pictures of my smashed-up car and said she'd be down to take care of me. I didn't even try telling her not to come. I wanted taking care of. I needed it. I'd been on an island by myself for too long and since that exile was self-imposed, I had only to look in the mirror to ascribe blame. I don't suppose I ever forgave myself for Katy's murder. It took seven years for Sarah to absolve me and the rest of the universe either didn't know or didn't care. If there was any persuasive argument for the existence of God, it wasn't in the biology of things, but in emotion, in feelings. I couldn't quite see how guilt and forgiveness had evolved from the primordial stew. I don't know, maybe the "adult" relationship I'd been sharing with Pam over the last two years was just part of my self-inflicted exile. I let her in, but not inside. Suddenly, I wanted off the island and I didn't care why.

When I refused treatment or to go to the ER, the EMTs told me to go home, rest, and to make an appointment with my regular physician if the pain in my neck didn't clear up or if any new symptoms arose. It'd been weird, sitting there, talking to them, and not asking them questions about Alta and Maya. I wouldn't have known what to ask, really. What could I have asked them, what could they have said to change the essential facts of the case? Maya Watson and Alta Conseco had simply stood by and let a man die. A month later, someone stuck a knife into Alta Conseco and killed her.

It truly was a fool's errand I had taken on. Even if I stumbled upon all the right answers and found out every gory detail of how this tragedy had unfolded, so what? Neither Lazarus nor Lady Lazarus would be coming back from the dead. Justice would not be served because there is no justice for the dead, only for the living and sometimes not even then. Had every murderous Nazi son of a bitch been captured, convicted, and put to death, the innocent dead would not have risen. The dead are beyond the reach of justice. And the truth wasn't going to bring justice. It was my experience that where tragedy was involved, the truth made things worse. Always. What naïve fool was it, I wondered, who had made the specious connection between truth and justice in the first place? One thing I knew about him, whoever he was, he wasn't nearly as big a fool as me. If he had known what I knew, he would have closed up shop and gone home. Not me. I meant to get to the bottom of this if for no other reason than I was a curious bastard and didn't want to leave loose ends behind me.

I called up one of those rental places that delivers the car to your door. My taste in cars ran to the small, sporty side, but this one time, I went big, really big. Given that someone, probably a crazy fireman, had just tried to run my ass off the road, I would have rented a city bus if I could have. A Chevy Suburban was the best the rental company could do on short notice. That suited me fine. I met the woman who delivered it downstairs and didn't bother going back up. I wanted to leave before Pam got there. She had keys and I would let her take care of me when I got back, but I needed to finish what I started.

Kid Charlemagne's wasn't exactly a bucket of blood, but not for lack of trying. In the seventies, the East Village was a mess, a perch from which junkies, artists, punks, and pretenders could both watch the world go down the toilet and go along for the ride. Kid

Charlemagne's wrecked and dingy décor was meant to capture a sense of those long-ago times when Joey Ramone and Jean-Michel Basquiat roamed these self-same streets. It failed miserably. To begin with, naming a faux punk restaurant—whatever the fuck that was supposed to be—after a Steely Dan song was less than genius. Steely Dan was almost as antithetical to the ethos of punk as Emerson, Lake and Palmer. And as if to make the whole thing even a bigger farce, Lady Gaga was playing when I walked in. God, it was so self-consciously dreadful that it almost seemed to be the point. It didn't hurt that the hostess wore a purple and magenta Mohawk wig and was dressed in a ripped Sex Pistols T-shirt, studded leather pants, and red Chuck Taylors. Her lipstick was black, her eye shadow a thin rectangle of red powder that was splashed across both eyes and the bridge of her nose.

"Oi! What can I do for ya, rude boy?" she said in an affected low-rent British accent.

I was tempted to bust her balls about her not having been born until New Wave was old hat and hair bands had gone bald, but I didn't figure on that making much of an impression. Instead, I asked to see the boss or the manager.

"Get lost, granddad."

"Oi, Siouxsie, go play with the Banshees and stop wasting my time. Granddad is a copper," I said in a far better accent than hers, showed her my badge, and quickly put it away.

Her eyes got big. "Sorry, I was just—"

I cut her off. "Forget it. Just take me to the office."

The fake punk hostess kept apologizing—her accent far more Bronx than Brixton now—as we cut past the bar and through the dinning room. Strangely enough, the crowd was much hipper than the place merited. There were even some faces among them I recognized: the novelist who'd dissed Oprah, some painter I remembered from when I was looking for Sashi Bluntstone, and an actress who'd spent more time in rehab than on her syndicated superhero show. Christ, I even saw Lou Reed coming out of the men's room. I was at a loss to explain it. I felt like the one person at a comedy club who didn't get the joke.

"Give me a second, okay?" she said as we stopped outside an unmarked door on the other side of the restrooms. She knocked and the door buzzed open. Not smart, I thought, just buzzing someone in who might be armed with bad intentions and a gun. Then I noticed the closed circuit camera above me and to the right. She stuck her head in the office and then quickly back out. "The boss says for you to go right in."

"Thanks," I said, sliding past her, into the office, and closing the door behind me. When I turned around, I nearly shit.

"Hello, Moe," he said, an embarrassed half-smile on his face. It was Nathan Martyr.

Nathan Martyr was a collapsed super nova: an artist who exploded on the New York art scene one day and then imploded in short order. After his fast fifteen minutes, he devoted his wretched life to making bad art, shooting heroin, and blogging about Sashi Bluntstone. Martyr was one of Sashi's most ardent critics. It was on his blog that I found Photoshopped images of Sashi's nude body being crucified, flayed, and tortured. In the end, Martyr'd had nothing to do with Sashi's disappearance, but I loathed the asshole just the same. It was Martyr's ex-cop doorman and toady who had tried, nearly successfully, to put me in the grave. If Pam hadn't zapped the prick with her handy little Taser, my oncologist would have had one less patient to worry about now.

Still, Martyr seemed different somehow. He had been a twitchy bastard when we first met, but now his demeanor was calm, if not quite Zen-like. He'd been junkie-skinny back then. He'd put on a few pounds since and while he was by no means heavy, his face was fuller. He sported a tan. A tan! Jesus, talk about breaking the New York artist protocol. He was expensively and stylishly dressed. The last time I'd seen him, he smelled like he'd been wearing the same clothes for a week. Now he smelled of money.

"You clean these days?" I asked.

"Clean and healthy. I guess I owe some of that to you."

"How's that?"

"That thing with Sashi, it woke me up finally."

"To what?"

"To the hole at the center of my being that I tried to fill in with hate and heroin," he said, his voice cracked and brittle with emotion.

"Forgive me if I don't get all choked up."

"Hey, look, I understand that you've got no reason to care, but you asked."

"I did. So, what happened?"

"Have you ever had something in your life that you thought defined you and you woke up one morning and it was gone, just totally gone and you couldn't get it back?"

"Yeah, I know what that's like."

"That's what happened to me. I was an artist one day and the next day I wasn't and no matter how hard I tried to get my muse to dance with me again, she wouldn't. I tried everything: all sorts of therapy, drinking—"

"—heroin."

"That is how I got started, out of despair. I didn't really hate Sashi Bluntstone. I hated myself."

"Good to know I'm not alone."

He laughed. "You are now. I don't hate anyone anymore, least of all me. Just look at me. I'm healthy. I go to the gym every day. I eat well and I've got the muse back on my side."

"Showing at the Brill Gallery again?"

"C'mon, Moe. You struck me as a bright guy when we met. You're inside the art right now. You're part of it today."

"The restaurant?"

"Is it a restaurant?"

"Yes and no," I said, catching on. "It's staged."

"Not staged, exactly, no. When I came out the other end of rehab, I had a vision. I saw how small and unambitious my earlier work had been, how by working in one medium at a time I was self-limiting. I also saw that the commerce of art is set up to fuck the artist. I produce a painting or a sculpture and depend on the largesse of some patron or decorator or collector or speculator to buy it. Then the gallery owner and the agent would feed on the money, leaving the scraps for me. Bullshit! I don't know about you, Moe, but when I get fucked I want to enjoy it. Being an artist used to mean getting raped and then having to say thank you to the rapist. This place was my vision. It's visual art, performance art, street art, participatory art. It's living art that changes from second to second. It's theater and chaos and it turns a big profit. Everything having to do with this place—from its seemingly inappropriate name to its kitsch and camp—was done on purpose with a purpose. Each decision was, at least to some degree, an artistic calculation. The only things left to chance are the people who walk through the doors to eat and drink."

"Genius," I said, not quite believing the word came out of my mouth. "You win both ways. The ones who get it get it, so it's like knowing the secret handshake and being in an exclusive club. They get to enjoy the art and calculation. They get to feel superior, to laugh at the people who come here for a meal and are oblivious to the fact that they're being messed about."

He flinched. "No one's being messed with here. If people come for a meal, they get a good meal. If they come because they think this is what the East Village was like in the time of punk, that's what they get. I'm no more exploiting the people who walk into this restaurant than a photographer is exploiting the people behind the faces in a crowd shot. But somehow I don't think you came here to talk old times or to discuss the philosophy of art. Why *are* you here?"

My answer was simple. "Robert Tillman."

"Oh, everybody's favorite stroke victim. Why do you want to know about him?"

"He's my favorite too. I'm a fan."

He laughed again. "You're pretty funny, but that's not an answer."

"I'm working a case and his name came up. He used to work here in the kitchen with a guy named Tino Escobar."

"Did you do all your homework this well when you were in school?"

"And I gave my teacher a shiny apple every day. About Tillman, why did you hire him?"

"Tillman was handsome in a rough sort of way. His looks appealed to my aesthetics and he was the best prep cook we've ever had."

"The eaters don't see the kitchen staff, so why does it matter how they look?" I asked.

"Everything matters. The art doesn't stop at the kitchen door."

"Whatever. So, Tino recommended Tillman to you?"

"You are a thorough bastard." Martyr said. "Yes, Tino recommended him."

"And why did Tillman leave?"

For the first time since I walked into the office, Nathan Martyr looked uncomfortable, his posture defensive. I repeated the question, loudly.

"Some of the staff . . . some of the women who worked here said he made them uneasy."

"That's pretty vague, Nathan. Uneasy how?"

"He was inappropriate with them."

"Inappropriate. God, for a junkie you sure are a squeamish motherfucker. What are we talking about here?"

"I don't know the whole story, but Natasha Romaine, one of our hostesses, quit abruptly and Abigail Dawtry, our head bartender, came to me and said Robert had cornered her in the bathroom after closing one night. She got out, but she said he scared the shit out of her, so I had to let him go."

"Abigail working tonight?"

He ran his finger along a schedule taped on the wall next to his desk. "Sorry. Abby is off tonight."

"Can I get her contact info and the info for the hostess that quit?"

"After what happened between us with Sashi, I suppose I owe you that much," he said, tapping at a keyboard. "It's printing."

"I don't suppose you know where Tino Escobar might be working these days? He left the High Line Bistro after Tillman's death."

"Sure, I know where Tino is," Martyr said, handing me the sheets that had come out of the printer. "I rehired him. He's in the kitchen. Come on, I'll introduce you."

I followed Martyr down the hall, back into the restaurant, and through the kitchen doors. No matter what Nathan Martyr had said about every decision in the restaurant being a calculation, the kitchen was a working kitchen and didn't look much different than any other restaurant kitchen I'd seen. I did, however, have to confess, that the cooks and even the guy at the dishwasher station were really a pretty attractive bunch.

"He's over there, at the grill station," Martyr said, turning to me.

Tino was coffee-skinned, about five-five and sturdily built, eyes facing the grill. He was handsome enough, but there was a distinct blankness to his face. It displayed the kinds of sharp corners and hard edges that only a rough life carves out of a man. Maybe it was the dance of the spitting flames that bathed his face or his stone-cold expression that gave me a chill, but whatever the reason, there are times when the cover tells you everything you need to know about the book inside. And what Tino Escobar's cover told me, what it screamed at me, was that there was only one soul between the two of us.

"Tino," Martyr called to his grill man. "Someone would like to speak to you."

He turned his eyes up. They were as black and empty as a shark's. Then everything happened at once. His expression went from icy to feral. I swore he sniffed the air for my scent like a wild animal checking if a rival predator had stepped into his territory. I may not have looked like a cop anymore, but I guess I still smelled like one. Escobar bolted, plowing right over the kid working the grill with him. As he darted through the kitchen to the side door, he made sweeping motions with his arms, knocking bubbling pots and full plates, glasses, and silverware behind him and in my path.

"Stop!" I shouted after him.

He didn't stop. Go figure. The surprise was that I ran after him, through the side door onto 7th Street heading west. For once, the cancer in my belly wasn't at issue. My surgically butchered knee, the arthritis that had developed in it, and my age all trumped the tumor. I didn't think about my knee much anymore. It was just another injury, another wound, some scar tissue picked up along the way. That's what aging is about: wounds and scar tissue. There were times it seemed that my life was not much more than a collection of both. But it was the wounds no one could see, the scars on the inside that were worst of all. Sometimes wounds are like a cascade and so it was with me. It was injuring my knee all those years ago that started the flood.

Escobar put more distance between us with each stride. Time was I could have reached around behind me and come up with something to make him think a little harder about running away. Problem was that in spite of my scent, I wasn't a cop and I wasn't going to pull out my .38 on a busy Greenwich Village street. For all I knew, this was a misunderstanding, that Escobar might have been an illegal alien and thought I was an immigration agent. Half a block into the chase, I stopped running and watched Tino Escobar disappear into the crowd and the fallen darkness. Even without Escobar, I had made progress. Robert Tillman was now something more to me than an innocent corpse and I had the contact information for the two women who worked at Kid Charlemagne's. I didn't know how things would play out or if it would help explain why Alta and Maya had let Robert Tillman die. I didn't know a lot of things, but for the first time since Carmella had asked for my help, I felt close to an answer. I felt it in my bones.

THIRTY-SIX

I knew something was up. Pam was standing just inside the door when I walked into my condo. It wasn't that she hugged and kissed me. It was the way she hugged and kissed me: tentatively, almost shyly, as if we had an audience. And when I stepped out from the little alcove between the front door and my living room, I saw Carmella. She was sitting on the couch, a half-finished glass of beer in her hand.

"You two have to talk," Pam said, heading for the bedroom door. "I've got some calls to make."

We waited for the bedroom door to close and for the other to speak. I wasn't in the mood for a test of wills or Carm's mind games, so I just spoke.

"You show up in New York unannounced. You leave without notice. Then you come to my house without letting me know you're coming. You're just full of surprises these days."

"Do you love her?" Carmella asked, but didn't wait for an answer. "She loves you, you know?"

"None of your business. Move on."

"You're mad at me."

"I've been mad at you for nine years. You left me, remember?"

"No, you are mad because I took Israel back home. I had to get him back to school. That's all."

"It's not why you're here, though, is it? You're not here to talk about why I'm mad at you or to talk about Israel or even about me and Pam."

"Then why am I here?" she asked, her tone smug.

"To tell me to forget it, to stop looking for Alta's killer."

Carmella wasn't very often speechless. She was now. I don't know that she was conscious of it, but she kept opening and closing her mouth, groping for something to say like a landed fish gasping for air.

I pressed her. "Isn't that right? You want me to stop, don't you?"

She couldn't look at me. "Yes."

"Why?"

"I also went away to think a little. I realize it doesn't matter if I find out who is responsible for killing Alta. It was a foolish idea. My sister is dead and I can't make things better between us. I cannot make right my turning my back on her."

"You were never much good at lying to me, Carm."

That pissed her off. She jumped up from the couch and got in my face, the faintly sour smell of beer strong on her breath. "Everything I just said is true."

"The words are true, but you're lying. That's not why you want me to stop looking."

"Don't be stupid, Moe."

"You want me to stop looking because you're worried I would find out that Alta was a lesbian. Maybe that her being gay had something to do with her murder and if I found out what happened, it would all come to light. You're too late," I said. "I went to Alta's old apartment and I spoke to her landlady. She told me you'd come by and taken your sister's things out of the apartment, so I went to the house on Ashford to talk to you. The old man across the way told me you left with Israel."

"That's not it," she said, again turning away.

"I couldn't figure out why you wouldn't want me to see her personal stuff. You were a detective, the best detective I ever knew, for chrissakes! Of all people, you would know how important personal stuff could be. A scrap of paper with a name on it, a phone number, a matchbook, whatever—anything could be crucial. Why, I wondered, would Carm ask me to do this and then tie my hands behind my back by hiding stuff? The only answer that made sense was that there was something you didn't want me to know about Alta. It didn't take me long to figure out what that thing was once I dug a little deeper. I actually should have recognized it sooner from the hate mail, from the things they called your sister. Did you really think it wouldn't come out? And why the fuck would it matter?"

"It's wrong."

"What's wrong?"

"The way Alta was. It's wrong."

"Say it, Carmella. Say it out loud, because I can't believe what I think I'm hearing."

"With women. It's wrong."

"Are you kidding me?"

"You didn't see the things she had—the letters from her girlfriends, the pictures of her doing things, the . . . It's wrong."

"You fucking hypocrite! *You're* ashamed. You're going to stand there and tell me you're gonna judge your sister because she was gay. Is that what you're saying? You, who turned your back on your whole family because you felt they were ashamed of you? You're just like them. No, worse than them, because you let their shame change your entire life. You know better than they did."

She was seething, her face red. "I could not help what happened to me."

"And you think this was a choice for your sister, that she woke up one day and said I'd rather be a lesbian? In 2009, you're going to stand there and say this was her choice like what clothes to wear? The only thing about this whole mess that was your sister's choice was letting Robert Tillman die untreated. You know, Carm, in my head I always believed that you couldn't know somebody else no matter how close you were to them. I believe that because I don't think people even know themselves. Still, you fool yourselves sometimes because otherwise you can't live in this world. I fooled myself about you. I don't know you at all."

Her whole body clenched. "Leave it alone, please."

"Maya told me that Alta never forgave herself for what happened to you as a girl, that she blamed herself until the day she was murdered because she felt she should have stopped you from being taken. Do you even care? But you cut her out of your life, so how could you know that? And now you're doing it a second time, cutting her out of your life, turning your back on her again. Suddenly you're not ashamed of her letting a man die, but of her fucking women. You *should* be ashamed . . . of yourself."

Carmella reared back and slapped me across the face. Now I was stunned and speechless.

"You did what I asked," she said, walking to the door. "For that I will always be grateful."

"I don't want your gratitude. I don't want anything from you, but I'm not leaving it alone. You have to know that, Carmella. I'm not leaving it alone."

She stopped in her tracks, about-faced, and asked, "What does it matter to you? Like you said, she let a man die. She's dead. Nothing will change that. Why do you care?"

"Maybe because no one else does. Someone has to care."

"And that's you, right, Moe? Always you. Moe is the heart at the center of the world."

"Not for much longer."

"What is that supposed to mean?"

"Nothing. Now, if you don't mind," I said, gesturing at the door. "I'll let you know what I find."

"I don't want to know," she said, her back to me as she walked through the door.

I waited for the door to close. "Liar."

. . .

Pam's being there was good for me on more than one level. I'd discussed aspects of the case with Fuqua, Nicky Roussis, Brian Doyle, and Carmella. What I hadn't done was discuss the case globally or unfettered and not doing so hadn't served me well. Pam was the perfect person to discuss it with: she was a top-notch investigator so she could see things from my perspective, but with the added advantages of emotional and geographic distance from the case. Sure, she had heard of the case, everybody had, it was big news. Still, she didn't have a horse in the race.

Okay, given my history with Carmella, I didn't think Pam could be completely objective, but that was fine. Objectivity is bullshit anyway. It's like calculating pi to the last digit. Humans are incapable of it. We all come to the dance, any dance, with too much baggage, conscious and unconscious. We judge. We prejudge. It's what we do. It's how we survive. I felt I was close to finally getting some answers, but close is sometimes more frustrating than far away because I didn't know how close or where to look next.

"There are days it feels like two or three cases, not one," I said, pretending to drink my wine. "There's Tillman dying at the High Line Bistro as Alta and Maya watch. There's Alta's murder and then there's all the other stuff."

"The other stuff?"

"Maya Watson's silence. Delgado trying to hire someone to hurt Alta. Someone trying to run me off the road. Fuqua warning me off Delgado. The deputy mayor being so sure Tillman's family won't sue and this new thing about Tillman and the women at Kid Charlemagne's. And why did Escobar take off on me like that? There's a lot going on here, Pam. I'm close to something, but I'm confused."

She didn't speak, not right away. Instead she sat there for a minute, sipping more wine, not looking at me, not looking at anything at all.

"Break it up," she said. "Break it up."

"Break what up?"

"You said this feels like this is more than one case. Then fine, treat it like more than one case. Instead of trying to squeeze everything into a box that seems too small, break it down into smaller bits. Get the easy answers first like when you were a kid taking a hard test. Get the easy answers, so you can build and move onto the hard questions."

"Okay, I get the idea, but how do you mean?"

"Look, re-ask yourself some questions you have about the case and find those answers one at a time. When you have enough individual answers, you'll probably understand the whole case. Have you tried that yet?"

"Re-asking myself individual questions? No."

"Then start asking and while you're asking, I'll be talking to the women from Kid Charlemagne's."

"Hey, wait a—"

"No, I'm not waiting. I'm not blind, Moe. I can see the toll this is taking on you even if you don't. I don't like it, but I know you. Carmella asked you to stop, but you won't stop. You won't stop because it's not in you to stop."

"Stopping's not an option."

"I didn't think so, but that's for tomorrow. For now, I want to go to bed."

THIRTY-SEVEN

It was something that Maya Watson had said about the type of women Alta was attracted to—*She liked military types, younger chicks, white girls mostly*—and about a name on a witness statement I'd read over a week ago. It was also about Pam's advice to break the case down into smaller pieces and to build from there. I think the minute Pam had said it, my mind began focusing on the Grotto and one of the first questions I'd asked myself about the case: What was Alta, who lived on the other side of Brooklyn from the Grotto, doing there in the first place? And when I woke up in the morning, I knew the answer.

Detective Fuqua was happy to humor me as long as I wasn't still on my Jorge Delgado kick. The latest saint of New York was getting buried today, anyway. Fuqua was probably thrilled to babysit me to make sure I couldn't do something outrageous like interrupting the funeral mass with wild accusations of Delgado's complicity in the murder of Alta Conseco. The brass had made me Fuqua's responsibility and my acting out would sabotage his career. No, that just wouldn't do, not for someone with Fuqua's level of ambition. That's why he had done as I asked and arranged the meeting without asking any questions.

We were stopped at the gate to Fort Hamilton by a sentry who looked barely old enough to shave, let alone vote, but clearly old enough to die. One of the first lessons I learned on the job was that nobody, nobody ever, was too young to die. Fuqua gave our names, flashed his shield, and told the sentry we had an appointment with Colonel Madsen.

"That building there, gentlemen," the sentry said, pointing the way.

Fort Hamilton dated back to the 1800s and its cannons had once fired on and damaged a British troop carrier during the Revolution. The fort had guarded the Brooklyn side of the Narrows at the mouth of New York Harbor. These days, it was darkened by the shadows of the Verrazano-Narrows Bridge, but it was still a lovely old fort.

Colonel Madsen was a gaunt gray man with serious blue eyes and a cool manner. Yes, he had arranged for us to meet privately with Lieutenant Winston. He said he was pleased to do it, but really seemed about as pleased as a plump farm turkey the afternoon before Thanksgiving. He asked again why we were there. When Detective Fuqua explained it was to go over a statement the lieutenant had given in relation to a homicide investigation, Madsen looked even less pleased than before. He felt compelled to remind us that we were on a U.S. Army base and were governed by its rules and not ours. He showed us to a nondescript room in the same building and told us to wait. Told us, not asked us.

There was a smart rap at the door and then it opened. The woman who strode into the room transcended her unflattering Army greens. With some makeup, she might well have been a for-mer beauty queen or head cheerleader or model. I didn't know any-one, man or woman, who wouldn't've been even a little taken with her, if not out of lust then out of envy. Lieutenant Kristen Jo Win-ston was an athletic five foot nine with legs up to here. Her jawline was softly angular and her cheekbones impossibly high. She had a pert nose, bobbed and bouncy strawberry blond hair, and violet eyes. They were the kind of eyes you could not help stare at or into.

We stood to greet her. I wanted Fuqua to do all the talking, at least to begin with. I just nodded, blank-faced, when the detective pointed to me and introduced me as his "colleague" Moses Prager. The lieutenant and Fuqua had met once before, on the night Alta was murdered. He had taken her statement, so she wasn't exactly unnerved by his request to speak with her again. That was my job, to unnerve her a little bit.

"Gentlemen," she said, her voice and demeanor pleasant enough but professional. "What is it I can do for you?" Her accent was deep south, Mississippi maybe or Alabama.

We waited for her to be seated before we sat. The table in the room and the chairs around the table were as nondescript as the room itself.

"Some things have come to light about the homicide of Alta Conseco, the woman who died at the Gelato Grotto on the night of . . ." Fuqua made a show of thumbing through his file.

"I recall," she said. Her expression remained unchanged, but something changed at the corners of her eyes. "What is it you think I can do for you, Detective Fuqua? I told you all I could on the evening in question."

"I'm aware of that, Lieutenant Winston, but there are times that, with some prodding, people can recall details they may have left out or remember after the fact."

"My daddy says that people who remember things long after they happen aren't very dependable witnesses. That most of the time their minds are just embellishing or trying to make sense of things that don't make sense to begin with."

"Your father is a wise man," Fuqua said. "What does he do for a career? An attorney perhaps?"

She actually giggled. It made her look very young. "Oh my, no, he hates lawyers. Daddy is a police detective down in Mobile."

She pronounced Mobile like MO-beel.

"Alabama?"

"Yes, sir, Detective, Mobile, Alabama." But just as she was begin-ning to relax, she reminded herself why she was here and stiffened up rod straight in her chair. "We aren't here, though, to discuss home or my daddy."

Fuqua ignored that. "You're a West Point grad."

"I am. Soldier's the only thing I ever wanted to be. Even as a little girl, I pictured myself in uniform."

That was my opening. "So you'd do just about anything to pro-tect your career, wouldn't you, Lieutenant Winston?"

"I don't see what this has to do with that night." She looked to Fuqua for help.

He obliged. "Never mind my colleague, Lieutenant. He has some very silly notions. It occurs to me that I failed to ask you what you were doing at the Gelato Grotto on the evening the Conseco woman was murdered. Would you mind telling me now?"

"I was hungry for pizza," she said with another giggle, but this one caught in her throat. "It's not all that far from the fort and some of the soldiers from this area are always bragging on it. We don't get pizza like that at home."

"So you went by yourself to the restaurant, not with other offi-cers?" Fuqua asked.

I didn't let her answer. "Bet you're happy to be away from home. I mean, I'm sure you miss your daddy and the rest of your family, but it's easier to be who you really are away from home. Am I right?"

She looked to Fuqua again, but this time no rescue was forthcoming.

"Why, Mr. Prager—I'm sorry, I never did get your rank—I could not possibly know what you mean."

"Oh, sorry, it was a kind of don't ask don't tell thing, Lieutenant Winston."

That did it. She held herself together, but there was real panic in her eyes. She tried playing for time, but I didn't let her.

"Look, Lieutenant, all we're interested in right here right now is the truth about what you were doing at the Grotto that night."

"As I've previously told you, gentlemen, I was hungry for—"

I kept at her. "If you cooperate, we'll walk out of here and you'll never hear from us again. You can go on and have the career you've always wanted and deserve. Or if we don't like your answers, we can all walk over to Colonel Madsen's office and have a nice chat."

"I don't know what you mean."

"Please don't make me do this," I said. "Please."

She jumped out of her chair. "Do what?" she asked, a slight quiver in her voice, the panic spreading. "I'm leaving now and I suggest you never contact me again concerning—"

Fuqua came once more to her rescue. "Please sit." He waited for her to do so before continuing. "We know why you were there, Lieutenant. We know you went to meet Alta Conseco and we fully realize the pressures you are under. We understand that you could not have said these things in your statement, that to do so might have risked the career you love. And while we are not interested in you, per se, we do have an unsolved homicide to deal with. I would ask you to help us, to be fully honest with us in answer to our next questions."

"Or what?" she asked.

"Or we'll have to produce witnesses who will testify to having seen you with Alta Conseco in places your commanding officer would most assuredly not approve of, and then there are the pictures." All of it was a bluff on my part, but especially the stuff about the pictures.

"I don't respond well to threats."

"Fine," I said. "Forget the threats. Tell us the truth because it is the right thing to do and because you owe it to Alta."

Tears rushed out of her, her body convulsing, but there was scarcely a sob. This had been a long time coming. Fuqua and I sat there silently and let it happen. When she was done, she was done. The lieutenant wiped her cheeks with the backs of her hands, then her palms.

"I was in love with her, yes," she said.

"Alta Conseco?"

"Yes."

"And you went there to meet her?"

"Yes. I had seen very little of her since . . . since the incident and it was killing me. I told her no one would recognize her, that people had moved on."

My turn. "So the Grotto was your idea?"

"Yes."

"Did she come, eat with you, then leave or had she not yet shown up?"

"I was getting up to leave because she was so late. I wasn't mad at her, just disappointed. I thought she had gotten scared about coming to such a public place and decided not to show. Then . . . that's when she—"

"That's okay, Lieutenant Winston," I said. "You're not a suspect and we really do understand how hard this is for you. What we're more interested in is what you and Alta talked about. What did she tell you about the incident at the High Line Bistro? What did she tell you about why she and her partner were there in the first place and why they let Robert Tillman die?"

Winston sat there, squeezing her hands together so hard the blood went out of them. There are times you can literally see people struggling with themselves. This was one of those times.

"I can't," she said, her voice shaking. "I gave my word."

I asked, "And you would sacrifice your career to keep your word?"

"If I had to, yes, sir, I would. How can you measure yourself if not by the value of your word?"

This wasn't the time for more pressure. She would have shut down. Instead, I took a picture out of my wallet and slid it across the table to her. It was a photo I'd carried for nine years. I hadn't looked at it for nearly as long. I saw the recognition in her eyes and there were more tears.

The lieutenant picked up the picture. "That's Alta's sister Carmella, Israel, and you," she said. "I didn't make the connection. Alta used to talk about missing her."

"That's right, Kristen, I'm Moe. I used to be married to Alta's little sister. So do you understand why I'm here and why it would be okay with Alta to tell me?"

The lieutenant never looked up, but kept staring at the photo. "Maya, Alta's partner, was being blackmailed. She wouldn't tell me about what because she had made a pact with Maya that she would never tell anyone, that they would never even speak about it."

"Blackmailed? Blackmailed by whom?"

"She never told me, but Alta said they had gone to the restaurant that day to confront the man who was doing it. Maya didn't want to go through with it. She begged Alta not to, but Alta said she wouldn't let Maya keep paying, that she would take care of things even if it meant killing him. That was Alta. She was really protective of the people she—" Winston put the picture down, finally.

I reached across the table and took her right hand in mine. "I'm sorry for the things I said before, but . . ."

"I understand. Just find the person who did this, please."

"Is there anything else, any other details you've left out about any of it?" Fuqua asked.

"No, I don't think so. Alta didn't give me any details. It was hard for her to even tell me what she did. Her word meant a lot to her too."

That's how we left her, sitting at the table, collecting herself, her thoughts, and her feelings.

Fuqua waited until we exited the fort before giving voice to what we were both thinking. "It was him, Tillman, who was the blackmailer."

"Looks that way to me, Detective."

"But to let him die . . . What could he have been blackmailing her about to let things get to such a point?"

"There's only one person who knows that answer," I said.

I excused myself, telling Fuqua I needed a restroom break. What I needed was to call Pam. When I got her on the phone, I related to her what the lieutenant had just told us about Maya being black-mailed and that it looked like the late Robert Tillman had some-thing to do with it. She said she didn't know when she'd get back to my condo and told me not to wait up for her.

Fuqua was in the car waiting for me just outside the door of the building. I got in. Neither of us spoke. No need. We knew where we had to go and who we had to speak to. Out of the fort, he turned onto the Belt Parkway east toward Queens and Maya Wat-son's condo.

THIRTY-EIGHT

We weren't quite to the Flatbush Avenue exit on the Belt when my phone buzzed in my pocket. I didn't recognize the number, but I'm such a curious bastard, I picked up anyway. It was a real flaw of mine that it was difficult for me to ignore a ringing phone or a knock at the door. Over the years I had done a lot of talking to Jehovah's Witnesses and kids selling fundraising raffles. Someone once said your biggest weaknesses are also your greatest strengths. Might have been Ben Franklin. Might have been Charles Manson. I forget. Well, curiosity was an abiding weakness of mine. I could never just stand back and let it be. Wasn't in my nature. I wondered about what would happen to my curiosity when I was dead. Where would it go? What happens to the energies that drive the engines that drive us? Do they just vanish?

"Is this Moses Prager?" a man's voice on the other end of the line asked.

"You tell me. You're the one calling this number."

He repeated the question. "Is this Moses Prager?"

"Who wants to know?"

"Detective John DiNardo, NYPD."

"And what's this in relation to, Detective?"

That got Fuqua's attention and he mouthed, "Who is it?"

I covered the mouthpiece and told him.

He shrugged his shoulders. "The name is not a familiar one."

I could hear the detective talking, but couldn't make out his words. I went back to him.

"I'm sorry, Detective DiNardo, I was interrupted there for a second. What's this in relation to again?"

"Do you know a Maya Watson?"

"I might."

His previously flat affect turned decidedly hostile. "What the hell's that supposed to mean?"

"It means I'll show you mine if you show me yours. What's this about?"

"This is a homicide investigation, Mr. Prager, and I suggest you stop fuckin' around with me and answer the questions."

"Is Maya Watson dead?"

There was silence on his end of the phone.

I covered the mouthpiece again and turned to Fuqua. "I think Maya Watson's been murdered."

He crossed himself, mumbled something in French, then asked for the phone. I obliged.

"Detective DiNardo, this is Detective Jean Jacques Fuqua of Brooklyn South Homicide, shield number 814. Mr. Prager is assisting me in an investigation that also involves Maya Watson. Mr. Prager will cooperate with you fully, I can assure you. Can you please tell me what happened? Oh . . . Suicide . . . Yesterday . . . How long had she been dead? . . . Three days . . . A neighbor . . . The One-O-Seven . . . On Parsons Boulevard . . . We will be there within the hour."

"Christ," I heard myself whisper.

Fuqua clicked off and handed back the phone. "Definitely a suicide, but you know procedure. It is treated as a homicide until other possibilities are eliminated and the ME makes the final determination. They found your number and messages on her cell phone. He was just doing his job."

"Did she leave a note?"

"He did not say, but we will know soon enough."

. . .

Detective DiNardo was a forty/forty man: forty years old with a forty-inch waist. He was counting the days until he could put in his papers, collect his pension, and move down to South Carolina. I knew a lot of John DiNardos when I was on the job. They were sort of the opposite numbers to ambitious guys like Larry McDonald and Jean Jacques Fuqua. For the DiNardos of this world, making detective third was as far as their reach extended. They were content to wear Walmart wardrobes, work the cases that came across their desks, and to get fat on fast food. That was fine. In the opera of the law, someone's got to sing in the chorus. And the fact that DiNardo didn't aspire to be Sherlock Holmes made him easier to deal with. To him Maya Watson's suicide was an easy case to clear, so he had no qualms about sharing information with us.

DiNardo handed Fuqua two plastic, amber-colored prescription bottles in an evidence bag. "She swallowed about fifty of those. This was no cry for help. She meant to do the job right."

Fuqua handed the bag back. "Why was there no report of her death in the media?"

"We didn't put two and two together at first," DiNardo said. "That thing with her and her partner letting that guy die, that was months ago. None of us made the connection. Only when I started digging a little did I put it together. It'll be in the papers tomorrow."

"Suicide note?" I asked.

"No need for one," DiNardo said, handing me another evidence bag. "That's the letter from the FDNY officially dismissing her. I figure it was the last straw and that was that."

I wanted to argue with him, but what he said made too much sense. I had seen the way Maya had shut herself in and closed herself off. I had smelled the cigarettes and seen the cups and cups and cups of coffee. I had heard her talk about her unending grief over what had happened to Alta. Sure, that day when we went to Coney Island, she seemed better, feisty even, but I was no shrink. People killed themselves for all sorts of reasons, sometimes not very substantial ones. No one could argue that that was the case with Maya Watson. Her reasons seemed substantial enough to me.

It struck me, though, that her suicide had shut the door on the only lead we had. We might now never know what she was being blackmailed about, if Robert Tillman had been the man behind it, or if the blackmail had anything to do with Alta's murder.

"Detective DiNardo, did you call all the other numbers in her cell phone in and out box?" I asked, not quite sure why.

"I did."

"And did you get everyone on the phone?"

"Nah. I couldn't reach one or two of them."

"Would you mind giving me those numbers and letting me keep trying?"

"Not a problem. Let me get them for you." He transcribed the numbers from the file onto the back of his card and handed it to me. "Anything else, gentlemen?"

Fuqua and I looked at each other and silently agreed that we had no more questions.

"Nothing I can think of," I said. "Thanks."

We all shook hands like captains at the center of a football field before the coin toss.

"Good luck with your case, Fuqua," DiNardo said. "What these women did was wrong, but I don't think either one of them deserved their fates."

I changed my mind about DiNardo. He wasn't like the guys I'd known on the job. None of them would have been thoughtful enough to look beyond their own gut reactions. The guys I had known would have looked at what had befallen Alta and Maya and said good riddance.

THIRTY-NINE

It was her apartment, but it wasn't, and we didn't need a crystal ball to know what we would find. She hadn't answered the door and she hadn't responded to our knocking at her windows. We knew all we needed to know when the foul stench of rancid flesh seeped under the door and around the window frames like fog. Old death's signature is as distinctive as John Hancock's. I knew that if the fog could get out, flies could get in. The image of her body as the hostess of flies made me sick to my stomach and I covered my mouth to hold back the vomit. That image would be as hard to erase as the stink that filled up my senses.

Fuqua handed me a cell phone. *Where was mine?* I punched in her number like a silent prayer. Silent or not, God said no, and the call went straight to voicemail.

"It is the Tonton Macoute," Fuqua said, his hands shaking. Then he turned and kicked in the door. It crumbled into dust as if it were made of chalk and a wave of thick black coffee came pouring out the empty doorway, thousands of cigarette filters riding the surf. Our clothes remained perfectly dry. "Watch out for the Tonton Macoute," he whispered, his index finger across his lips.

We walked into the apartment. The walls were papered in hate mail, the carpeting covered in tobacco stains and sticky brown resin. There was a makeshift altar in one corner of the living room. On it was a framed photo of Alta Conseco kissing Kristen Jo Winston. The photograph was surrounded by hundreds of Hanukah candles;

blue and white wax dripped into a two-foot high mound on the floor. Odd, I thought, this altar was just like the altar in John Tierney's house, the man who had been accused of kidnapping Sashi Bluntstone. But this wasn't his basement, or was it?

Fuqua nodded at the altar. "See, see?"

We were in her bedroom now. It was so thick with flies that we breathed them in like black air, but the beating of their wings was only a whisper. John DiNardo was now there with us. He pointed at the bed. Her body lay under a quilt that conformed perfectly to her outline.

"This is how we found her," he said. "She's still under there. Look!"

And when Detective DiNardo pulled back the quilt, nothing was in bed but a cell phone.

I didn't wake up screaming because I'd been complicit in my dream. It was as if I was rooting from the sidelines for me to keep moving ahead, to find what I was looking for, to find an answer. No, I woke up feeling like an old-fashioned percolator. Things were bubbling up inside me. Sure, there was regret over Maya Watson's suicide, but death had been her choice, a luxury I didn't think was going to be afforded me. Besides, I didn't hold with those people who believed that suicide was an act of cowardice. Those were the same people who saw addiction as a moral weakness, the same people who thought of posttraumatic stress as a disease for pussies. Suicide wasn't exactly an act of heroism either, not in my book. It was an act of control, the ultimate proof of propriety.

I rolled over in bed. Pam was there with me, asleep but lightly so. She was in that rested, semi-conscious state where a soft touch in the right place would lead us down the road to slow building, sleep-drunk sex. Pam was nude and with my body pressing against her back, it would have been easy to touch any number of sensitive spots and to let the dance begin. Instead I put my arm around her abdomen and held on for all I was worth.

"What is it?" she mumbled, rolling onto her back and brushing my cheek with the back of her hand. "What time is it?"

"It's either very late or very early." I dragged my thumb over her lips. "Lady's choice."

"Late is sexier than early."

"Then it's very late. What time did you get in?"

"Past midnight. We've got a lot to talk about later," she said.

"It's already later."

She pushed me over onto my back and straddled me. "Later later," she said. "Some things can wait. Others can't. Lady's choice, remember?"

I knew when to keep my mouth shut.

FORTY

It had taken Pam nearly the entire day to track down Abigail and Natasha, the two women from Kid Charlemagne's. She had had to tell them lies, different lies to each, but she had managed to have coffee with Natasha, the hostess who had quit, and a glass of wine with Abigail before her shift. Pam had a gift for lying. That was how we met, through a series of her lies. Although I too could lie with as little effort as it took to blink, I'm not sure I ever got completely over how Pam and I came to be together. Even after Pam saved my life, I couldn't forget her lies. Most of the time I was fine with it. She had just been doing her job. I knew that was true. True or not, it rang hollow, the way my words must've sounded to my first wife Katy when she discovered I'd been lying to her about her brother Patrick's disappearance since before we were married.

Pam's hard work had gotten her only so far.

"Abigail was very cooperative. She told me that a couple of months ago some of the crew from Kid Charlemagne's went to the bar next door to the restaurant for drinks one night after work. They did that sometimes, nothing unusual about it. As it got later and later, the crowd thinned out until only she, another bartender, one of the other cooks, and Tillman were left. She said she liked older men and Tillman was handsome enough. They had flirted around a little bit. Then she started feeling weird, not sick exactly, just light-headed, and she went to the bathroom to throw some cold water on her face. When she came out, Robert Tillman was standing there. He opened his

241

hand and there was a pill in his palm. He told her to take it, that it would make everything feel better. When she refused, he shoved her back into the bathroom and tried to force it down her throat. She spit it out, kicked him in the nuts, ran out, and caught a cab. Said she really doesn't remember getting home and woke up still in her clothes like twelve hours later. She told her boss and Tillman was fired."

"And the other woman, Natasha?"

"Nice girl, but fragile. She wouldn't talk. She was scared shitless. When I brought up Tillman's name, I thought she would snap in two."

"Doesn't make any sense. If Tillman was blackmailing her or even if he was just a pig and had pulled the same stunt with her as he had with Abigail, he's dead. Dead is dead."

"Maybe not," Pam said.

"What's that supposed to mean?"

"Listen, Moe, no matter how I tried to get her to tell me what was wrong, she wouldn't. Finally, when I saw I wasn't getting anywhere with her, I did a variation on Abigail's story and told her Tillman had tried it on me. She began shaking like crazy and when I put my hand on her to try and calm her down, I could feel she was cold sweating. She asked me if he was still threatening me too."

"What?"

"That's what she said, Moe. 'Is he still threatening you?' When she saw the confusion in my eyes, I saw betrayal in hers. She knew I was lying and ran out."

"This is nuts. The one thing we do know here is that Tillman is dead."

Pam smiled a sad smile. "Well, Natasha doesn't seem to think so."

"Holy shit!" I smacked myself in the forehead. "It's all right here."

"What's all here?"

"The answers," I said.

"To what?"

"To everything."

"Everything?"

"Almost."

"Did the Mafia kill JFK?"

I kissed her hard on the mouth. "I said almost everything, wiseass. I've got some calls to make."

FORTY-ONE

I don't think I'd ever fully grasped the concept of reverse engineering. There was more to it than just breaking something down into its component pieces and putting it back together. There were more subtle aspects to it. Even inanimate things are more than the sum of their parts. Pam understood that. Carmella understood it too. Me, Mr. Stumbler and Bumbler, I didn't get it until now. Alta's murder was proving to be a lot more than a series of connected events. I wanted to trace it back to its point of origin, to the first falling domino, and now I thought I knew where that domino had fallen.

It was a five-minute walk and a one-minute drive from where Maya Watson and Alta Conseco were stationed to Piccadilly. Piccadilly was the bar next door to Kid Charlemagne's and the chick behind the bar recognized Maya's face immediately.

"Used to be in here all the time."

"Used to be?"

"Haven't seen her in here since February maybe. She was so hot and so cool—guys used to be all over her like flies."

"Hot and cool. How do you mean?"

"Come on, man. With those mixed-race looks and that long lean body, are you kidding me? But she was also aloof, you know?"

Yeah, I knew. She was now as aloof as aloof could be.

I hadn't had to search for a picture of Maya to show around because it was on the front page of all the local dailies. Detective DiNardo was right, word of her suicide had become news. And with the news of her suicide came the nightmare, the public rehashing and communal hand-wringing over the death of Robert Tillman. It was a field day for the pundits and talking heads, a second bite at the apple. But this time around Alta and Maya, and even Robert Tillman, were like deep sea dwellers, beyond the reach of the tempest roiling the surface.

So now I knew where it had all started, where Maya Watson and Robert Tillman had crossed paths last February. And given what Abigail had told Pam, it didn't take a rocket scientist to figure out that Tillman had probably slipped something into Maya's drink. It was the mechanics of what followed that I was curious about and there was only one person who could help me find that answer.

. . .

Pam had to cajole her way into meeting with Natasha. I took a more direct approach and badged my way into her building. I told the doorman to call ahead to let her know I was coming up. Would it freak her out, the notion that a cop was coming up to her apartment? Maybe. That was the idea.

Natasha Romaine, dressed in cut-off jean shorts and a pastel pink tank top, was waiting at the door for me when I got off the elevator. I could see what Pam meant about her fragility. No older than twenty-one or -two, with wispy red hair, freckled, almost translucent skin, watery blue eyes, a button nose, and pale lips, she was pretty in a delicate, hothouse flower sort of way. She was very slight of build and couldn't have weighed more than ninety pounds. She'd probably always played an angel in her church's holiday pageants. I felt immediately protective of her, a reflexive reaction that I imagine she elicited from most men. Most, not all. That reflex was going to make what I knew I had to do even harder.

"I don't have to talk to you," she said, girding herself, thrusting out her chest. Her breasts were evident, but as small as the rest of her.

"You don't even know what I came to talk about."

"Yes, I do," she said, staring into my eyes, "and I don't have to talk about it."

"I guess you don't have to, no, but part of you wants to. May I come in or are we going to have this talk out in the hallway so all your neighbors can hear?"

Her apartment was typical Manhattan fare: a cluttered studio that was probably not much bigger than her bedroom back home— wherever that was—and probably more money per month than most folks' mortgage payments. But the clutter was of fine things. Her computer, an Apple desktop, had a huge monitor and every peripheral known to mankind. The futon and chairs were high end. No IKEA in here. The clothing and shoes strewn about were SoHo boutique, not Aéropostale. The art on the wall, mostly pieces from famous street artists like Banksy and Shepard Fairey, was either original or a signed and numbered print. Any one of the things in the studio cost more than a restaurant hostess could afford. Natasha came from money. Helps when you're being blackmailed.

I sat on the futon. The delicate flower pinballed back and forth from the front door to the bathroom door like a trapped fly banging against a closed window. Just my being here had raised her anxiety level into the red numbers.

"What do you want?" Natasha fairly barked at me.

I opened the paper, but hid the headlines. "Do you recognize this woman?"

Her eyes got gigantic and she buried a trembling hand in her armpit. "No." She was lying and she knew I knew it.

"Listen, Natasha, let's stop lying to each other, okay? I used to be a cop, but I retired a long time ago. I'm a private investigator now and not a very good one anymore."

"Get out!"

It was my turn to say no. "I'm not going anywhere until you talk about this, about what happened to you. I have a daughter a little bit older than you and I would hope that if she had trouble in her life and couldn't talk to me about it, that she would be able to talk to someone else, someone who would listen, who would care and not judge."

The steel was going out of her, but she wasn't at the point of surrender. "Please go."

I showed her Maya Watson's face again. "Do you recognize this woman?"

"Yes."

"That's all, just yes?"

"Why is she in the paper?" Natasha asked, a lot of fear in her little voice.

I ignored the question and pushed her harder. "How do you know her? Have you seen her in the papers before or on TV?"

Natasha tilted her head at me like a confounded puppy. "What?"

"She committed suicide a few days ago," I said, answering the earlier question. "She couldn't take the secrets and the lies anymore. Swallowed two bottles of pills. They found her in her bed in a hot apartment. The insects had gotten to her."

She bent over at the waist, letting out a strangled gasp, and began dry heaving. She covered her mouth as I had in my dream.

I kept at her. "You knew her from Piccadilly, right?"

She nodded yes.

"She drank there sometimes after work like you and the other people from Kid Charlemagne's. That's how you met, right?"

She nodded again.

"You knew that she was one of the EMTs who let Robert Till-man die at the High Line Bistro."

She nodded.

"He had been blackmailing you and he had been blackmailing Maya and probably a lot of other women too."

Now Natasha fell to her knees and the heaving was no longer dry. She vomited up whatever she had eaten in the last few hours, but she kept heaving. I got down beside her and held her head, stroked her hair and hugged her like I used to do with Sarah. When she was finally done, I laid her down on the futon, and got her a cold bottled water out of her fridge. I wiped her face and put a cold cloth on her forehead. After cleaning her floor, I sat in a chair across from her as she napped for about half an hour. When she got up, she didn't say a word. Instead she went into the bathroom. I listened to her brush her teeth, gargle, and take a quick shower. She came out of the bathroom in a robe, went directly to her computer, and began tapping at the keyboard.

"Can you please come here." She uttered her first words in nearly an hour. "See this email?" She pointed to a line in her inbox. It was from RT6969@constop.com. Didn't take Einstein to figure out who RT6969 was. The subject heading was *Ebony and Ivory*.

"Uh huh, yeah."

"I'm going to get dressed and leave for about an hour because I just can't be here. When I leave, click on the links in the email and then you'll understand."

That was it. She gathered up some clothes, disappeared back into the bathroom, and was gone. As she closed the door behind her, I opened the email and clicked on the first link.

The link was to a video. I pressed the play arrow and knew imme-diately that Natasha was right: I understood, maybe more than I wanted to. In the video, a man I took to be the now late Robert Tillman and three much younger men took turns raping and sodomizing both Maya Watson and Natasha Romaine individually and in groups. I didn't recognize the younger men in the video. Maya and Natasha were obviously drugged up, but not unconscious. They were pliable, not cooperative, but not uncooperative either, sort of will-less. Then things got weirder.

The women were dressed in fetish wear—leather and latex— and posed in several positions with each other, sometimes with sex toy props. A lot of it seemed totally staged, but in some of the footage, a third woman joined in. She was thin and muscular, clad in a black latex bustier, super high-heeled black stilettos, and a black latex mask. She wasn't drugged or, if she was, it was a very different drug cocktail than Maya and Natasha had been fed because this woman didn't seem to need any posing or prompting. She was active, enthusiastic, and none of what she did seemed forced or involuntary. Some of the things she did to Maya and Natasha were very disturbing and had probably been very painful for them.

The second link was to another video featuring much of the same footage, but it had been professionally edited. No longer did the things that had seemed so obviously staged seemed staged. A cheesy synthesized soundtrack played in the background. The sort of low moans, probably from pain and bewilderment, that Maya and Natasha had emitted during the nightmare, had been enhanced so that the women sounded like they loved what was going on and couldn't get enough. Gaudy pink lettering was superimposed over the video to make it look like an advertisement for Ebony and Ivory Escort Service. Numbers flashed up on the screen and a disembodied voice promised that there wasn't anything Ebony and Ivory wouldn't do to make their clients happy. The footage that went along with that particular promise featured a montage of the most disturbing scenes from the earlier video.

The third link was to another video and, in some ways, the most chilling of all. In it, a man's hand went through both women's bags and clothing pockets one item at a time. An unusual amount of time was spent on shots of a BlackBerry, an iPhone, an address book, and two sets of keys. I clicked off, but forwarded a copy of the email with the links to my computer.

Okay, I thought, I understood a lot of it. Robert Tillman had drugged Maya and Natasha at the bar, gotten them back to a location where things were set to go, and probably kept feeding both women drugged drinks until he was done with them. And it was no wonder the women were willing to pay their rapist to keep that video footage away from the public. In this day and age, once video is out there, it is out there forever. Even if your parents or fiancé would believe your story about being drugged and raped, there might always be some level of doubt. But the fact was, Robert Tillman was dead and the other guys in the video didn't strike me as criminal masterminds. They seemed more like three frat boy jocks who were promised a good time and were just drunk enough not to give a shit about at whose expense that good time came. So what was Natasha still so scared of and why couldn't either Maya or Natasha breathe a sigh of relief after Tillman's death?

Then, as I was staring at the line on Natasha's email account, two things hit me so hard I was almost breathless. The date of this email was last week. Natasha certainly and probably Maya had continued to be blackmailed four months after Robert Tillman's death. Now I couldn't help but wonder if it really was the termination letter that pushed Maya over the edge and into eternal sleep. One piece of the puzzle was clear enough: Tillman hadn't returned from the dead. He had left behind a very live partner. Of course he had a partner. How else had he managed to get both women to where the footage was shot? How had he managed to round up the frat boys and run the camera? Tino Escobar! No wonder he took off when I went to talk to him at Kid Charlemagne's. It made perfect sense. He and Tillman worked together in both places. Convenient, huh?

The other thing that struck me was that there was no money demand anywhere in the email or buried in the video that I could see. I forced myself to watch them again, looking for something I might have missed. I hadn't missed anything.

I think Natasha half-hoped I would be gone when she returned, but only half-hoped. The other half hoped I could make the black-mail finally go away. I told her that I thought I could, that she would need to trust me, and do as I asked, no matter what I asked. It couldn't have been easy for her to agree, but she did just the same.

"I don't know your name," she said, as I headed for the door.

I took one of my ancient cards out of my wallet and wrote down my cell number.

"Moses," she whispered to herself and then, looking up at me, "Why are you doing this?"

I opened up my mouth to give her a quick, meaningless answer, but held my tongue. This wasn't as simple a question as it seemed. I thought about it for a moment. Why *was* I doing this? Was it because of the history between Carmella and me or because I was sick and working the case was a form of denial? Was it as simple as my curiosity or as complicated as my guilt? Was I trying to make up for the hurt and damage I'd done, to put one more check in the good column before I died? Or was it just because it was the right thing to do?

"I'm not sure," I said at last. "I'm really not sure. Does it matter?"

"No. I just want it to be over."

I was careful not to mention Tino Escobar. I didn't want her getting more freaked out than she already was. Besides, I needed more proof than convenience and coincidence to connect him to this. I took a long last look at Natasha before leaving. Suddenly, she didn't seem quite so fragile. To see that almost made it worth it.

I thanked the doorman on the way out. He nodded goodbye, not quite sure what to make of me. That made two of us. I was a sixty-something eighteen-year-old who didn't know himself any better now than he did when he really was eighteen. Sometimes I fooled myself that I knew more about my nature and the nature of things than I did, but I guess what I actually understood was how little I understood. People always say that when you are near the end, you get religion. Not me. The louder I heard the coffin lid closing, I believed less and less. What I wanted was to know things before I died, to know things for sure. Maybe that's what I should have said to Natasha, that I wanted to know things, something, anything for sure before the metastatic golf ball in my belly ate me alive, that I was working the case because I was tired of questions and wanted answers.

I got some when I called Fuqua on the way to my car, though not exactly the kind of answers that would make dying much easier.

"Anything?" I asked.

"Your instincts were right about Robert Tillman."

"How so?"

"Robert Tillman was an alias. His real name was Roland Sykes. He was born in Vestel, New York, July 22, 1972. And he was not a very nice fellow. When he died, the city had no luck in contacting his next of kin through the usual methods. In most such cases, the city would have kept him on ice for a respectable amount of time and, if his body remained unclaimed, they would have stuck him in Potter's Field. But this was too high profile for that, so they ran his prints *et voila*, Roland Sykes! A pity that poor Roland had a criminal record."

"When you say he wasn't a very nice fellow, how do you mean?"

"Most of his arrests and convictions were for forging checks, running scams on old women, even extortion. But he was also convicted of statutory rape with a sixteen-year-old girl. It was a class E felony and he did the full four-year bid. Got out two years ago. He kept up with his reporting responsibilities for a year and then disappeared from the radar screen."

"So this was the city's hold card. If any of his real family members came forward to sue, the city would play hardball. It would be tough to find even a civil jury or judge sympathetic to the family of a convicted sex offender. No wonder everyone was so tight-lipped about it. The city just wanted it to all go away and be forgotten. No harm, no foul."

"Just so. Now we both know why my superiors were so adamant about you not pursuing Jorge Delgado as a suspect. The publicity would have been impossible to contain. You are aware, I hope, it wasn't easy for me to discover these things, Moe. I had to call in many favors and I have not been a detective long enough to have many favors to ask."

"I don't suppose my gratitude will be enough to satisfy you."

He laughed. "It will be a fine starting point."

"We're not done quite yet," I said. "Find out who his cellmates were during his last few times inside. My guess is you're gonna run across the name Tino Escobar somewhere in there. See if Tino or any of them worked with video equipment."

He didn't ask why. I liked that. I enjoy most those moments early in any relationship when you know the other person has begun to trust your judgment. So it was with Fuqua. His ambition made it impossible for me to trust him quite so much as he seemed willing to trust me.

FORTY-TWO

Brian Doyle was about the last person I expected to hear from, but that's life, isn't it? It's not the things we expect that makes it both wonderful and impossible to bear. Think how dull it would all be if things went according to plan. Frankly, there were times I could have done with a little more boredom than some of the unexpected and unwelcome surprises I'd been dealing with lately. For instance, I think I might have welcomed my oncologist saying something like, "April Fools!" or "Sorry, Moe, wrong chart." Those would have worked much better for me than his, "Look at it this way, it's treatable." That it-could-always-be-worse kind of rationalization was lost on me. No one had to tell me it could always be worse. I had a lot of firsthand experience in that area.

Mostly, I was surprised to hear from Doyle because he had washed his hands of the whole Jorge Delgado mess. I'd seen Brian in a lot of moods, but I'd only seen him scared a few times in all the years I'd known him. And when he appeared at my condo the other day, he was scared. He tried not to show it, playing up the brawl and how he'd given better than he got. I always admired that about the Irish cops I worked with over the years, their love of a good fight. Jews, even tough Jews, tend to fight as a last resort. For some of the guys I knew, fighting was more like foreplay, just a way to get their blood up, a kind of a pinch to let them know they were still alive. And I was surprised, not so much by Doyle as myself. After learning of the blackmail and of Maya's suicide, I had more or less turned my attention away from Alta's murder, the reason I had gotten involved in this in the first place. It was a reminder to me that even at my age, I had no clue of what I was doing or where I was going. Here I was again, stumbling around in the dark.

It was a good thing Brian called me when he did, because if I'd gotten across the Manhattan Bridge and into Brooklyn, I'm not sure I would have gone back. I was tired, very tired, and my head was swimming. I was focused on the blackmail, on Natasha, on the dream of Maya in a room of black flies, on putting an end to it. I was thinking of Pam, of Sarah, of my own guilt over leaving them behind. The last thing I was interested in was the recently interred, New York saint-elect, Jorge Delgado. Besides, I no longer believed for a second he really had anything to do with Alta's death. He was just another macho schmuck who had acted foolishly and impulsively when he went to Nestor Feliz and Joey Fortuna to have Alta hurt. I'm sure the parents of the little girl he saved wouldn't have cared if Jorge was an axe murderer. Who knows, maybe it was his own guilt over what he'd done that made him jump in front of that car? I didn't particularly care.

Doyle was leaning against the fender of a midnight blue Corvette coupe when I pulled onto West 11th Street in the West Village.

"Like it?" Brian asked, gesturing at the 'Vette.

"You must be doing well for yourself these days."

He winked at me. "I make a nice living for an ex-cop."

"Not exactly inconspicuous, though."

"Just like you and Carm taught me, I drive a vintage shitbox when I do surveillance."

"Nice to know someone listened to me."

"It was really Carm who taught me," he said. "I just didn't want you to feel left out."

"Fuck you, Doyle. I see your face is healing up. So what are we doing here?"

He didn't answer directly. "You ever wonder why Delgado wasn't cleared of Alta's murder from the get-go and why everybody was so big on warning people off?"

"It crossed my mind, yeah."

"I mean, all the guy had to do was give the cops a solid alibi and that was that, right?"

"Right."

"So it's gotta make you wonder why he didn't. To me, there's only two possible reasons a suspect don't give a rock-solid alibi. He either committed the crime or he thinks the alibi is more trouble than it's worth. Like a guy wouldn't say *I can prove I definitely didn't kill X in Brooklyn because I was too busy killing Y and Z in the Bronx.* Or maybe he knew that even if he was a suspect, that the cops couldn't prove it and his rock-solid alibi would have been so embarrassing he was willing to take the heat."

"Is this going somewhere, Brian?"

"Yeah, apartment 5S."

"What's going on? I thought you were done with this case."

"For about five minutes," he said, pressing the vestibule buzzer for apartment 5S.

I grabbed him by the shoulder after we were buzzed in. "I don't know what I'm going to find up there, but thanks for not giving up. You know this means a lot to me."

"No offense, Boss, but I didn't do it for you. I've never let myself get scared off anything in my life and I wasn't gonna start now. You back down once, there's no telling when it'll stop. You let yourself get scared and it never goes away. It fucks up your judgments."

We shunned the elevator and walked the five flights up the pink marble stairs of the old pre-war building. The steps were so well-used that there were actually smooth ruts worn into the stone treads. The walls in these buildings were thick plaster and made for good neighbors the way stone walls and high fences made for good neighbors in the country. In a city of probably ten million people, New Yorkers held dear their small, private niches.

At the door to 5S, Doyle slapped me on the shoulder and handed me a slim digital voice recorder. "What you need is already on there," he said, "but I think you'll want to hear this for yourself. You can take it from here, Boss."

I watched Brian walk away. He disappeared down the stairs, but his footsteps echoed around the stone and plaster. I rang the bell to the apartment and waited.

When the door pulled back, I was greeted by a slight but fit young man, maybe thirty years old. Shirtless and dressed in gym shorts, he was about five-seven and likely weighed no more than a hundred and thirty pounds. There wasn't an ounce of fat on him and his muscles were cut and ripped without being ridiculous on someone his size. He was by any standard a handsome man. He had hazel eyes, flawless, perfectly shaven skin, and close-cropped light brown hair.

"Please," he said, sweeping his arm back in a welcoming gesture. "Step in."

I did and listened as the door closed behind me.

"I'm Marco and you must be Moe."

"I am."

"Something to drink? Wine? Bottled water?"

"Bottled water would be good," I said. "It'll be fine to leave it in the bottle."

"Okay, look around. I'll be right back."

I took his suggestion to heart and stepped into the living room. The apartment was as perfectly groomed as Marco: neat and very well appointed. In one corner of the apartment was a rolltop desk used more as a mantel than a desk. A host of framed photos covered what would have been the writing surface and in those photos were the illustrated story of why Brian Doyle brought me here.

When Marco returned from the kitchen, he had a glass of red wine in one hand and a bottle of Perrier in the other. I took the bottle from him.

"Cheers."

"Cheers."

I clinked bottle to glass and picked up one of the framed photos. At a glance, it looked like a shot of Cher on stage. "You?" I said. I didn't wait for an answer. "Very good."

He smiled proudly with all his perfectly straight white teeth. "*Gypsies, tramps, and thieves, that's what the people of the town would call us,*" he belted out in quite a good imitation of Cher's voice.

There were photos of him as Barbra Streisand, Marlene Dietrich, Joan Rivers, Elizabeth Taylor, and Liza Minnelli. They were remarkable.

"Liza, that's who I'm known for. She's even come to see me."

And there it was, a picture of his Liza and the real one standing cheek to cheek. It was signed by her with the inscription: *If only I were this young and pretty and talented. Love, Liza.*

"She's such a doll."

But none of the photos of Marco as other people interested me nearly as much as the photo of Marco as himself, clutched in the thick, powerful arms of Jorge Delgado. He noticed my gaze.

"We met when he was working on the pile at Ground Zero," Marco said, taking hold of the photo and sitting down on the couch. "God, I was such a child back then. I had been in the city for about a year from Denton."

"Texas?"

"Yes, not exactly a place that had much use for someone like me."

"I wouldn't think so."

"But after the attacks, I went down there to the Trade Center to help anyway I could. Georgie and I just struck up a kind of odd friendship to begin with. We both loved working out and though you can't tell it, I'm half Argentinean. I speak fluent Spanish. Georgie liked that and my sense of humor. That's all it was for years, a friendship. He would come to see me do my act on occasion. Of course, he could never tell anyone about me. My goodness, he would have never heard the end of it on the job. And his family . . . forget it! They would have been horrified. In some ways, I think that helped him to finally give into it. He had to hide me anyway. Over the years, when he would drink a little too much, and I was still in costume, we would kiss sometimes, but nothing more. Then one night, about two years ago, it didn't stop with kissing. I loved him very much."

"Not to burst your bubble, Marco, but your lover over there had a funny way of dealing with being with you. He basically tormented Alta Conseco because she was a lesbian. Did you know he tried to hire a guy to break her bones?"

"Guilt," he said without a moment's hesitation. "Moe, I didn't say it was all bliss with Georgie. In some ways, it was easier when it was only kissing and I was in drag. He could maintain the pretense that way, but once we were together, his world crumbled. It's always more difficult with men like him, the married macho types who can never accept themselves for what and who they are. He was jealous of Alta, someone who could be out in the world as a gay woman. Georgie resented it and was repulsed by who he was. What's the old saying? We hate those things in other people we detest most about ourselves."

"Why come forward now?"

"I didn't exactly come forward, did I? Your Mr. Doyle found me."

"Come on, Marco. I've been around the block a few times myself. Brian wouldn't have found you if you didn't want to get found."

"Georgie died fretting over whether he would have to tell the cops the truth to clear his name. He was afraid that if that happened, it would all come out. He didn't want to hurt his family. He also forbade me from coming forward. He was like that."

"And now?"

"He's dead and buried, a hero. I need the doubts erased. I couldn't live with myself if people continued to whisper that Georgie had anything to do with that woman's murder."

"You were with him that night and you can prove it?" I asked.

Marco didn't answer. Instead, he stood up, and went into what I supposed was his bedroom. He came out holding a nine-by-twelve envelope and handed it to me.

"I can prove it and so can a hundred other witnesses. He was at both shows that night. It was a very special night, the anniversary of the first time we were together. It was also the night I premiered my Lady Gaga routine. Look for yourself."

Sure enough, there was Marco on stage as Lady Gaga. And at one of the front tables in the time-and-date-stamped shots was Jorge Delgado's smiling face. I put them back in the envelope and made to hand the envelope to Marco.

"No. Keep them. It will help. I want those whispers to be done with. Brian tells me you'll know how to make that happen."

I stood up. "I'll try."

He walked me to the door and thanked me for making this last gift to his lover a possibility.

"Can I ask you one thing, Marco?"

"Sure."

"Why Delgado? It couldn't have been easy."

"We love who we love," he said. "We love who we love."

I had a sick feeling in the pit of my belly, not because of the cancer and not because of what had transpired between Marco and Delgado. On the contrary, I agreed with Marco's view: we love who we love. The older I got, the less all the old rules mattered to me about the rights and wrongs of love and relationships. I thought about how destructive Carmella's attitude was and who it really hurt in the end. What did any of those stupid *shoulds* and *shouldn'ts* accomplish except to ruin lives and crush hope? It was just that I was uneasy, that somehow I knew what Marco had given me as a gesture of love and absolution would be perverted into a weapon and that I would be the one to wield it.

When I got downstairs I realized I was only a block or two away from the High Line Bistro, a restaurant, frankly, I wish I had never heard of.

FORTY-THREE

In all things, success breeds complacency. It is dangerous and unavoidable. This was equally true for blackmailers and baseball players and bartenders. When you're so sure things will go smoothly in the future because they have in the past, you're bound to get bitten in the ass. Complacency, that's what I was counting on as I drove Natasha around the Upper West Side in my rented Suburban, killing time until I had to drop her off.

She had been true to her word, cooperating fully without a word of complaint. As I instructed her to do, she had gotten in touch with her blackmailer as she always had, sending him an innocuous email: *Package ready. Just need an address.* Then, within twenty-four hours, she received a call giving her instructions. No, she didn't recognize the voice. She never could because he used one of those voice distortion boxes.

"The first two times," she said, "he had me mail the cash to different PO boxes. After that, he had me drop it in garbage cans or leave it on a bench."

"How much?"

"The first payments were for three thousand dollars each. Now they're a thousand bucks each time."

Clearly, the blackmailer—who I couldn't help but see as Tino Escobar—wasn't as trusting of the mail as his late partner. That and he was impatient for his money. That was good, a nice compliment to his complacency. His focus would be on the money.

"How much are you into him for?"

"Eleven thousand."

I didn't press her about it, nor did I ask her about how she felt when she heard Tillman was dead or when she found out that his death seemed to be beside the point. I didn't ask her why she hadn't gone to the cops immediately. I didn't ask her where she was getting the money to pay. I didn't ask her a lot of the questions it had occurred to me to ask. What did any of it matter now?

"I was tested," Natasha whispered.

She could see the puzzlement in my eyes.

Tears were rolling down her freckled cheeks. "For HIV. I'm okay. I had the test the porn stars use when they get checked, the one that tells you right away. And I've had follow-ups."

Neither of us commented on the irony in that. I'd been so focused on the nuts and bolts of the case, I hadn't even thought about it. What an awful burden, I thought, as if the rape and blackmail wasn't enough. As bad as I wanted to get this guy before, I wanted him much more now.

"Okay," I said, handing the brown paper lunch bag to Natasha. "Just do what you always do. It's okay to be nervous. He expects you to be, so if he's watching you, he won't see anything unusual. Make the drop like he told you and I'll handle it from there. Just get off the train and wait upstairs."

"Are you sure about this?" she asked. "The bag is awfully bulky."

"I did that on purpose. It's in small bills because I don't want him to feel comfortable enough to take the money out of the bag and put it in his pockets. It's easier to spot that way. Now go ahead, you should have plenty of time to walk from here to the 79th Street station."

I didn't follow Natasha. I knew where she was going and when she had to get there. Besides, Pam was already in position. I hadn't told Natasha about Pam because no matter how much an amateur wants to cooperate, too much information makes them act in dumb and unnatural ways. The only thing I wanted Natasha to focus on for the moment was making the drop. When Natasha reached the corner, I put the Suburban in gear and drove over to the station.

The instructions were simple and it wasn't hard to figure out the mechanics of how things would work. Natasha was to walk onto the downtown platform for the number 1 train and find the southern-most trash can on the platform. She was to wait until she saw the first number 1 train after two A.M. pull into the station, then she was to drop the lunch bag into the trash, and get onto the first car of the train. That was it. All very easy, quick, and clean. The black-mailer would either be on the platform or the train itself. The latter was the more likely because he wouldn't risk being spotted before the train arrived. When Natasha got on the first car, he would get off the second or third car. He'd wait until the train pulled out of the station, walk over to the garbage, collect his money, and leave. There was a chance he might wait for the next train, but that seemed unnecessarily foolish and risky. He'd be a sitting duck. No, he would grab the sack and head right up to the street, grab a cab, or get to a car he'd parked close by earlier in the day.

I pulled over by a fire hydrant and kept the SUV running. I texted Pam my exact location. All things being equal, it would've been better if I could have been the one in the subway. Pam was a New Englander and though she had worked cases in New York City before and had spent a lot of time here since we began seeing each other, she didn't know the lay of the land like a native. But all things weren't equal. Natasha would have seemed way too comfort-able with me close by. And the fact was, I'd been working the case for a while and many of the players, especially Escobar, knew me, knew my face. I'd also gotten a lot of press during the search for

Sashi Bluntstone. I couldn't risk blowing it all. Anyway, I'd given Pam a full description of Escobar. She was a total pro and could handle herself. I'd witnessed that myself.

I checked my watch: 2:03. As I did, Pam texted: *On second car. Wrong choice. No Escobar. No men.* I texted back that he was probably on the third or fourth car and not to worry. I was no fan of technology, but you had to love the fact that between cell phones, laptops, iPads, Kindles, digital video cameras, et cetera, it was impossible to tell if someone was just listening to music or doing surveillance. Even if Pam was the only person texting in that subway car, no one would give her a second thought.

Next text: *Pulling into 86th St.*

Next text: *Man on. Not Escobar. Young. Black. Black hoodie, jeans, Nikes. Walking 2 back of train.*

Next text: *Pulling out. On way 2 79th. No men on car.*

Next text: *Slowing for 79th.*

Next text: *Stopped. Doors open. Out. No men! Young woman at can. Got it. Coming up.*

A woman! Maybe Escobar was smarter than I'd given him credit for. It was wise of him to insulate himself, to give himself some deniability. And here I was thinking that using the 79th Street station had been a mistake. It had very limited street access and no access between north and southbound platforms. There were only two choices for escape: up the stairs to the street or to risk life and limb by crossing the tracks to the northbound platform.

In the brief instant that I did a double-take at Pam's last text, I missed the woman coming out of the subway. When I gazed back up and into my rearview mirror, all I caught was a glimpse of long black hair, a bare leg, the bulging paper bag in tapered fingers, and a cab door slamming shut. What an idiot I'd been. I was the complacent one. I'd been so sure it would be Escobar making the pickup himself, so sure he would grab a cab on the avenue, that I had left myself in exactly the wrong position. Pam opened the Suburban's passenger door and jumped in.

"I almost missed her completely," I screamed. "She got in a cab."

Pam didn't need to be told twice; I was already moving before she closed the door and belted in.

"What about Natasha?" Pam asked.

"Call her and tell her that we're following the money. Don't mention anything else. Tell her to take a cab home and that we'll be in touch."

But as Pam made the call, I knew our cause was lost. The Suburban was facing south down Broadway and the cab had headed west along 79th. At that time of the morning, much of the traffic in the city was yellow cabs and spotting one from the other was like sorting through a penny jar. I raced down Broadway and cut west as soon as I could, but it was no good, no good at all. Even if I could have isolated each of the thirty cabs I'd seen on the way and the ones I was looking at now, I would have no way to pick which one I wanted to follow unless I could see the backseat passenger. Talk about fucked.

"We'll just wait for the next payoff demand," Pam said, trying to console me. "Now that we know he has a woman helping him, we can be alert for that. We can bring in help next time."

"There's no time for a next time."

"Of course there is. Blackmailers don't stop. Sooner or later, they want another taste. Natasha will understand. After Sarah's wedding we'll—"

"Pam, it's not Natasha I'm worried about. It's *me* that doesn't have time for a next time."

"What's that supposed to mean?"

267

I barely heard the question because my mind was processing something. I closed my eyes and thought back to the glimpse I'd seen of the woman getting into the cab. There was something familiar about her, the color of her hair, the shape of her calf. It's amazing how little we need to see of someone to recognize them. I knew her, but from where? Then, all at once, it came to me, and it made a sickening kind of sense. I pulled to the curb and slammed my hand hard against the steering wheel.

"What are you doing—and what was that crack about having no time?"

"I know her," I said.

Pam was confused. "Know who?"

"It's not Escobar. It never was."

"Who's not Escobar?"

"The girl in the cab."

"Who is she?"

"Wrong question. It's not who she is. It's who she used to be. Call Natasha and tell her we're coming over."

FORTY-FOUR

When I described her, Natasha said she knew who I was talking about. She said she worked as a bartender at Kid Charlemagne's, but didn't know what happened to her.

"She's a very beautiful girl."

I agreed.

"Do you remember her name?"

"It was an interesting name, foreign sounding," she said.

"Was she at Piccadilly the night . . . you know?"

Natasha closed her eyes for a moment. "I think so, but I can't be sure. I don't remember a lot of it. Why?"

I didn't have to answer the question for her. I saw the answer in her eyes.

. . .

It had been easy enough to get her address from Nathan Martyr and to confirm it with Chef Liu. It was no shock that the address matched Tillman's. Of course they had lived together. Now it was only a matter of waiting outside her apartment, the top floor of an unremarkable house in the Long Island City section of Queens.

"If she was extorting more than two women, she could do better than this," Pam said, staring up at the house for a second before returning her gaze to the passenger's sideview mirror.

"Tuition."

"What?"

"Tuition costs a fortune at SVA," I said. "And she's put her film education to good use."

"Funny fella. I don't think Maya Watson would have seen it that way."

"None of them would."

Pam tensed. "Here she comes. My side of the street, half a block down. You're sure you want to do this?"

"Are *you* sure?"

"It's not me you should be worried about," she said. "Are you sure *he's* going to go for it?"

"If he is who I think he is, yes. If not, we're all fucked."

On that cheery note, I got out of the SUV. Hiding behind the side of the Suburban, I dialed the number DiNardo had given me from Maya's cell phone, the same number Natasha had given me: her blackmailer's number. I heard the muffled ringing of a phone just as she passed me. I stepped out from around the Suburban, phone in hand.

"Hello, Esme," I said.

She wheeled around. She knew immediately who I was, but pretended not to. "Do I know you?"

I waved my cell at her, smiling. "Why don't you answer your phone?"

She ignored that. "Who are you?"

I clicked my phone off and the ringing in her bag was silenced. "Aren't you curious how I got your number?"

"Not really, no. Who are you again?" Now she was just stalling for time, trying to make sense of the situation.

"Maybe you don't recognize me without my old badge or a drink spilled all over me."

"Oh, I remember now, yes. From the High Line." She smiled at me, running her tongue over her lips as she had the second time I spoke to her. "How did you find me?"

"Finding your address was simple, almost as simple as blackmail."

"You are crazy. I do not know what you are talking about."

"Weak, Esme. That was weak. And you were doing so well up to then. See, I know all sorts of unexpected stuff about you, like how to email you at RT6969@constop.com."

That chased the flirtatious smile right off her lips. Her face hardened and her eyes busied themselves burning holes right through mine. That was good because she was so focused on me she never even heard Pam come up behind her. Only when Pam pressed the tines of the Taser to Esme's neck did she realize the tables were about to turn on her and turn hard.

. . .

I would have dismissed it as a scene out of a bad movie—a woman duct-taped to a chair in a semi-dark room in a warehouse. Only the warehouse belonged to my brother and me, and it wasn't a movie. There were times when there weren't very many options and this was one of those times.

When Esme stirred, she tried shaking herself fully awake. She tried moving her arms and legs to no avail and then looked down at the strange clothes she was wearing.

"You shit yourself when you got zapped," I said, straddling a chair directly across from her. "It happens sometimes."

"I'm gonna fuck you up for this."

I clucked my tongue at her. "Sorry, Esme, but your fucking people up days are over."

"You think so?"

"What's the matter? Not so much fun when you're not in control, is it?"

"Fuck you!"

"I'm not the one who's fucked here."

"What are you going to do, kill me, old man?"

"It's a distinct possibility."

I stood up and reached under my jacket for my .38. I opened the cylinder and emptied the cartridges onto the floor. I picked a lone bullet up and made a show of putting it back in the cylinder. I walked over to her and spun the cylinder very close to her right ear. Then walked behind her, spun it again and snapped the cylinder shut. "Click, click, click, click . . . I love that sound. This is a trick I learned to play as a cop, Esme. Now let me teach it to you. You see, it's stupid beating a confession out of someone. Too messy, too much potential fallout. In any case, we don't really need you to confess, do we? No we don't. Keeping that cell phone on you, that was really sloppy, and picking the money up yourself was just plain stupid. And sorry, but we've got your computer here, all your little sex toys and outfits, and all your video equipment too. I'm sorry. I'm getting off the point. Where was I? Oh, right. The trick.

"Yeah, like I said, it's dumb hitting a suspect. And you know, I was always in uniform, so I never got to learn how to ask clever questions in that manipulative way detectives ask them. Some of those guys were amazing. They could get real hard-case motherfuckers to confess to terrible things, but sometimes it took hours, days sometimes. No, see, out on the street, we had our own way of interrogating suspects and we also got hard cases to confess to all kinds of shit, but it never took more than two minutes. That's where the trick comes in. It worked every time too, 'cause no matter how different people are from each other, tough or weak, brave or cowardly, sane or psychopath, they all have one thing in common: they don't want to die. And, Esme, I bet you think you're different. I bet you always think that, huh? That you're gonna be the exception to the rule. Well, you keep thinking that, okay?

"So here's how it would work if you were a hard case. I would take this gun here with the one bullet in it and I'd jam it against the back of your fucking head or press it to your temple." I lightly brushed her hair with the muzzle of the .38. "Then I'd start asking you for where the video footage is stored, for all your access codes, and the master codes for your accounts. I'd ask you for a list of names, addresses, and phone numbers of the people you've been blackmailing. And the minute you stopped answering or started lying to me, I would pull the hammer back and squeeze the trigger and I would keep doing it until I got the answers I was looking for. See how it works? But here's the trick," I said, walking around in front of her and showing her the bullet in my left hand. "The trick is that I palmed the one bullet you thought was in the cylinder the second I moved out of your line of sight. The gun's empty." With that, I pressed the muzzle up to my temple, pulled the hammer back, and squeezed the trigger. I did it over and over and over again. "See?"

The look of utter horror on her face was astonishing. The cop who taught me this trick many years ago told me it would work just this way.

"It scares 'em more if you put the empty gun against your own head or put it in your own mouth and keep squeezing. That really scares the shit out of them. They're already scared to begin with, but seeing that makes 'em think you're just crazy enough to really kill them if you have to. And that's the whole point."

It went off perfectly, but I wasn't feeling particularly proud of myself. Nor was I quite done, not yet.

I leaned over her and put my lips very close to her ear and whispered, "Someone is going to come talk to you now. He's a real cop, a detective, but if you don't cooperate with him and give him all the things we talked about, including your bank account and pin number, I'm gonna come back in here and we're gonna play that game again. Except this time, I won't palm the bullet. I'm dying, Esme. I have gastric cancer and, unlike you, I've got nothing to lose."

"You are full of shit," she said, trying unsuccessfully to keep her voice steady.

I stepped back from her far enough so she could see my face. "Take a good look, Esme. Look in my eyes and tell me I'm full of shit. Tell me!"

She was silent.

I turned to go.

"What is this to you?" she called after me. "Why should you care what I do?"

I kept walking.

When Fuqua came out of the room, he handed me the cartridges I'd left scattered on the floor in front of Esme. I hadn't done it out of carelessness.

"Here is the information," he said, giving me a sheet of paper. "How long will you continue to hold her?"

"A few more hours. I have a computer guy who used to work for me. He'll check this stuff out and wipe the videos."

"Now, I believe you have something for me, *non?*"

I didn't say a word as I handed him the fuel to feed the furnace of his ambition: a nine-by-twelve envelope and the digital voice recorder. I had that sick feeling in my belly again.

FORTY-FIVE

Empty.

Empty, that's how I felt.

It was over.

Done with.

And who was better for it? Carmella? Maya? Pam? Natasha? Yes, Natasha. Maybe Natasha and the fourteen other women Esme had blackmailed. Pam and I checked their names against phone numbers, emails, addresses, and videos. Fourteen was the number, not counting Maya Watson, of course. It was hard to watch all the videos, even in fast forward, although there was a horrible, mind-numbing sameness to them. I didn't hold out any hope that these women who had been drugged and raped and blackmailed would find an ounce of comfort in the fact that they weren't lone victims. They were alone in every way that mattered, far removed from solace, though not quite as far removed as Maya. At least part of the nightmare was over for the survivors, but how much solace would there be in that? I felt like the doctor outside the triple amputee's door preparing a speech about looking on the bright side. None of these women, I thought, was apt to see any silver lining.

Empty because I had seen the son that was taken from me nine years ago, but whose loss I was fully feeling only now.

Empty because Pam had gone back to Vermont to wash away the stink of this mess. I thought she'd have to scrub long and hard in very hot water from now until I came up for the wedding to even make a dent.

Empty because I'd failed at the whole point of this. I had even less of an idea about who had killed Alta Conseco than I had before I got involved. This was it, the last good chance, and I'd blown it.

Empty because I'd made deals and compromises that weren't mine to make.

Empty because the clock was ticking.

Empty because that famous luck of mine had run out.

. . .

I went to the house on Ashford Street. I didn't know if Carmella had stuck around or if she'd run back up to Toronto, covering her eyes and her ears so that she could ignore the unpleasant truths. If she wasn't there, I'd call her. If she didn't answer the phone, I'd fly up to Toronto. She had gotten me into this and she was going to hear me out.

No need to go to the airport. Carmella answered the door. She read the look on my face and invited me in. She'd said she wanted me to stop working the case and maybe she even meant it when she said it, but Carm had been a cop, was still a cop. You never stop being one, badge or no badge, retired or not. You never stop being one on the inside. Whether or not she had better come to terms with who her sister was since our argument, I couldn't judge.

She offered me a drink, which I refused. I needed to get this out.

"How did you know to come, Moe?"

"What?"

"I am leaving tomorrow and I won't be coming back. I have rented this place out since I inherited it. I could not stand to let it go. It means the only happy memories I have of my family. But now . . . it is time. I have arranged for an agent to sell it and I have someone coming to take the furniture away. I have been hanging on to hopes and ghosts for too long. My life is with Israel in Toronto. It is not here. I am not sure it ever was."

Only when she finished did I notice the phantom images of picture frames on the bare walls and the stacks of cardboard boxes neatly lined up in rows.

"I always liked this place. Even now I can feel your grandmother's presence. I'll be sorry when it's gone."

"It is already gone, Moe. So what have you come to say?"

"I don't know who killed Alta, Carm. I don't think we'll ever know. I suppose it might have been a pissed-off fireman. That's still my best guess. I thought I had someone for it, but that didn't pan out."

"It is not a surprise. I have already come to terms with that, I think."

"But I did find some stuff out that you'll want to hear, stuff you need to hear."

She took a deep breath, girding herself. "Go ahead."

"I know why Alta and her partner didn't treat Robert Tillman at the High Line Bistro. The short version is that Tillman raped Maya Watson and was also blackmailing her. At Alta's urging, they went to the restaurant to confront Tillman. It was their bad luck that he happened to pick that moment to stroke out. Alta never got over what happened to you, the thing that blew your family apart, and this was her chance at redemption. It wasn't only Tillman she went to confront. It was the man who did what he did to you when you were little. It was her own guilt and regret she went to confront. Do you understand? Do you see why she couldn't help him?"

"I understand," she said, trying to hold herself together.

"It was all about you, about you and her. What might have been, what should have been between two sisters."

Carmella cried with her whole body so that I felt it through the floor up from the soles of my shoes. I let her cry. I didn't try to comfort her. The time for that had long passed. That old bond between us was finally broken.

"It seems like you've done a good job of raising Israel," I said when her jag had quieted.

"Thank you."

"Does he know—"

"—about you? No, but one of the things I am going to do when I get back home is explain."

"I'm glad, Carm. He should know and about his biological father too. A kid needs to know where he came from so he can know where he's going."

"You are right, Moe."

There was a moment of awkward silence before I stood to leave. Carmella walked me downstairs. We didn't speak, not at first, but then I hugged her long and hard. It was a last hug goodbye. Just before I left, I handed her a slip of paper with Lieutenant Kristen Jo Winston's contact information.

"Who is this?"

"Someone you need to sit down with and speak to before you go home."

"Why?"

"Because if you don't, Alta really will be lost to you forever."

I turned and didn't look back.

FORTY-SIX

Since I was in tying-up-loose-ends mode, I decided to stop in at the Roussis Family Restaurants, Incorporated, corporate offices in Downtown Brooklyn. I wanted to thank Nicky for his help and to say that we should keep in touch. He was a good guy, Nicky, and if I came out the other end of my treatment, I'd need some friends. Truth be told, going back to an empty apartment with only my thoughts for company wasn't exactly ideal, given my state of mind.

Sarah's wedding was only a week or so away. Three days after the wedding Sarah and Paul would be strolling through the Guggenheim Museum in Bilbao, Spain, and my surgeon would be slicing through my kishkas. Yeah, somehow, I didn't want to go home and contemplate those stark realities. It's one thing to ponder your own mortality as an eighteen-year-old who's just smoked a bowlful of Thai-stick and quite another to do it as a sick old man. So it took little effort for me to turn off Ashford Street and aim my car down along Atlantic Avenue.

In the lobby of the building, I had trouble finding the number of the offices. I guess it was pretty foolish—or desperate—of me to think that Nicky and his family had kept their offices in the same place all this time. It had been nearly fifteen years, after all, since Carmella and I had worked the case for them. New York commercial real estate was like an expensive game of musical chairs. Companies moved all the time to get better deals after their leases ran out. A security guard, a real old-timer, noticed me staring at the board.

"Can I help you, son?"

Son! I liked that. No one had called me that in a long while. "I was looking for the Roussis Family Restaurant offices, but I guess they moved, huh?"

"Not moved exactly," he said.

"I'm not following you."

"Money troubles," he whispered. "About three years back, they were . . . er . . . shown the door."

"Really?"

"Shame too. Killed the old man."

"Spiros?"

"Kind man. Generous man. Always with a warm greeting. Always with a nice gift on the holidays. Never forgot to ask about the wife and kids. Even gave me a savings bond for each of my grandkids. You knew 'em?"

"I was on the job with Nicky back in the day and I did some work for the family when I went private."

"Nicky, a good man like his dad. It was that other son, that Gus that was the bad seed."

"How so?"

"Can't say, really, but you know how you can just tell sometimes? I just know it."

"Thanks." I shook his hand.

"Need anything else, let me know."

"There is something. Is Spiegelman, Abbott, Bobalik and Cohen still—"

He smiled. "Moved to bigger offices. They take up the whole eighth floor these days."

I rode up to eight and the elevator opened into the reception area. The receptionist smiled a practiced smile at me and asked if she could be of assistance. I wondered if Steve Schwartz was around. She buzzed him and he told her to send me down.

"Corner office. I'm impressed."

"Don't be," he said, his eyes on a monitor, his hands at a keyboard. "I look out onto Atlantic Avenue, not Park Avenue. Okay, done." Steve, a slender man a few years my senior, stood to greet me. "Moe Prager. What are you doing here?"

"A farewell tour," I said only half-kiddingly.

Never a barrel of laughs to begin with, Steve looked at his watch to indicate his patience was already wearing thin.

"Roussis," I said.

He understood immediately and shrugged his shoulders. Spiegelman, Abbott did corporate and commercial real estate law. They had represented the Roussis family business when Carm and I worked the case in '95.

"You know I can't give specifics although we don't represent them any longer," he said.

"Not asking for any. I'm just surprised. I've reconnected with Nicky lately and he didn't mention the troubles."

"Nick's a proud man."

"But . . ."

"Gus," he said as if his name explained it all. Maybe it did. At least Steve and the old-timer were on the same wavelength. "The kid was a fuck-up. They gave him a position he wasn't ready for and he ran the ship aground. But they got a big influx of cash somewhere and seem to have rebounded. More than that, I can't say."

I thanked him and left. In the elevator on the way downstairs I went over it in my head again and again, that first conversation I had with Nick when I ran into him at the Gelato Grotto. He'd definitely said that he went into the office a few times a week. I couldn't figure out why Nicky would've said that. Maybe Steve had already answered that question for me. Nick, he had said, was a proud man. I could see that, but it still bugged me a little. Funny how a man like me, a skillful and practiced liar, could be so bothered by what was clearly an innocent, self-protective lie. Or maybe it was that I needed to focus on something other than my impending surgery.

Detective Fuqua couldn't have known the favor he was doing me when he called.

FORTY-SEVEN

Fuqua looked like he hadn't slept since he walked away from me two days ago with the ammunition he would need to do a little blackmailing of his own. Marco's detailed description of his love affair with and his alibi for Jorge Delgado would have been powerful enough, but to have photographs of New York City's most recently sanctified hero at a notorious drag queen show was like the plutonium core at the center of a chocolate-covered H-bomb. Given that the city and the media had just spent weeks touting Delgado as the perfect family man, fireman, self-sacrificing hero—the anti-Alta Conseco, if you will—and thrown him a five-star funeral, those photographs gave Detective Fuqua the power to demand just about any bump-up in rank or assignment he wanted. With this type of ammunition, my old friend Larry Mac could have had himself declared a prince of the realm. Fuqua looked like a prince all right—Hamlet.

"It is a great hypocrisy, is it not, Moe, that almost anyone else could have gone to such a club as Delgado went to without fear of recrimination? You or I could go to such a club and say we went on a dare or just for fun."

"We don't have enough time, ink, or paper to list the great hypocrisies, and as they go, there are far greater ones than this. Besides, Delgado was as big a hypocrite as they come. He tried to hire a hitter to take out Alta Conseco in part because she was gay. He tormented her with his phony macho bullshit, so don't ask me to

283

weep for him. If there's anyone I have sympathy for here, it's Marco. He gave me this stuff to save Delgado's rep and I'm the one who's perverted it into leverage for you."

"Here," he said, sliding the voice recorder and envelope across his desk to me, "take them back, please. They are of no use to me. I thought I was ambitious enough to use them, but I cannot."

"Look, Fuqua, the stain is on me, not you. I'm the one who offered you this stuff so you would help us with Esme. If you hadn't played the heavy and gotten her to cooperate, those videos would have gone public either in court or as payback. The only other way to have stopped her would have been to—"

"Do not say that in here!"

"Okay, but you know it's true just the same. Maya Watson killed herself over this and it hadn't even gone public. Can you imagine the fallout if these videos started appearing on the web? Some of these women are married and have families. It's bad enough that they were raped and blackmailed. Do you know what hell their lives must have been? I wasn't about to let it go any further. I'm the one who compromised himself by betraying Marco, not you."

"Still, I have no wish to use them. I will feed my ambition with accomplishment, not leverage."

"Are you sure? You realize that this leverage has a limited shelf life and with every day that passes these pictures lose some potency. Two weeks from now, a month from now, they will lose all their power altogether. Once the city moves on, and it always moves on, no one will care or even remember Jorge Delgado. The brass will no longer have a stake in protecting his rep. If anything, they can run this stuff up the flagpole when they need to distract the media from some real scandal or fuck-up."

"I am quite certain."

"There's hope for you yet, Icarus."

284

But if I thought returning the alibi and photos to me would unburden Hamlet, I was wrong. If anything, Fuqua looked more miserable than when I came in.

"What is it?" I asked. "Something else is bothering you."

"Let us go for a walk."

Outside it was August in June. Though the mist was so thick that the top of the Parachute Jump had vanished with the sun, the temperature hovered above ninety. Sheets of roiling black clouds from the south moved up slowly behind us as we walked up Mermaid Avenue. For now the only rumbling we heard came from the subway terminal at Stillwell Avenue, but from the dark hues of the clouds at our backs it was obvious the rumbling song of the subway would soon no longer be a solo. As we turned right on Stillwell toward the ocean, even the breezes told tales of the coming storm. The light winds seemed almost to conform to the folds of my face like hot barbershop towels. We made it all the way to the near-deserted boardwalk before Fuqua uttered a word.

"I fear I have made a very grave mistake," he said, his eyes looking out to sea but unseeing. "A terrible mistake."

"How so?"

"When I was with Esme the other day, something about her bothered me very much."

"You mean other than the fact that she was a blackmailing sociopath who had been living with a convicted rapist?"

He winced when I said it. "You have a sharp sense of humor, Moe, but this is not a thing to laugh at."

"Sorry. So what bothered you?"

"I was not certain. She was too cooperative too quickly, but it goes beyond that."

"You know, I meant to ask you about how you got to her," I said. "I figured she would give in eventually, but that it would take all night. You were in and out of that room in less than an hour. I just assumed she was smart enough to recognize that you were a serious man and that you weren't fucking around. What *did* you say to her, anyway?"

"I told her that I would pin Alta Conseco's murder on her if she did not cooperate. She had motive, after all. Alta had let her live-in lover die without treatment. I supplied the means," he said, removing a plastic evidence bag from his suit jacket pocket and handing it to me. "That weapon conforms exactly to the knife used to murder Alta Conseco. I wrapped Esme's palm around it. *Voila!* The murder weapon. I told her I would make sure to defeat any alibi she might produce. When she protested a bit, I informed her that you were not only a former policeman and PI, but one of her victims' fathers and that you were very probably going to kill her regardless. Dead suspects, I said to her, need no alibis. 'When you are dead, Esme, I will have someone call my office with a tip and I will find this knife conveniently hidden in your closet. Case closed.' She then gave me everything you asked for."

"That was the idea, right? So what's the problem?"

"I could not sleep that night. I went over it time after time and her attitude bothered me more and more. Yesterday morning I realized finally what was bothering me."

"Which was what?"

"I saw that video you showed me. Horrible. Horrible. I suppose I was as outraged by it as were you. I was blinded by my outrage and ambition. I thought, why not help you? I would help rid the city of this parasite. I would do good and myself good all at once with only a small risk to my shield. So when I went in that room to threaten her, I was not actually thinking of Alta Conseco's homicide in any sense but as a tool. What I realize now, what I came to realize was that the case I made against Esme to pressure her to cooperate—"

Then it hit me so that I was almost breathless. "Holy shit!"

"Yes, Moe, you see now. She very well might have been the person who killed Alta Conseco. She was the best suspect I have had and I did not think to look at her twice."

"Wait a second. Wait a second. We're getting way ahead of ourselves here," I said as much to convince me as him. "Tillman or Sykes or whatever his name was, was a con man. I mean, come on, Fuqua, he was a shitbird convict and she was a sociopath who probably jumped from lover to lover like bees go from flower to flower. When she was done sucking up the nectar, she moved on. Who says they were in love? She probably didn't give him a second thought when he dropped dead. She would move on, not avenge some clown she didn't give a shit about."

"That is what I thought as well. Then I made inquiries."

"Inquiries?"

"First I checked with both restaurants at which Esme was employed. She was not scheduled at either the evening Alta Conseco was murdered."

"So what?" I said. "Half the pissed-off firemen in New York City were off that night too."

"It gets better . . . or worse, depending upon your perspective. You recall that Tillman was convicted of statutory rape, *non*?"

"Yeah. He did four years, right?"

"Would you care to speculate as to the identity of his teenage victim in that case?"

I got that sick feeling again. "You're kidding me."

"Esmeralda Marie Sutanto of Goshen, New York—Esme. I spoke with the DA that prosecuted the case. Tillman was working a home improvement scam in Goshen when he met the Sutantos, a divorced mom with a teenage daughter. The mother and Tillman started seeing one another. While the mom was at work, Tillman would stop over and keep young Esme company after she came home from high school. The mom caught wind of it and went to the local police."

"Let me guess," I said, "Esme refused to testify against Tillman."

"The DA says that they claimed to be in love and he believed them, but with the mother pushing him and an election that year, he had no choice but to prosecute and go for the maximum. When Esme graduated from high school, she left home. Would you like to guess the identity of Tillman's only regular visitor during his years in Bedford Hills? His only visitor? I had a training officer who told me when I first got on the job that only fools ignore the obvious."

"So bring her in. I'll call in a tip from a pay phone and you can get a warrant."

"Too late," he said.

"She's gone?"

"With the wind. I paid her apartment a visit yesterday evening. She took only a bag with some of her things and did not bother with her furniture. No matter, we gave her time to destroy any evidence she had not already gotten rid of. I fear my training officer was right. I am a fool."

And with that, the sky opened up on us. Two fools in the rain.

FORTY-EIGHT

There were at least two sleepless men in the borough of Brooklyn that night. I didn't know what Fuqua was doing about his insomnia, though I was tempted to call and ask. Me, I had no intentions of staring up at the ceiling. I'd tried to get to bed early as a means of escaping the various spiders in my head. I'd even stooped to taking a pill to help me drift off. Yeah, I used to get high and drop acid when I was in college and until my recent adventures through the looking glass of oncology, I drank enough scotch and red wine to float the Spanish Armada. Yet somewhere in the bizarro mélange of cognitive dissonance that was my moral compass, I'd become downright puritanical about narcotics. But puritans have their breaking points too and I'd reached mine. Of course, all the damned pill did was make my head cottony and got me no closer to sleep than counting sheep.

I took a shower—my second in the last several hours if you counted the earlier drenching I got on the boardwalk—and considered doing something I hadn't done in a very long time: driving over to the Grotto for a dish of pistachio gelato. Perhaps I'd risk a slice of mediocre pizza, I thought, as I took the ten-minute ride from my condo to 86th Street. One of the reasons for the Grotto's continued popularity was that it stayed open late. The place was crowded as ever. There were no spots on 86th, so I drove around back and parked on West 10th Street at the foot of the entrance to the loading dock.

As I walked back around the corner, I noticed that June had pushed August back into the future where it belonged. The day's vengeful storms had given way to cloudless, star-saturated skies and the dampness of the afternoon had been replaced by dry, gentle breezes. It smelled like June again and the temperature was very Goldilocks—just right. All this and the lingering cotton in my head were nearly enough to keep thoughts of Esmeralda Sutanto from ruining the glory of the night. Nearly.

After Fuqua and I parted, I'd tried convincing myself that he was wrong about Esme and that he was building a case out of his own demons. That he was horrified by the nakedness of his ambition and the lengths he had almost been willing to go to feed it. That his guilt over looking past Esme was driving his need for self-flagellation. While all of that may have been true, it was more true that Esme really was the perfect suspect for Alta's murder.

I decided I'd have a slice of pizza and got on that line first. Even if I somehow managed to survive the surgery, chemo, and radiation, I knew that my days of eating whatever I wanted to eat whenever I wanted to eat it were dwindling to a precious few.

"Slice of Sicilian and a Bud," I said to the kid at the pizza counter.

When the kid slid the tray my way and handed me my change, I asked if Nicky was around. I doubted he would be at this time of night, but I would have felt like an idiot if I hadn't asked. Although it still bugged me a little that he'd lied to me, I owed him a thank-you for trying to help me with the case. I also wanted to let him know that it was good to reconnect. Over the years, I had shed so many friends that I felt like a snake that'd molted once too often and now had nothing left to replace its old skin.

"Sure," he said. "He's in back. You wanna talk to him?"

"Tell him Moe is here when you get a chance, okay? I'll be sitting over there." I pointed to a corner table by the railing.

I pulled the cell phone from my pocket, stared at it as if it might make the decision for me, and gave Fuqua a call. He wasn't asleep nor was he terribly enthusiastic at hearing the sound of my voice.

"Come have a beer with me, a slice of pizza," I said, after he got done grumbling. "I'm at the Grotto."

"It is well after midnight."

"You're not gonna sleep tonight and neither am I. We can do it alone or together."

"It would take a half hour for me to get there from Canarsie."

"So what? We can have a beer here and then go somewhere else."

"I am exhausted."

"Look, I'm here. You wanna come, come. You don't wanna come, don't."

I was done with my slice by the time Nick Roussis came to my table. Although the pizza lived down to its usual standard, I enjoyed it more than I had ever enjoyed any pizza. I was struck by the revelation that the menu for a condemned man's last meal is almost beside the point. What matters in the scheme of things is that it is a last meal.

Nicky looked tired, but there was something else too. He seemed out of sorts, distracted.

"What's up, Nick?"

"What? Oh, what's up? You tell me," he said. "I hear you were at the old offices today."

"News travels fast."

"Steve Schwartz called as a professional courtesy. Told me you was poking around."

"Not poking around. Actually, I was coming to say thanks for the assist with the case. That's all."

Drumming his fingers on the table, he asked, "How'd that pan out?"

"Not like I hoped," I said.

"That's too bad. Listen, Moe, can you excuse me for a minute? I've gotta delivery comin' in and—"

"Don't worry about it. Go ahead. I'm gonna get a gelato."

"Good. I'll tell the kid to take care of you. It's on the house."

"Thanks."

"No problem, Moe. Just don't go nowhere."

"I'll be here."

The pistachio gelato was just how I remembered it: rich, buttery, but not too sweet. I hated things that were so sweet that the sweetness obscured the complexity of the flavor and texture. Savoring the gelato, my mind drifted off to the other food experiences that defined old Brooklyn to me: the pineapple ices at Adesso's Bakery on Avenue X, the pastrami at Max's Deli on Sheepshead Bay Road, the ruglach from Leon's Bakery, the roast beef from Brennan & Carr on Nostrand, the french fries at Nathan's.

"Earth to Moe. Earth to Moe." Nicky had returned, snapping his fingers in front of my face.

I looked at my watch. Twenty minutes had passed as if in a second. Who says time travel is impossible?

"Sorry. Just lost in the past."

Nick sat down across from me. We chatted for a few more minutes, neither of us really saying anything. I was feeling tired at last and Nick was even more distracted than he had been earlier. We shook hands and agreed to have dinner again soon, but this time it was a hollow promise. My prognosis notwithstanding, it was Nick who seemed uncomfortable at the suggestion. It was a familiar story. Rekindling long-dormant friendships doesn't usually work unless both parties are equally committed. Otherwise, it's like a one-armed man trying to start a fire by rubbing two sticks together. I remembered thinking the very same thing twenty years before. I guess I'd been hemorrhaging friends for a very long time.

When I looked around, I noticed that most of the tables were empty and that the red and green neon Gelato Grotto sign had been shut off. Closing time. I walked back around the corner, tired but sated, my head much less foggy than it had been since I'd taken the pill. When I got back to my rented SUV, I realized that I was parked in exactly the same spot Alta Conseco had parked in the night she was killed. A lot of things were suddenly clearer to me and I stopped stone still in my tracks. It got quiet—no, not quiet, silent. Silent so the only thing I could hear were my own thoughts in between the suddenly quickening beats of my heart.

I looked at the rear of the Grotto and, sure enough, a van was backed up to the loading dock. But the van didn't have commercial license plates and the doors were unmarked. There was no company name on the doors, no DOT number, no company logo, nothing. Anyway, who gets a food delivery after midnight? And why did the owner have to be here to take in a simple food delivery? It made no sense. Then, in a single breath, I went from clear-headed to light-headed, as a thousand images and questions rushed to mind all at once.

I walked twenty feet back toward the corner, the spot where Alta's blood trail began. I tried to remember details from the coroner's report Fuqua had shown me. Alta was stabbed once in the back; the remainder of the wounds were to her right side and the front of her torso. She had many defensive wounds on her arms and hands. I returned to where I was parked, tried to time how long it might take someone running from the loading dock to catch up to someone walking around the corner. I flashed back to the night Nicky had invited me back to his office, the night we left through the prep kitchen onto the loading dock. I pictured the wall of the prep kitchen—rows of knives neatly lined up on magnetic strips.

Fuqua's training officer had been right all along: only fools ignore the obvious. And I was the biggest fool of them all. I saw Nicky's eagerness to reconnect, to go to dinner, to help with the case in a new light. Who had so conveniently supplied me with a witness against Delgado? Who kept calling me to see how things were progressing? What was one of the first questions out of Nicky's mouth tonight? I thought back to Nick's silly lie about going into the office a few days a week. I thought about what both the security guard and Steve Schwartz had said about the family business nearly going under and that sudden infusion of cash.

I laughed. It was a laugh disconnected from joy. I reached for my cell phone to call Fuqua. He would be relieved, I thought, to know that Esme might have been a blackmailing sociopath, but not a murderer, not yet anyway. I stopped laughing when I felt the cold steel press against the nape of my neck.

FORTY-NINE

My first thought was that I was going to avoid surgery after all. I smiled. My second thought was about missing Sarah's wedding. I wasn't smiling anymore.

"I'll take that, asshole."

I didn't recognize the voice, yet there was something vaguely familiar about it. Powerful fingers grabbed the cell phone out of my hand, but I wasn't sure the guy pressing the gun to my neck was the same guy who took the phone. I sensed there were two, maybe three of them. If I was wrong and there was only one, I still didn't like the odds. A gun to the neck counts for a lot.

"He's probably carrying." This voice I knew. It belonged to Nick Roussis. Hands were patting me down; one reached under my jacket and yanked my old off-duty piece out of its holster. "Come on, let's get him off the freakin' street and into the van." The headlights of a car turning the corner cast our own shadows ahead of us. "Come on, come on."

I counted the shadows. There *were* three of them: Nicky and two other guys. The muzzle of the gun was pushed hard into my neck, urging me forward so that I almost tumbled head first. The car flashed past. I wasn't hopeful that the driver would see or understand what was going on. Even if the driver had been looking right at us, it was too dark for him or her to see much. Now we were at the side door of the van. The muzzle eased off my neck. My arms were pulled backwards, my wrists pressed close, and taped behind me. I was shoved face first onto the van floor and rolled over on my back. Nick crawled in beside me and sat across from me with his back against the van wall. He was pointing my own .38 at me. His two friends got into the front seats and we were moving.

"You just couldn't leave it alone, could ya?" Nicky said. "When did you know?"

I didn't answer immediately. Instead I stared at the man sitting in the passenger seat and at the driver. The guy in the passenger seat was squat, thick-necked. His hair was more salt than pepper and I couldn't make out much of his profile except that his left cheek was scarred and pitted. I had a better angle to see the driver. He was a twitchy bastard, but he looked like a skinnier, younger version of Nick Roussis.

"Aren't you going to introduce me to your brother?" I mumbled.

Gus jerked his head back at me. "Shut the fuck up or I'll kill you right here."

Nick screamed at his little brother in Greek and not the kind of Greek Aristotle or Socrates were known for. Gus screamed back at Nick. I didn't fool myself that this dissention was going to help me. I didn't let it breed any hope. They were brothers and that's what mattered. I was being taken to die, to be shot in the back of the head and dumped in a shallow grave or thrown in the ocean for fish food. I used their distraction to work myself onto my knees and then flop back into a sitting position. Through all the screaming the passenger sat stoic and unmoving, not once turning his head.

When the brothers quieted down, Nick turned his attention back to me. "I asked you a question. When did you know?"

"About three seconds before the gun was shoved into my neck."

Nick shook his head at me. "Why couldn't you just leave it alone?"

"That's the funny thing," I said.

"There's something funny about this?"

"I guess I mean ironic, not funny."

"What's that?"

"It wasn't me who couldn't leave it alone. It was you, Nicky. You made a big show of giving me the security footage. You were the one who made noise about us getting together. It was you who treated me to dinner. You who served up Jorge Delgado up on a silver platter for me. If you had just shaken my hand and said goodbye that first time I stopped by the Grotto, we wouldn't be here now."

"I guess that was pretty dumb, huh? But I always did kinda look up to you when we were on the job and I was honestly happy to see you when you came to the Grotto that day."

"For all the good it's gonna do me now."

"Sorry, Moe. I got no choice. We work for him," he said, pointing his free hand in the direction of the passenger, "not the other way around."

"You're not a killer, Nicky. It's not in your nature. That's why you quit the job. You said it to me yourself. You couldn't stand the bodies and the blood. You hated the smells: the piss, the shit, the decay."

"Don't fool yourself, Moe. I'll do what I have to."

"I know that. You'll do anything to protect your family. That's what this is all about, right? You protecting the family business, you saving your fuck-up brother. He is a fuck-up. That's right, isn't it, Gus?"

Gus, half-turned, one hand on the steering wheel, a Sig Sauer pointed at my head. "Keep talking, motherfucker and I'll—"

Gus never finished his threat because the stoic passenger slapped him across the face. The sharp smack was amplified by the metal walls of the van. "Shut up mouth and drive van. Pay attention."

Slavic accent, I thought, but not Russian.

"You'll kill me. I know that, Nick." I tried sounding calm, but I wasn't. I thought I would have been okay with dying, with avoiding the pain of surgery, of recovery, and loss of pride that was sure to come with the treatments, but I never wanted to live more than at that moment. "No, I'm talking about Alta Conseco. I know it wasn't in you to kill a woman like that. That had to be your brother."

Nick didn't say a word, hanging his head in shame. That was answer enough.

"But what did Alta see that made Gus chase her down the block, stab her in the back—that was really brave of you, by the way, stabbing a defenseless, unsuspecting woman in the back—"

"That's not how it happened!" Gus yelled, half-turning again. "I didn't want to—"

"You didn't want to, but what, you fucking coward? Your mommy made you stab her in the back?"

"Shut up! Just shut up, Moe!" Nick yelled, shoving the short barrel of the .38 into my chest. "Shut up, Moe!"

"No! Let him speak," the passenger ordered.

"Serbian?" I said. "No. Bulgarian, maybe."

"Very good, smart man. Not idiot like Nick or moron brother. Maybe I get rid of them and keep you alive." He had a good laugh at that. He was the only one laughing. "Go ahead vit you story. I am entertained."

"Alta saw something or you thought she saw something she shouldn't have, like one of these late night deliveries of yours. And I'm thinking there aren't many things even an asshole like Gus would think was worth killing a woman over. Drugs come to mind. Heroin?"

Gus confirmed it. "That's right, asshole."

"Keep quiet, Gus," Nick warned half-heartedly.

"Why? He knows we're gonna kill him. What the fuck does it matter?"

There, he said aloud what we all knew. Don't ask me why, but I wanted to thank him. I could deal with it now. With no hope I was less tormented, calmer. If I was about to die, though, I didn't want to die curious.

"The Pizza Connection all over again," I said, referring to how the Mafia had distributed heroin through New York pizzerias from the mid-seventies to the mid-eighties. "It's Afghani heroin, isn't it?"

The passenger applauded.

"How could you know that?" Nick asked.

"Look at a map. Bulgaria has access to the Black Sea and the Adriatic and it's not really that far away from Afghanistan. You could transship it through Greece, Turkey, the Balkans. I hope that protecting your fuck-up brother is worth helping finance al-Qaeda."

"Enough!" The passenger turned around, a Glock 26 in his hand. The rest of his face wasn't much prettier than his profile. "Enough!"

"We're here anyways," Gus said, the van rolling to a stop.

The Bulgarian and Gus flung their doors open. Nick crawled past me, keeping a bead on me as he slid open the van's side door. "Get out, Moe. Come on."

We were all standing along the shore of Coney Island Creek; the not too distant buzz of cars from the Belt Parkway and the rumble of the subway from Shell Road would have covered the firing of a howitzer let alone the loud *pop, pop, pop* of a 9 mm. I knew very well that my body wouldn't be the only one in the creek, but I took little comfort in that.

"Did you know there's a scuttled submarine in here?" I heard myself say.

They all looked at me like I was crazy. I was crazy, crazy with fear. That calm I'd had in the van only moments before was gone, evaporated.

"Okay, asshole, let's go," Gus said, pushing my shoulder, poking me in the neck with his Sig.

It was then I realized I wasn't as crazed with fear as I might have been because I dropped to the moist, rocky ground and kicked Gus's legs out from under him. He fell into the creek. "Fuck you! You fucking coward!" I screamed at him.

The Bulgarian barked at Nick, "Kill him. Now!"

Nick fired without hesitation, but not at me. The Bulgarian grabbed his throat, fell to his knees, then toppled face forward onto an old tire, stone dead. I struggled to my knees.

Gus came up out of the creek. "What the fuck, Nicky! We're dead. Do you know what they're gonna do to us? Wait a second. Let me—I know." Gus reached down and took the dead man's Glock, aiming it at me. "We'll kill Moe with Iliya's gun. Then we'll put the .38 in Moe's—"

"Drop your weapons! Drop them down on the ground and kick them away." It was Fuqua. Sirens were blaring in the background. "Do it. Do it now!"

Gus wheeled on Fuqua just as an F train pulled into the station a few hundred feet away. It was the last stupid thing he would ever do. Three flashes lit up the night and Gus Roussis collapsed to the ground, his body rolling back into the creek. His head was covered by black, filthy water. Reflexively, Nicky raised the .38, but I lunged forward off my knees, my shoulder connecting with the back of his legs and Nick crumpled backwards over me. By the time he collected himself, Fuqua was there and Nicky had no choice but to drop the gun.

"It wasn't Esme. It was him," I said, nodding at Gus's body.

Ten minutes later this dirty, mostly forgotten patch of Coney Island was swarming with blue uniforms. Crime scene tape seemed to appear as if by magic. I was rubbing the feeling back into my wrists as I sat on the back deck of an ambulance.

"Thanks, Fuqua. I take it that was your car that came around the corner and passed us as I was getting shoved into the van."

"Good for you I could not sleep and I was in the mood for pizza."

"Not really. The pizza at the Grotto stinks."

"Are you all right?"

"For now. I have stomach cancer."

He crossed himself. "I am so sorry."

"Don't be. My daughter's getting married next weekend and now I'll live to see it. You gave that back to me: the last best gift I'll ever get."

EPILOGUE—IFS AND MAYBES

It was a single column on page twelve of the paper:
BODY IDENTIFIED

A week earlier I'm not sure I'd have seen it. I would have been too busy puking my guts up after chemo or too tired to lift my head. I was on the cancer diet, all right. Sometimes I think it wasn't so much that I was nauseous all the time—a lot of the time, yes, but not always—as much as I was so exhausted that I barely had the energy to eat. Don't think for a second there weren't moments I didn't wish that Gus or the Bulgarian had just shoved me out of the van and put one in my ear. As I anticipated, death wasn't the tough part. It was the dying that was murder.

I'd gone up to Vermont on the Tuesday before the wedding, but plenty had happened in the interim. Nick Roussis ignored his attorney's advice and spoke to federal prosecutors, the cops, and the Brooklyn DA for nearly twelve hours straight. From a pragmatic standpoint, it was a very stupid and dangerous thing to do. From a moral standpoint, it was the only thing to do. Nick could have used his knowledge of the Bulgarian crime gangs as a bargaining chip to reduce his sentence or as an entrée into witness protection, but soul cleansing isn't about wheeling and dealing.

The story of the collapse of the Roussis family business into the abyss of organized crime was an old and painfully familiar one. Gus, a junkie and a gambler, had made some bad investments with company funds and had helped himself to other assets. He'd done such a good job of covering his tracks—addicts are expert at covering tracks—that by the time the accountants caught wind of it, it was too late. The business was fucked. Gus vowed to make it right and to save the family. Of course, trusting a gambler and a junkie to save the family business was tantamount to trusting Hitler to be the Shabbos goy. What Gus Roussis did was borrow money, a lot of money, from the people who supplied him with junk and who held his markers.

Like I said, it's an old story. The Bulgarians, who were looking for a foothold in New York City, knew Gus would never be able to keep up with the payments even at zero percent interest. With the vig they added to the loan, forget it. Within months, the wolves were at Gus and Nicky's door and the choice was a very simple one: immediately pay the loan in full, let the Bulgarians launder money through the business and use the restaurants as distribution points, or watch the Bulgarians murder their families. On the Monday before I left for New England, I got a call from Fuqua that Nicky wanted to see me.

He was being held in a high-security section of the Brooklyn House of Detention, the Brooklyn Tombs as we called it when I was on the job. It was on Atlantic Avenue, within walking distance of both Bordeaux in Brooklyn and of the PI office at 40 Court Street that I once shared with Carmella, Brian Doyle, and Devo.

I talked into the cubicle phone. "Hey, Nicky."

He could barely look at me through the Plexiglas, a guard standing a few feet over his right shoulder. He picked up the phone. "Thanks for comin'."

"You did the right thing by talking, but how is your family?"

"They're safe for now." Tears rolled down his face. We both knew what for now meant. "If my testimony ends up convicting enough of them, we'll get into the program. But these guys, Moe, they ain't like the old Five Families. They will never stop looking for me and they'll do anything it takes for payback."

I didn't think this was a good avenue for either of us to explore. "What did you want to see me about, Nick?"

"Those things you said about Gus being a coward, they're not true."

"Yeah?"

"I wanted to tell you what happened, really. The Bulgarians used to hide their heroin in plastic-wrapped bricks inside sacks of flour. The night that women, that Alta, was killed, she parked right by the loading dock. Gus was helping one of the Bulgarians off-load flour and he slipped. He screamed when he fell and she came over to see if anyone needed first aid. The sack of flour had busted open and there were four bricks of heroin laying there in the flour. She took off. The Bulgarian pulled his piece, but Gus grabbed his arm. Then the guy turned it on Gus and told him it was him or her. If only she had run for her car, she mighta had a chance. See, Moe, Gus had no choice."

"There's always a choice. Not always a good one, but there's always a choice."

He shook his head in denial. "You don't understand. He had no choice."

"Why'd you even get involved with these guys? You had to know that letting Gus try to fix things was gonna get you fucked tenfold."

"You said it yourself when you came to the Grotto that first day. How you and your brother had done some stuff to keep your business afloat, stuff you weren't real proud of. Remember, you said that business was a strange kinda creature, a predator and prey animal and scavenger all at once? To keep it going, you said, you had to use what worked even if you had to hold your nose while you did it."

"I didn't mean it literally, Nicky."

"If you had my brother instead of yours and the Bulgarians knockin' at your door, you'd see it that way."

That's where I wanted to leave it. I moved to put the intercom phone back in its cradle.

"I saved your life twice, Moe. Don't you think you owe me at least a goodbye?"

"Twice?"

"Yeah, I shot Iliya, but that was as much for me and the hell they put my family through as for you. See, once the Bulgarians found out you were snooping around about Conseco's murder, they were gonna just kill you. Instead I got them to let you talk to Joey Fortuna to throw you off the trail. I figured you'd give up sooner or later and they would leave you alone."

"Thanks, Nick, but they tried to kill me anyway, tried running me off the Belt Parkway a few days ago."

He laughed at that. "You don't know the Bulgarians, Moe. They don't go in for shit like that. They don't like ifs and maybes. When they want to kill you, they shoot you or hack you up or blow you up. They don't run you off the road. Whoever did that is still out there. Looks like that makes two of us who have to watch our backs."

And that was how we left it.

I called Carmella immediately after getting out of the B-Tombs to explain exactly how Alta had died, who had done it, and why. The irony of it wasn't lost on her. She thanked me for everything. I asked if she had gotten in touch with Kristen Jo Winston before she left Brooklyn for home. She said she hadn't, that she couldn't be somebody else. The irony in that wasn't lost on me. She asked me to pass on her best wishes to Sarah at the wedding and I said I would. I didn't tell her I was sick. Suddenly, I didn't want her sympathy. I no longer wanted anything she had to give. There was a time when we both would have had so much much more to say, but that was ancient history now.

The wedding was amazing. I don't think I even enjoyed my own wedding to Katy that much. Life is pretty fucking amazing when you take the time to actually let it in and wash over you. I danced like a madman with Pam, with Sarah, with my brother Aaron and my sister-in-law Cindy, with my little sister Miriam, with my nieces and nephews, with Paul's mom, with his dad, with Fuqua. At the last moment I'd added him to the guest list and he accepted. Paul's parents didn't say boo. They weren't about to say no to the man who had saved my life. For how long was anybody's guess. Not once during the whole day was I tempted to tell Sarah about my health. The dark realities in our lives catch up to all of us and they didn't need an assist from me. My daughter would find out about me soon enough. When she got home from her honeymoon, the surgery would be over and then we would all deal with things from there.

Pam had her own notions on the subject. After we threw the rice and waved goodbye to the limo, Pam took me by the arm and marched me to a quiet corner of the country club.

"You're sick, Moe, aren't you?"

I didn't bother denying it. "How'd'ya know?"

"You mean other than the fact that you constantly seem distracted, that you're too pale and thin, and that you only pretend to drink wine when we're together?"

"Other than that, yeah."

"It was something you said when we were in the car following Esme after she picked up the money at 79th Street. You said there wasn't enough time for another time. I asked you what that meant and you ignored me, but I didn't forget."

"It's bad," I said.

"I figured. Let's get back to my place and talk about it when we come up for air."

She hasn't left my side since.

On the strength of his arrest of Nick Roussis and for playing a part in breaking up a major drug ring, Fuqua is scheduled to get the bump to detective first and will receive a high departmental honor for saving my worthless ass. His instincts were right. It was better to feed his ambition with accomplishment than leverage. I'm very proud of him for that and I'm almost positive Larry Mac would have been too.

Sarah or Paul or both come down every weekend to visit and Klaus has taken over my responsibilities at the stores. My brother comes to visit, but he won't talk to me. Cindy says he's furious with me for not telling him that I was sick, but I know the truth. He's frightened I'll abandon him. So he sits across from me when he comes and doesn't say a word. That's okay. I hope his anger is strong enough to keep us both alive. Fuqua comes by and so does Flannery. Sometimes they visit together. I enjoy watching them drink in front of me. The deal is that when my treatments are over, they're taking me to Nathan's. I mean to hold them to it.

My oncologist says he's cautiously optimistic, whatever the fuck that means. Talk about hedging your bets! Unlike the Bulgarians he seems perfectly comfortable with ifs and maybes.

The body I read about in the paper that morning was identified as Esmeralda Marie Sutanto, twenty-two years old, of Long Island City, New York. She had been found a few days earlier by a lost hiker in a state park in Orange County. Although the body wasn't in the best of shape, there were signs she had been tortured before being suffocated. The cops weren't very specific, but Fuqua had all the details when he called me later in the day.

"They used a black latex mask to suffocate her," he said. "It was designed so that one might cut off the air supply to the wearer. From the shape of her, they did her a favor by killing her. Her murderer was very angry with her. The upstate authorities are putting it down to a sexual assault and homicide."

"You sound unconvinced."

"The homicide did not happen where the body was found, yet the murderer left Esme's suitcase with her body."

"So."

"I have gone over the inventory of the things in the suitcase. They were mismatched. It was as if someone else packed the bag for Esme to make it appear as if she had left her apartment in a rush."

Even in my frail state, I could read between the lines. I had no part in contacting the women Esme and Tillman had raped and blackmailed. Natasha said she would handle that. But none of us, not Pam nor Natasha nor Fuqua nor Devo nor I believed that simply getting Esme out of town would be the end of it. Devo said it to me straight, that there were no guarantees the videos wouldn't resurface, that there were billions of hiding places in cyberspace and that any half-assed kid could embed videos in places no one would think to look. Basically, we'd all chosen to ignore the eight-hundred-pound gorilla in the room. What Fuqua was saying was that one of us had decided not to it ignore it at all.

"What are you gonna do about it?"

"Do?" he puzzled. "I will do nothing."

"I thought all victims were equal in murder."

"Not all victims," he said. "Not all. It is not my job to increase the pain in the world. It is my job to stop it."

I let Fuqua hold on to that myth because as long as humans walked the earth, the pain would be there and we would go on doing what we could not help but do: inflict pain on one another as easily as we breathed. People can change, but they cannot change their essential natures. We were hurt machines and whether we evolved into them or God made us that way seemed beside the point.

THE END